Cuthbert Bede

Little Mr. Bouncer and his Friend Verdant Green

Also Tales of College Life

Cuthbert Bede

Little Mr. Bouncer and his Friend Verdant Green
Also Tales of College Life

ISBN/EAN: 9783337023362

Printed in Europe, USA, Canada, Australia, Japan

Cover: Foto ©Andreas Hilbeck / pixelio.de

More available books at **www.hansebooks.com**

LITTLE MR. BOUNCER

And his Friend

VERDANT GREEN

ALSO

TALES OF COLLEGE LIFE

BY

CUTHBERT BEDE, B.A.

AUTHOR OF

"THE ADVENTURES OF MR. VERDANT GREEN, AN OXFORD FRESHMAN"

WITH ILLUSTRATIONS BY THE AUTHOR

BOSTON
LITTLE, BROWN, AND COMPANY
1893

University Press:
JOHN WILSON AND SON, CAMBRIDGE, U.S.A.

CONTENTS.

CONTENTS.

CHAPTER VI.

CHAPTER VII.

CHAPTER VIII.

CHAPTER IX.

CHAPTER X.

CHAPTER XI.

CHAPTER XII.

CHAPTER XIII.

CHAPTER XIV.

CHAPTER XV.

CHAPTER XVI.

CHAPTER XVII.

CHAPTER XVIII.

CHAPTER XIX.

CHAPTER IV.

CHAPTER V.

CHAPTER VI.

CHAPTER VII.

CHAPTER VIII.

A Long-Vacation Vigil.

CHAPTER I.

CHAPTER II.

CHAPTER III.

CHAPTER IV.

CHAPTER V.

CHAPTER VI.

CHAPTER VII.

CHAPTER VIII.

CHAPTER IX.

CHAPTER X.

The only Man left in College on Christmas Day.

CHAPTER I.

CHAPTER II.

ILLUSTRATIONS IN THE TEXT,

BY THE AUTHOR.

LITTLE MR. BOUNCER

AND

HIS FRIEND VERDANT GREEN.

CHAPTER I.

LITTLE MR. BOUNCER MAKES A CALL ON HIS FRIEND VERDANT GREEN.

"ULLO, Giglamps!" It was the unmistakable cheery voice of little Mr. Bouncer. He had crossed from his own rooms in the grand old College of Brazenface, Oxford, and had stopped on a certain landing, before a door over which was painted the mono-syllable "GREEN." His battered College cap was on his head, but, as no under-graduate's gown was upon his shoulders, it was to be presumed that the little gentleman had not come from lectures, or returned from a stroll through the streets of Oxford, or from any other place where the wearing of

full academical costume would have been demanded by
the authorities of the University. Though, if the full
costume required by the statutes had been rigorously
enforced, Mr. Bouncer would have cheerfully bowed to

destiny, and would probably have imitated the gentleman who suspended his pair of bands under his coat
tails, because the law had not expressly stated on what
part of the body they were to be worn.

But Mr. Bouncer's sole academical attire on this occasion was his battered " mortar-board ; " and, in place of
carrying a Livy, or Euripides, or Euclid, or any other
book that would have betokened a recent attendance at

the rooms of Mr. Slowcoach or the Rev. Richard Harmony, and the other tutors whose delightful task it was
to teach the young ideas of the Brazenfacians how to
shoot '— instead of any tome of learning, little Mr.
Bouncer bore in his hand his long tin post-horn, from
which he invoked unearthly sounds, that re-echoed from
the staircase to the outer quad. He particularised this
performance as " sounding his octaves," and summarised
it as " going the complete unicorn." In addition to this,
Mr. Bouncer was smoking a cigar — that " Nicotian
herb " the consumption of which is so strictly forbidden
by another of those Oxford statutes, which every student,
at his matriculation, is solemnly required by the Vice-
Chancellor most strictly to observe. He was, moreover,
accompanied by two living creatures, who would not, by
any possibility, have been admitted to a college lecture.
These were his two famous bull-terriers, Huz and Buz;
most villainous-looking pets, with ponderous heads and
savage teeth and corkscrew tails, who, at every blast of
the horn, barked and howled, either in sympathy with
the noise, or in direct antagonism to its defiant summons; for, it would be difficult to interpret the feelings
of Huz and Buz when they heard their master's carica-
ture imitations of Kœnig's performance in Jullien's Post-
horn Galop, which, just at that time, was in the height
of its popularity, and was hummed or whistled in every
quad in Brazenface and the University.

The inmate of the rooms over the outer door of
which was painted the monosyllable "GREEN," had
" sported," or securely closed that outer door or " oak; "
and this not only prevented little Mr. Bouncer from
gaining immediate admission, but also caused him to
prolong the fanfares on his tin horn and furnished Huz

and Buz with a pardonable excuse for indulging in· a canine chorus; all of which was most detrimental to the peace of mind of Mr. Sloe, the peripatetic reading man in the garret above, whose study of Aristophanes had already been disturbed by the doleful performance of " Away with Melancholy," given on the cornet-à-piston at an open window on the ground-floor, by a gentleman whose love for music surpassed his power of expression and execution.

"Hullo, Giglamps!" shouted little Mr. Bouncer, after his Post-horn overture; " open sesame, old fellow; and let the forty thieves come in. Blow, warder, blow thy sounding horn; and never say blow it; but, thy banners wave on high. Why don't you wave your banners, Giglamps? here's the warder calling till he is hoarse. He's in, is n't he, Robert?"

Mr. Robert Filcher — the scout, who, as servant, waited on Mr. Verdant Green and the gentlemen who were on that staircase — was coming along the passage with a supply of eatables from the Buttery, and replied, " I know he 's in, sir; for he 's took out a *Æger*, and I 'm just taking him his Commons. He 's not had no sober-water this morning, and I 'm not aweer as he were pleasant last night; but, he 's sported his oak, not wishing to see nobody."

As Mr. Filcher spoke these words, the outer door was opened by a tall, benevolent-looking, smooth-faced gentleman, in spectacles; and Mr. Verdant Green gave admittance to his new friend, little Mr. Bouncer, and also to his scout, who laid the supply from the Buttery on the table, and, on hearing " there 's nothing more that I want, thank you, Robert," made his exit from the room.

.It was halfway through the first term of Mr. Verdant Green's University existence, and he was still, in every sense of the word, an Oxford Freshman. It was not so very many weeks since that memorable day on which he and his father had travelled up from the Manor Green,

Warwickshire, and, on the outside of the Oxford coach, had formed their first acquaintance with little Mr. Bouncer and other Oxford men, some of whom were destined to be better known to him in his University career. In the interval since that day, the casual acquaintanceship of the coach-journey had ripened into an intimacy that was fast settling into firm friendship. Mr. Verdant Green had gone through his intuition as an Oxford Freshman so meekly and with such good humour, that Mr. Charles Larkyns, and many others besides Mr. Bouncer, had taken very kindly to him, and were disposed to spare him when the temptation offered itself to make fresh attempts upon his credulity. But, although he had gained a certain amount of experience that would prove of great value to him in his future life, he had abundance yet to learn in that most difficult yet useful study; and it was fated that little Mr. Bouncer should be one of his preceptors.

"Hullo, Giglamps!" he cried, as Mr. Filcher left the room, "here we are again! how were you to-morrow, as the Clown says in the Pantermine? You look peakyish. What's the row?"

"I did not feel quite the thing; so, I thought I would not go to Chapel or Lectures; and Robert sent in an Æger for me," replied Mr. Verdant Green.

"What! cut Chapel and posted an Æger, for the second time in one week; and you only in your first term!" cried little Mr. Bouncer, with something like admiration in his tone. "'Pon my word, young 'un, you're coming it strong. Perhaps it's a deep-laid scheme of yours to post a heap of Ægers while you're a Freshman, and then to get better and better every term, and make the Dons think that you are improving the shining hours by doing Chapels and Lectures more regularly. Artful Giglamps!" Here Mr. Bouncer's attention was distracted by his dogs. "Huz! you troublesome beggar, lie down, and don't worry the gentleman's calves and make yourself generally disagreeable. Buz! drop that, you little wretch; or I'll know the reason why."

"Never mind," said Mr. Verdant Green; "it's only a slipper that my sister Mary worked for me. He won't hurt it."

"Won't he?" cried little Mr. Bouncer, who evidently knew his dog's propensities. "It's Berlin wool, ain't it? If so, he'll soon make it like Uncle Ned's head, and it'll have no wool on the top, just the place where the wool ought to grow. But, it's his education that does it. Once bring up a dog to worry rats out of a Wellington boot, and it demoralises him for his place in society as a companion and friend of man. He thinks that every slipper contains nothing less than a mouse. Now, Buz! drop it." Little Mr. Bouncer reduced his dogs into a state of comparative subordination; and then, turning to Mr. Verdant Green, who was looking somewhat disconsolate, said, "I say, old fellow, how peaky you seem! You look as if you had been at a tea-fight or a muffin-worry, and had taken more hot toast than was good for your digestion. What's the matter?"

"Oh, nothing very particular," replied Mr. Verdant Green, although in a tone that implied the contrary to be the case.

"What! not tell it to its faithful Bouncer! Oh, what base ingratitude is here! Make a clean breast of it, old fellow, and then I'll see if I can minister to a mind diseased, as some cove says in Shikspur."

And little Mr. Bouncer puffed at his cigar, hit the obtrusive Buz with his post-horn, and awaited Mr. Verdant Green's explanation.

CHAPTER II.

LITTLE MR. BOUNCER EXTRACTS FROM MR. VERDANT GREEN THE CAUSE OF HIS DESPONDENCY.

"NOW then! spit it out, Giglamps!" said little Mr. Bouncer, as he sat on the edge of a table, and puffed his cigar.

Thus encouraged, Mr. Verdant Green made a sudden and desperate plunge into the deep waters of his trouble. "I 've been persuaded to make a book."

"What! to come the literary dodge and do the complete author? Well! I did n't think it was in you, any more than rat-hunting is in a lamb. And what is it to be called? Is it to be the Whole Duty of Man style, as applied to Freshmen in general and Verdant Green in particular? or, is it to be something facetious, 'Grins by Giglamps,' or something of that sort? What 's the book about?"

"It 's about the Derby," said Mr. Verdant Green, with a heavy sigh.

"About the Derby! Oh! that 's the sort of book, is it? I see, now, which way the wind lies." Little Mr. Bouncer gave a meditative and prolonged whistle, which, being mistaken for a signal by Huz and Buz, immediately sent them on a vain quest for rats in every corner of the room. "A book about the Derby!" said the little gentleman, when, by the aid of thwacks from his post-horn, he had reduced his dogs to a deceitful tranquillity similar to that of a volcano before eruption; "why Giglamps, you could just as soon write ' Paradise Lost,' like that mute, inglorious Milton did."

"I 've lost my paradise — at any rate, my peace of mind," groaned Mr. Verdant Green, too occupied by his own thoughts to take notice of the false application of his friend's quotation.

"Tell me how it all came about, and I 'll see if I can help you," said little Mr. Bouncer, after some thoughtful pulls at his cigar. "Two heads are better than one, although mine 's but an addled one. The fact is, I 'd too much pap when I was a baby, and it got into my noddle. But, how was it?"

"You know Blucher Boots? — the Honourable Blucher Boots, son of Lord Balmoral?" added Mr. Verdant Green in explanation.

"Know him!" cried little Mr. Bouncer; "yes! who does n't know him? Although he 's Honourable by name, he 's not by nature. He 's as genuine a cad as was ever pupped; and if some feller would give him a good licking, and take the conceit out of him, it would be a public benefit. And did he help you to make your book on the Derby, Giglamps?"

"He did," replied the other. "At least he made it all himself; for I did not understand anything about it. I never saw a horse-race, and have never been accustomed to read much about them; and I am quite ignorant about taking bets, and laying odds, and all that sort of things; so Blucher Boots undertook to make what he called a book for me."

"I see!" said little Mr. Bouncer; "it's like the old rhyme — 'Who'll make his book? I, says the Rook.' And Blucher Boots is a regular rook. He'd bet with his own grandmother, if he could, and would cheat her out of every penny if he could get on her blind side. He's a nice young man for a small tea-party, I don't think. The less you have to do with him the better, Giglamps. Now let's hear all about it. Where did you tumble up against him?"

"I met Mr. Flexible Shanks, Lord Buttonhole's son, at Fosbrooke's wine party," replied Mr. Verdant Green, "and he very kindly asked me to come to his rooms, and I went; and there I met Blucher Boots, and he invited me to breakfast with him the next morning, and I accepted, and went."

"That little pig went to market, and this little pig stayed at home!" sang little Mr. Bouncer, in a voice that was almost too much for the feelings of Huz and Buz, who gave vent to their emotions by smothered growls. "It would have been better for you, Giglamps, if you stayed at home with this little pig — meaning me — and not have gone to Blucher Boots's breakfast."

"I went," said Verdant, simply, "because I thought it a great compliment to be invited to the rooms of two sons of noblemen, when I was not previously known to them, and was only a Freshman."

"Precisely!" rejoined little Mr. Bouncer, "I'll say nothing against Flexible Shanks, for he's a regular brick; but I expect it was because you were a Freshman that Blucher Boots asked you."

"But, at any rate, it was very friendly and polite of him to invite me to breakfast," argued Mr. Verdant Green, who would have wished it to be thought that the attentions of Lord Balmoral's son were due solely to his personal merits, and were not to be attributed to the fact of his being a Freshman.

"And so you went," said little Mr. Bouncer, "with the tear of gratitude in your eye, and a burst of loyalty in your bosom. Well, and what then? Cut along, my hearty."

"After breakfast," continued Verdant, "the men gradually went away; but he asked me to stop, and have a weed with him; and I did so, because I was all right for Lectures, having posted an Æger."

"Posted an Æger!" echoed Mr. Bouncer. "My gum, Giglamps, you're coming it, for a Freshman. You pretend to be Æger, or sick and peaky, when you're in robust health. And then, after your Æger breakfast — where, of course, you behaved yourself like a sick man ought to do, and had nothing but tea and dry toast — what came next?"

"Then Blucher Boots and I were left alone, and he was very friendly and pleasant, and asked me about Warwickshire, and places that I knew; and his claret-cup was very nice; and he talked a good deal about horses and races, and the odds."

"Odd if he wouldn't!" said little Mr. Bouncer, puffing at his cigar; "I know his horsey proclivities. And then he offered to make your Derby book?"

" Well," replied Mr. Verdant Green — as people often do when they are speaking of something that is not at all well, but bad — " something like it. He told me that he had a friend who had been kind enough to tell him, quite in confidence, which horse is to win the Derby. It is not the favourite; but it is a horse that, at present, is not much talked about. He said it was a dark horse; but whether a black or a brown, I don't know."

Little Mr. Bouncer involuntarily winked his eye, and smiled, as though he would direct an imaginary companion's attention, and say, " Oh, here 's a go ! " but his Freshman friend was too much engaged in his narrative to notice the action.

" And Blucher Boots' friend," continued Verdant, " has kept his eye on the horse for a long time, and has seen him tried on a private course, and is in a particular position to obtain correct information on the subject. And Blucher Boots himself has seen this dark horse, whose name I may tell you — but of course, in the strictest confidence."

" Of course ! the very strictest of the strict, Giglamps ! I 'll be as dark as the horse."

" His name is ' The Knight.' "

" That Knight ought to be ridden by Day, ought n't he? Oh, Day and Knight, but this is wondrous strange ! 'as Shikspur says."   And the countenance of little Mr. Bouncer, as he watched Mr. Verdant Green, was quite a study.

" And," continued that innocent gentleman, " Blucher Boots, to use his own expression; is sweet upon The Knight, and is firmly convinced that no other horse, not even the favourite, has the slightest chance to win the race from him. So that he is going to support him to the best of his ability, and said that he should put a pot of money on him — an expression that I do not fully comprehend."

"It means," explained Mr. Bouncer, "that the money he will bet on the dark horse will go to the pot — that is, will be all U. P. and done for; like classical parties, who, when dead, were burnt, and had their ashes put into pots or urns." The little gentleman knocked off the ash of his cigar, and asked, "And what did B. B., which stands for Bad Boy, do then?"

"Why, then he spoke about having made his book for the Derby, and that he had done it so cleverly, and on such a sure plan, that he must be a gainer even if The Knight did not win; although he thought such an event. was an impossibility. And then he offered to show me how to make a book; and I tried to comprehend him, but I could not do so; although I fear that I gave him to understand that his explanations were quite clear to me. And he rather confused me by referring to a sweep; and although I knew that, on a race-course, people must meet with all sorts of queer characters, yet I thought it rather odd that a nobleman's son should appear to be so familiar with a sweep. And he strongly advised me to do what seemed to me a very strange thing; and that was, to join him in a sweep."

Little Mr. Bouncer chuckled to himself, and said, "I suppose, Giglamps, you took him for a cannibal of the Fa-fe-fi-fo-fum species; and, if you did, old fellow, you'd not be very far off the mark; for Blucher Boots would pick your bones as clean as a chicken, and get every shilling out of your pocket. He's so hard up that he can scarcely rub two half-crowns against each other, and a sovereign might dance in his pocket without breaking its shins. Did he get anything out of you?"

"I am sorry to say he did," sighed Mr. Verdant Green, with a retrospective glance at his past conduct. "He talked to me so much about my Derby book, and joining him in the sweep, and other things which I could not properly understand — and he put it to me in so many ways about the great advantages that I should secure by backing The Knight at long odds, — I think that was his expression — that, at last, when he asked me if I could oblige him with change for a five-pound note" —

"I 'm interrupting you," said little Mr. Bouncer; "but, did you see that five-pound note, Giglamps?"

"No; I did not."

"If you had, you would have seen what his creditors have not yet been privileged to witness, much less to handle," observed Mr. Bouncer. "Well, young 'un, go ahead!"

"And I told him that I could not change him the note; for, curiously enough, I myself wanted change for a five-pound note; my papa — I mean, my Governor — having, that morning, sent me, in a letter, three five-pound notes. And, when Blucher Boots asked if I had got the notes with me, I said 'Oh, yes!' and pulled them out of my pocket-book. And he said that they had been sent most opportunely, and that I could n't do better than to let him lay them out for me; and that they would bring me in ever so much more. And he, in fact — that is to say," stammered Mr. Verdant Green, as he somewhat hesitated to make a full disclosure of the truth, even to his friend — "in short — I — at last I handed them to him."

"What! you gave Blucher Boots the three five-pound notes? My gum, Giglamps!" Little Mr. Bouncer did not say much. Perhaps, like the monkeys, he thought the more. There was a silence for a few minutes. Mr.

Verdant Green sat in a dejected posture, with his head leaning upon his hand. Mr. Bouncer puffed savagely at his cigar; flung the stump out of the window; hit Buz abstractedly, yet sharply, with his post-horn, causing that canine monster to show his teeth in a highly threatening way; and, at length, said, "I don't wonder, Giglamps, that you look in a blue funk!"

Although Mr. Verdant Green attached very indefinite ideas as to the nature and sensations of a "blue funk"

— a subject on which Gainsborough's "Blue Boy" might have been able to throw some light — yet, the phrase sounded ominously in his ears, and, if possible, plunged him yet deeper into the deep waters of his trouble.

CHAPTER III.

LITTLE MR. BOUNCER TAKES MEASURES TO BEFRIEND MR. VERDANT GREEN.

ECOVERING somewhat from the prostration of that "blue funk" with which, according to little Mr. Bouncer, Mr. Verdant Green appeared to be overcome, the Oxford Freshman resumed his explanation, mingled with an apology for the conduct both of himself and Mr. Blucher Boots.

"He only borrowed those three five-pound notes: they were not for himself, you must understand; but were for my own Derby book, and were to be used in bets on my behalf. Blucher Boots said that he was quite sure of winning. He had calculated the odds according to mathematical rules; and, whether The Knight won or lost, he himself would be a winner, and, of course, I should go shares with him. And, it seemed to be such a good chance of gaining twenty or thirty pounds, which, he said, would be the very least that I should receive — although there was every probability that I should win as much as seventy or eighty pounds if The Knight came in first, which Blucher Boots said he would be sure to do — that," continued Mr. Verdant Green, somewhat incoherently, "I saw it was such a good opportunity — and the money would have been so nice — and I could have bought such handsome presents to take home to my sisters — and, you must remember, that I had all the benefits of Blucher Boots' superior knowledge — and he is Lord Balmoral's son, you know — and he said something about my being just the sort of man that his father would like to be introduced to — and he hinted at my coming to see them at Wellington House in the Long Vacation — and he seemed so civil and friendly — and it is for me that he is investing the fifteen pounds, and not for himself, you understand " —

" Oh! I understand perfectly," said little Mr. Bouncer, cutting his friend short; " and Blucher Boots shall find it another pair of shoes before I 've done with him. Oh, Giglamps! what would your respected parients say, if they knew that you 'd made a book on the Derby, and been and gone and done it after this fashion? Your Governor don't bet on races, does he? "

" Oh, no! I 'm sure he does not!" responded Mr. Verdant Green, heartily, as his thoughts fled back to his home at the Manor Green, Warwickshire, and pictured the form of his father, sitting tranquilly, after breakfast, and reading his letters and morning newspaper in slippered ease.

" And," continued little Mr. Bouncer, assuming the air of a Mentor, " I 'm equally sure that he would n't like his only son and heir to do so."

" I 'm quite sure about that," said Verdant, confidently; " and I 'm very sorry now that I have given away those three five-pound notes, and have been induced to make bets on The Knight. And the fact is, that it is fretting me very much."

"Well, don't fret yourself into fiddle-strings, old fellow!" said little Mr. Bouncer, encouragingly; "that won't mend matters. I'll see what can be done to pull you out of the mire. You trust to your faithful Bouncer to get you out of the pickle, if it can anyhow be managed."

"Perhaps I had better go to Blucher Boots, and see what can be done?" timidly suggested Mr. Verdant Green.

"Perhaps you had better do nothing of the sort," promptly rejoined Mr. Bouncer. "If you open your mouth, you are sure to put your foot into it. No, my tulip! you leave it to yours truly; and I'll do my possibles, as the Parley-voos say, to act as your confidential agent and go-between in setting matters straight. But, I tell you plainly, Giglamps,

if this sort of thing goes on, it can only end in one way."

"What way?" asked Verdant, anxiously.

"Why, this way! you'll run a fearful mucker," replied Mr. Bouncer, sententiously. "Come along, Huz and Buz, and I'll shut you up in the little shop for coal, while I go and see Blucher Boots. Ta, ta! Giglamps! Keep up your pecker." And little Mr. Bouncer took himself, and his dogs, and his post-horn, out of the room, with no small noise from his canine pets, and with a piercing fanfare from his unmusical instrument, which was heard sounding octaves all down the stair-case, and out into the quad.

Left to his solitude, Mr. Verdant Green made himself a very strong cup of tea — an accomplishment in which he was now tolerably perfect, thanks to the lessons in the science that he had received from his old bedmaker, Mrs. Tester; and as he sat over the steaming beverage, it painfully occurred to him that he also, like his tea, was, metaphorically, in a stew and in hot water. He did not attach any very definite meanings to those two phrases of little Mr. Bouncer, which had reference to his being in " a blue funk," and hinted at the probability of his " running a fearful mucker; " but although he was unable to grasp the full signification of the Oriental imagery of his friend's expressions, yet, undoubtedly, they sounded far from reassuring, and did not tend to add to his comfort. Nor did he feel any happier when he conjured up a gloomy series of mental pictures, which passed before his mind's eye in fantastic phan-tasmagorias, and showed him what the inhabitants of the Manor Green would think, and feel, and say, and do, if they only knew the course that the hope of their house was pursuing; and that, in his Freshman's term, he had already begun to bet on horse-races and make a book on the Derby. What would his father say to those three five-pound notes being handed over to the custody of Mr. Blucher Boots? What would his good mother think of his backing a dark horse — supposing that she could understand such 'a phrase? Would his sisters be disposed to exculpate his conduct, in con-sideration that it had made him the friend of a noble-man's son, with a possible introduction to Wellington

House? 'And would his aunt, Miss Virginia Verdant, be able to comprehend the darkness of the case when she was told the startling intelligence that her nephew had "joined in a sweep"?

Alas, that sweep! it was an *atra cura* to Mr. Verdant Green — a black care that rode behind the horseman and crouched astern the jockey on the crupper of "The Knight." He began to feel that he was indeed beginning to run that fearful mucker of which Mr. Bouncer had spoken; and he knew that such a race would be one that would be all downhill in facile descent to Avernus, and to a

precipice of danger and disgrace. Who should tell to what conclusion his book on the Derby would lead, and what would be its Finis? Could he look with pleasure to the last page of its third volume, or anticipate its end with satisfaction? Better to shut up its pages, and to fling the book into the fire, lest his own fingers and pockets should be burnt!

As such reflections coursed through his mind, he felt as miserable as he did when, not many weeks before, he had sat by his window, after his father had left him, while the strains of " Home, Sweet Home," from a German band playing just outside the college gates, were borne to his ears, and reduced him to a melting mood; 'so that, when Mr. Robert Filcher came into the room, he found his new master busily engaged in wiping his spectacles. Although it could not be affirmed on the present occasion that when the scout returned to take away the breakfast things, he discovered Mr. Verdant Green in the act of removing tears from his glasses, yet that gentleman's eyes certainly seemed to be somewhat moist, and, altogether, he looked like a knight of the rueful countenance. But, as yet, he was only a Freshman; and he had many things to learn, not only in a pleasant Oxford college, but also in the stern school of Experience, whose discipline, though hard, is salutary.

Meanwhile, little Mr. Bouncer was as good as his word, and at once took active measures to extricate his

friend from the pitfall into which he had been lured by one who had proved himself to be too astute and cunning for the simple nature of the other who had so readily fallen into his toils. Placing Huz and Buz in the coal cupboard just outside his door, and giving them, for their amusement, an old Wellington boot, out of which, during his absence, they could h u n t imaginary rats, Mr. Bouncer put up his post-horn, and thrust his arms into that ragged and scanty garment, furnished with a lappet and two streamers, which the little gentleman called his " tail-curtain," but which the academical authorities would have termed his undergraduate's gown. It was needful for him to assume this elegant costume as he had to leave Brazenface and walk up the High Street before he could reach the particular college which Lord Balmoral's son honoured with his presence; and, as the time had not yet reached the afternoon's hours, when caps and gowns might be dispensed with in public — the members of the various Colleges being then supposed to be leaving the city for a country walk, or for the river and cricket-field and other sports — including the hunting of rats and the shooting of pigeons and rabbits — Mr. Bouncer was compelled, through fear of being proctorised, to " sport a tail-curtain." If it did not improve his appearance, that was not his fault, but was a matter for the rulers of the University to rescind their statute " *De Vestitu.*"

In less than half an hour after he had left Mr. Verdant Green's rooms, little Mr. Bouncer was knocking at a certain door on a particular staircase, where, as he had ascertained from the porter at the lodge of the College, the person of whom he was in quest " hung out; " so, at least, Mr. Bouncer phrased Mr. Blucher Boots' tenancy of the rooms in question.

" If he thinks it 's the woodpecker tapping, he 'll be slightly deceived," said Mr. Bouncer to himself.

" Come in ! " was shouted from withinside the room; and Mr. Bouncer went in.

CHAPTER IV.

LITTLE MR. BOUNCER TROUBLES THE HON. BLUCHER BOOTS FOR AN EXPLANATION.

THE room into which little Mr. Bouncer passed was not a room that was " hung around with pikes and guns and bows," like to that of the famous Fine Old English Gentleman of the national song, but it was furnished after the fashion of a room belonging to a young English gentleman of the modern time — more especially of that particular species of gentleman which is known as the Oxford Undergraduate. There certainly were " bows " in the room; for archery was then in fashion, especially at those colleges that possessed extensive lawns; and the Hon. Blucher Boots, as befitting a son of Lord Balmoral, was not to be behind in the fashions of the day. But, instead of "pikes and guns," there were pipes and meerschaums arranged on either side the fireplace, on fanciful shields carved and emblazoned by Margetts. And there were numerous sporting prints, and coloured hunting scenes, and Landseer's animals, and pretty feminine inanities, all in elegant gilt frames, from Ryman's or Wyatt's; and there were handscreens and fancy articles in *papier maché*, on which the artists of Messrs. Spiers and Son had drawn the glories of Oxford from their most picturesque points of view; and there were Parian statuettes, and vases, and china; and there were handsomely-bound volumes on rows of oaken book-shelves; and there were two or three pairs of antlers (convenient for the support of riding-whips, walking-sticks, and such like), the owners of which had fallen to Mr. Blucher Boots' unerring rifle, at Glen-slipper, his father's shooting-box in Perthshire.

The furniture of the room was an evidence that the occupant was a person of æsthetical tastes; and that he was either wealthy or was in a position to obtain unlimited credit for the various articles that he had gathered around him. If the son of a Commoner has facilities for doing so, the son of a Peer finds himself indulged to an extent that is seductive and dangerous; and Oxford tradesmen are almost the last persons who should be blamed for the evils of the credit system. Very often they themselves are the sufferers, and find that they have fallen victims to one who is, legally, " an infant."

The Hon. Blucher Boots himself was one of these legal infants, and, physically speaking, was a tolerably fine specimen of the infant race. When, in compliance with his call " Come in ! " little Mr. Bouncer entered his room, he was sitting in one of his numerous easy-chairs, " in gorgeous array," like Villikins' Dinah, with a scarlet Turkish fez on his head, and a crimson-and-blue-striped dressing-gown belted round his waist, the while he smoked a short black pipe and consulted a " Racing

Calendar."   He was by no means an ill-looking young
man, although during his interview with Mr. Bouncer,
his countenance could assume an expression that was
the very reverse of prepossessing.

"Good morning!" said little Mr. Bouncer, as he

closed the door behind him.   "I 'm lucky to find you
in ; and not only in, but alone."

"The luck 's all on your side," sharply rejoined the
other, who seemed to sniff a coming breeze.

"Then I 'll make the most of my luck," said the
intruder, as he flourished his battered cap by its tassel.
"My name is Bouncer on the Grampian Hills, and also

in' Oxford — see Gazetteers and County Directories, *passim*. Henry Bouncer is my name; England is my nation; Brazenface is my dwelling place. You may have heard of me in the pages of History, although you don't seem to know me."

"Don't know you from Adam," said Mr. Blucher Boots, stolidly.

"Did you mention the name of Adam? I'm not acquainted with that party, so can't tell if there's any likeness between us," replied little Mr. Bouncer.

"You're a cool card," observed Mr. Blucher. Boots, as he puffed, somewhat savagely, at his short black pipe.

"Perhaps so. I was n't born in a hurry; so I've had time to look about me. But sitting's as cheap as standing; so, if it's all the same to you, I'll sit down while we have our talkee-talkee — unless you charge for your chairs, like those fellows do in the Park ; a penny to sit down on one, tuppence to put up your legs on another, and no reduction on taking a quantity."

As Mr. Blucher Boots kept silence and went on smoking, little Mr. Bouncer sat down, and said, "You could remember me, I dare say, if you chose to do so. We met ; 't was in a crowd — at Fosbrooke's rooms — and I thought you had done me; I've come, and you don't move, though your eye is upon me. I'd my eye upon you, that night; for I dropped the best part of a fiver to you, at Van John, when you were slightly lucky in turning up aces."

"Do you mean to insinuate "—— began Lord Balmoral's son, with a flushed face and angry scowl.

"Oh, dear, no! don't put yourself about, and get waxy, and make yourself as red as your fez; I don't

insinuate anything," said Mr. Bouncer. "Some people
have a certain person's luck ; and that seemed to be
your case. But, it was not so much the aces as the
betting. You're a first-rate hand at laying odds; I'll

give you credit for that; for I like to give every man his
due. And that's the business that's brought me here.
I think you know a Brazenface man of the name of
Verdant Green?"

"A Freshman?"

"Something like one. He is a particular friend of
mine."

"I can't compliment you upon your acquaintance," sneered Mr. Blucher Boots.

"Never mind that; I don't care for empty compliments," replied little Mr. Bouncer, sticking up for his absent friend. " Verdant Green 's not at all a bad sort, though a trifle fresh — as you have found out. And, to come to the point, it seems to me that you have been taking an undue advantage of his freshness and inexperience."

" I don't know by what right you intrude into my rooms, and read me a lecture," said Mr. Blucher Boots. " But before I kick you out "——

"Kick me out? " echoed Mr. Bouncer. " Two can play at that game, my beauty; and I don't think your shoemaker will ever become acquainted with my tailor."

" —— you may as well enlighten me," continued Mr. Blucher Boots, puffing at his pipe, " as to the supposed advantage that I have taken of your friend's freshness."

" With all the pleasure in the world," said Mr. Bouncer. " You have persuaded my friend, Verdant Green, who knows nothing whatever about horse-racing, to make a book on the Derby, and you have taken his money to invest on a certain dark horse."

" What of that! " exclaimed Mr. Blucher Boots. " Though the horse is a comparative outsider, yet he 's entrusted with good money, and has some big bets written in his name. His stable companion has been backed for a good amount; but he 's the better horse of the two, and I have certain private information about him on which I can rely. I 've put a lot of money on him myself; and if I 've put your friend up to a good thing, I 've done him a kindness."

" I don't see it in that light," said Mr. Bouncer; " and,

on Verdant Green's behalf, I have come to request you
to return to him the three fivers that he handed to you."

" I decline to do anything of the kind."

" You do ? "

" Most decidedly I do !" cried Mr. Blucher Boots,
angrily. " And it's like your impertinence to force
yourself into my rooms and to make such a proposition."

" Very well, then, my beauty," replied little Mr.
Bouncer, coolly, as he rose to leave the room; "then,
having fulfilled my errand, and got my answer, I'll go,
and leave you to look out for squalls. Betting isn't
allowed in college, as you are aware; and, all that's
done in that way is *sub rosâ*, and unknown to the Dons.
In their eyes, bets on cards would be bad enough ; but
bets on races and books on the Derby would be·looked
upon as something more than peccadilloes. As you
don't choose to hand back Verdant Green's three five-
pound notes, I shall go at once to Dr. Portman, the
Master of Brazenface, and lay the whole affair before
him. I shall do the same by the Head of your own
College. My friend will get off very lightly, because
he's a Freshman and inexperienced, and was led on by
you; but it will be a different thing with you; and if,
to-morrow you don't hear something about Rustication,
then my name's not Bouncer. It'll be a nice thing,
won't it, for Lord Balmoral's hopeful son to be sent
down to the country for getting a raw Freshman's money
out of him? There are unkind people in the world who
would, perhaps, say that it was as bad as fleecing a
Freshman; but, whatever they may say, you've only
yourself to thank for it. Ta, ta! my beauty. Look out
for squalls." And little Mr. Bouncer left the room.

" Hi ! here ! wait a moment, you sir !" called out Mr.

Blucher Boots, as he went to the door of his room, after a momentary hesitation. "If your Freshman friend don't choose to avail himself of my disinterested kindness, he's a fool for his pains. It isn't every one who could have had such a good thing offered to him. If he don't like to post his money of course he can have it back again; but he will be throwing away an opportunity that may never fall in his way again."

"I hope not, with all my heart," said little Mr. Bouncer; "so if you like to give him back the money he'll be quite content to lose his chance of making his fortune by your investment. That's about the size of it, I think." And they went back into the room.

"There are the notes," said Mr. Blucher Boots, as he took them out of his pocket-book; "and I hope I may never see your face again."

"That will be your loss," replied little Mr. Bouncer; "and it shows that you are no judge of pretty pictures. Your mug is none too handsome, I can tell you. But, adoo, Samivel! I've got the three fivers, so I'm satisfied. You can have a proper receipt for them, if you like."

The Hon. Blucher Boots made use of unparliamentary language, under cover of which little Mr. Bouncer made good his retreat, and returned to Brazenface.

CHAPTER V.

LITTLE MR. BOUNCER GIVES A BREAKFAST PARTY.

ERE are the notes, Giglamps," said little Mr. Bouncer, as he re-entered his friend's room at Brazenface, on his return from the interview with the Hon. Blucher Boots. "I had a squeeze to get them; for the fellow cut up rather rusty. But here they are, and joy go with them."

"Oh, thank you, so much!" cried Verdant Green, heartily, as he once more handled the three five-pound notes that had been entrusted to the charge of the son of Lord Balmoral. "You are a real friend. What can I do to repay you?"

"Why you can do this," replied Mr. Bouncer. "In the first place, you must cut that fellow's acquaintance; he's a bad lot, and will do you no good. In the second place, you must give me your word and honour, as a Brazenface man, that you'll never bet again in a similar way."

Verdant Green readily gave the required promise.

"I'm not over wise myself in some things," continued the little gentleman; "especially in reading and all that, and in those sort of things that the Examiners stump you with at the beastly Examinations. My first years must have been passed in healthful play, and not in books and works, as Dr. Whats-his-name says; and, I daresay, that what you call the intellectual faculties had n't a fair chance, and were kept dormouse, and all that sort of thing. But, in other things, I 'm wide awake and up to snuff, and not quite such a fool as I look; and I 'm wise enough to know that if you take to betting on horse-racing — of which you know no more than a kitten, and especially with men like Blucher Boots — you 'll soon make ducks and drakes with your money, and will go to the bad like a house a-fire. If you want to do it at all, it 's quite sufficient to keep to a little mild betting at Van John and Three-card Loo; not but what you may overdo that. But, as for horse-racing, keep clear of it, old fellow; and, if you take his advice in that particular, you 'll bless yours truly, Henry Bouncer. And now, I vote we do some bitters. My throat 's rather dry with so much speechifying."

So little Mr. Bouncer holloa'd " Robert! " and on Mr. Filcher's appearance ordered him to bring them a big pewter of that Buttery ale for which the College of · Brazenface has a deserved reputation. " That 's the stuff to make your hair curl," he said, as he reluctantly took his lips away from the pewter. " Who was the cove who sang something about dipping his beak in the Gascon wine? Here, Giglamps; you dip your beak in that, and it will do you more good than any Gascon wine."

" I can't help thinking how kind you have been to me," said Verdant, who was now looking more cheerful than he had done when his friend had first entered the

room on that morning. It was evident that the " blue
funk " had nearly cleared away, and that the Freshman,
having worked himself up to a state of feverish anxi-
ety, was now experiencing the delightful sensation of
unexpected relief.

" There ! never mind about the kindness," replied Mr.
Bouncer. " We 'll say no more about it. But, don't
you ever bet on horse-racing again — more particularly
with Blucher Boots."

" Indeed, I never will. This has been a lesson to me."

And it was something more than that ; for this little
episode in his life's history greatly helped to cement the
friendship that Mr. Verdant Green already felt for little
Mr. Bouncer. It showed him that, under all his pecu-
liarities of language and manner, Mr. Bouncer was a
person who was capable of giving him good advice and
was ready to keep him from falling into those snares and
temptations that beset every young man on his entrance
into life, and none more so than a home-nurtured, inexperienced youth who is suddenly removed from a
well-ordered household to the mixed society of a throng
of undergraduates, in a beautiful city where he can freely
procure all that he desires without troubling himself to
think of present payment.

A fortnight after, when the memory of The Knight
and the book on the Derby was beginning to fade from
Mr. Verdant Green's mind, little Mr. Bouncer entering
his room with a newspaper in his hand, said, " Giglamps,
old fellow ! your dark horse has been scratched."

" How cruel of them ! why did they scratch it ? "
asked the Freshman.

" Oh, you sweet innocent ! " laughed Mr. Bouncer.
"The Knight's name has been scratched out of the list

of horses for the Derby; so your fifteen pounds would n't have made your fortune. However, there was a good end to that business; and we 'll let bygones alone. What a splendiferous weedcase this is!" he said, as he took a cigar out of a blue velvet case that had been presented to him by Verdant Green, as a *souvenir* of the Blucher Boots transactions. "I think I was the only gainer by your book on the Derby."

"I gained experience and a lesson for life," said Verdant.

"So you did; and that 's worth something," replied Mr. Bouncer.

The days went by, and the end of the Term 'had arrived; but Mr. Verdant Green had not received another invitation to breakfast with Mr. Blucher Boots, nor had Lord Balmoral's son in any way condescended to notice him; in fact, when he next met him in the High Street he stared him full in the face, and cut him dead; the which Verdant by no means took sadly to heart, but ate his dinner that day in Hall as heartily as usual. But if he did not further cultivate an acquaintance with the Hon. Blucher Boots, he had made other friendships that would be more agreeable to him; and on the last morning but one of the summer Term he found himself at a breakfast party in little Mr. Bouncer's rooms, in company with his old friend Charles Larkyns, Mr. Flexible Shanks, Mr. Smalls, Mr. Blades, Mr. Fosbrooke, and others — in all a goodly company, blessed with good appetites and animal spirits. Perhaps there are no breakfasts more enjoyable than a College breakfast at the close of a Term, when the guests have not to run away to Lectures, and to prematurely part with their provisions in order to assume a forced acquaintanceship with Greek and Latin writers, or, still worse, with Euclid and mixed mathematics. On the present occasion, at little Mr. Bouncer's breakfast, they were able to partake of the good things provided for the occasion, and to linger over them with pleasurable zest.

The table presented the usual medley of eatables and drinkables, in which coffee and beer-cup, chickens and claret-cup, moselle and pigeon-pie, mutton cutlets and sardines, curaçoa and potted char, beef-steaks and grilled fish, cocoa and caviar, devilled kidneys and ome-lettes, anchovy toast and sangaree, found a place among various other refreshments, both heavy and light, that were fast disappearing before the attacks of the bevy of hungry undergraduates. Through the open windows was caught a glimpse of the City of Colleges, bathed in the radiant streams of summer sunshine, every turreted tower and soaring spire standing out clear and sharp against the blue sky. The grand avenue of limes for which Brazenface is celebrated, was filled with a murmur of bees. Below was the smoothly-shaven turf in the centre of the Quad, with the Hall on the one side, the Chapel on the other, and on either hand the rows of mullioned, heavy-headed windows, at some of which the unaccustomed sight was seen of young girls peering into the court below — an unusual but pretty look-out at Brazenface. For it had been the Commemoration week, when the feminine element puts in a strong appearance in Oxford, and for a few days in the year enlivens the old grey colleges with pretty pictures of beauty and fashion, and brightens up the rooms of happy under-graduates, of learned tutors, of stately dons, and miser-able Fellows, whose tantalising lot it is to look and admire, but not to marry, under pain of resigning their incomes. So at many windows there were pleasant visions of dimpled cheeks and rosy lips and flashing eyes, and through many a casement came the sound of girlish laughter; but these sights and sounds were absent from Mr. Bouncer's rooms.

"I couldn't get the Mum and Fanny to come," he said, referring to his mother and sister; "though I held out, as an inducement, that I would introduce them to you, Giglamps. That will be a treat in store, won't it? You must come and see us during the Long at our little shop in the country." In another day the Long Vacation would begin; and just at the time when the chief

portion of its population was about to run away from it,
Oxford was looking at its best.

The confused talk at Mr. Bouncer's breakfast-table
was somewhat settling down into more regular conversation, as pipes and cigars were lighted, and a perfumed
cloud began to float through the room and mingle its
scent with the aroma of coffee and spiced ale. Huz

and Buz were making themselves happy with platefuls
of chicken-bones, and their master was lolling at his
ease, with his legs stretched over the arm of his easy-
chair. Verdant Green and the greater portion of the
guests lingered at the table, while others looked out of
the windows, enjoying a smoke and the prospect — the
latter including pleasant glimpses of the young ladies
who appeared at the opened windows of rooms whose
owners were, in that respect, more fortunate than was
little Mr. Bouncer.

But what was said on that occasion by himself and
his friends must be told in another chapter.

CHAPTER VI.

LITTLE MR. BOUNCER ENTERTAINS HIS FRIENDS, AND IS ENTERTAINED BY THEM.

YIELDING themselves willingly to the pleasures of the hour and the enjoyments of the breakfast-table, little Mr. Bouncer's guests made themselves happy in each other's company, knowing that on the morrow they would all be leaving Oxford, and would be travelling north, south, east, and west, preparatory to making more extensive (as well as expensive) tours on the Continent and elsewhere, and otherwise beguiling the months of the Long Vacation, until October should once again see them reassembled in their beautiful City of Colleges.

In the interval, Brazenface would be given up to scouts and bed-makers; and while Mr. Robert Filcher would stand as umpire at a scouts' cricket-match, Mrs. Tester would preside at a tea-party in the porter's lodge. Workmen would also be whistling and shouting for " mortar " in the passages and on the staircases where the " mortar-boards " were daily seen during Term-time; the necessary repairs would be effected; the burnt plank where a lighted cigar had been dropped, and whereby the College had been nearly set on fire, would be replaced; the yellow coruscation would be removed from the wall where an egg that had been playfully shied at a Freshman's head had missed its mark but left a stain; whitewash would also obliterate the various works of art, executed in burnt cork, on the

staircase walls, by little Mr. Bouncer and other ame-teurs, in which grandeur of effect and satirical expression were sought for, rather than delicacy of execution and flattery of portraiture; the smashed panel, through which a small but highly obnoxious Freshman had been propelled, would be made good; twisted gas-pipes would be repaired, and Brazenface would be put into apple-pie order.

Though it seemed to stand in little need of improvement, as it looked at the present moment, with the bright June sun shining full upon it, and with the unwonted bits of gay colour gleaming here and there from the dresses of the ladies, as they appeared at some of the mullioned windows, or strolled across those grass-plats which might not be trodden on by the feet of undergraduates. Cheery talk and laughter were also borne to the ear from Quads and rooms; and a due proportion of it came from the room of little Mr. Bouncer. Huz and Buz had finished their breakfast of chicken-bones, and had been much annoyed by Mr. Smalls, who had been vainly endeavouring to teach them to sit up and hold short pipes in their mouths — a proceeding which they had resented with much dudgeon.

"They think it low," said their master, "to do tricks like Circus dogs, even though you held out the inducement of acting as Clown. You 'd better let them alone. They 've a long journey to take to-morrow, and it won't do to upset their feelings to-day. Help yourself to liquors, Smalls, and don't interfere with the enjoyments of the animals. I shall be glad to hear your views on things in general, particularly on the political condition of Europe." And little Mr. Bouncer made himself comfortable, with his legs over the arm of his easy chair.

"Well; you know old Peter?" replied Mr. Smalls, as though he were hastening to comply with his host's request.

"What! Peter the Great? Yes; I 've known him from a baby. Fire away, my boy," said Mr. Bouncer.

"Old Peter, the cake-man, is the party referred to," explained Mr. Smalls — "the old fellow who is allowed

to come into the men's rooms. Well, the other day,
Tom Higgins was in his bed-room, and heard old Peter
come into the other room. Tom kept quiet, and old
Peter evidently thought that there was no one at home.
Presently, Tom heard old Peter taking the stopper out

of a decanter that was on the table, and holding a
monologue dialogue — if I may use the expression —
the while he helped himself to the port. But he did so
in a very original way. All the while the performance
was going on, old Peter was saying, ' Take a glass of
wine, Peter.' ' Thankee, sir; I 've no objection; here 's

your health, sir.' 'Do you like this wine, Peter?' 'Very much indeed, sir, thank you.' 'Then take another glass, Peter.' 'Much obliged, sir.' 'Take another glass, Peter; it won't hurt you.' 'Well; I don't think it will, sir; so I drinks to-wards you.' Here Tom thought it time to interfere; or, perhaps, old Peter would have kept up the imaginary dialogue until he had finished the decanter; so he knocked down a chair in his bed-room, and, under cover of the noise, old Peter bolted."

"The old rascal!" exclaimed Charles Larkyns, who was puffing at a long "Churchwarden" which he considered to be the very king of pipes, and that every inch of its "yard of clay" — if it were a true Broseley — was priceless. "The old rascal! But they are all alike, whether cake-men or scouts. It was only last week that I missed some of my best weeds, and I fancied that Robert had bagged them. I did not quite like to tax him with making free with them; but, at a venture, I said, 'How do you like my tobacco, Robert?' Instead of being taken aback by the question, he at once replied, with admirable coolness and self-possession, 'Not so much as the last lot you had, sir; they're a trifle too strong for summer smoking.' Now, I call that slightly cool. Perhaps the next thing will be that we are expected to supply our scouts with cigars."

"And submit the brands to them before they condescend to make a selection," suggested Lord Buttonhole's son, Mr. Flexible Shanks. "What a cheesy idea!"

"That reminds me," said Verdant Green, "that I intended to ask you if it was the custom to do what Mrs. Tester, my bed-maker, has done. The lock of my tea-chest has been out of order for some time; in fact,

ever since Mrs. Tester used it in showing me how to
make tea. I told Robert to get it mended; but I suppose that he forgot to do so."

" His memory would be safe to be bad on that point,"
observed little Mr. Bouncer. " It's an amiable weakness of his."

" So," continued Verdant, " as I found that I got
through my tea very rapidly, I shut up the tea-chest in
my cupboard. But Mrs. Tester said that the cupboard
must be dusted; so I let her dust it; but when I looked
in the chest all the tea was gone."

" I suppose that she had dusted that also," interpolated
Charles Larkyns; " without leaving you even the tea-
dust."

" I thought it better to mention it to Mrs. Tester, and
asked her if she knew anything about it. She said, oh,
yes! she had taken it, because 'gentlemen in general
liked their tea-chestes to be cleared out, so that they
might begin afresh next Term.' Is that the case? "
asked Mr. Verdant Green.

" Well, I expect it is — with Freshmen," replied
Charles Larkyns; " but you will be able to begin afresh
next Term, old fellow, without being a Freshman; and
you can then be quits with old Mother Tester, and wide
awake to her pickings and stealings. Has she got much
brandy out of you lately, eh, Verdant? "

" Not much," replied that goodnatured gentleman.
" Her spasms began to be somewhat of a bore; for, she
was always attacked by them whenever she found me
alone in the room; and as I did not like to refuse her
request to ease them with three drops of brandy on a
lump of sugar — which was the remedy that she was
accustomed to take whenever she was suffering from

an attack — I have tried, lately, to avoid her, and to go out whenever I thought she was coming in."

Nevertheless, on the following morning, when Mr. Verdant Green had " tipped " his scout and bed-maker, before setting off home- wards, Mrs. Tester was opportunely s e i z e d with spasms, as she was bidding him farewell. And as she pressed and thumped her sides in a terrific manner, and made every out- w a r d demonstration that she was suffering from internal agony,  Verdant benevolently inquired what was the matter.

" It's the spazzums, my good young sir ! " groaned Mrs. Tester, dropping courtesys at every sentence, like the beats of a conductor's *baton*. " To which you be'old me a hafflicted martyr. And can only be heased with three spots of brandy on a lump of sugar. And how I am to get through these spazzums doorin' the veccation. Without a havin' em heased by going to your cupboard. For just three spots o' brandy on a lump o' sugar. Is a summat as I am afeerd to think on, my good young sir."

Whereupon Mrs. Tester was so completely overcome by the mingled pain of spasms and the prospect of losing Mr. Verdant Green's source of relief, that the Freshman was weak enough to present her with an extra half-sovereign for the express purpose of supplying her, during his absence, with the means of obtaining her accustomed medicine.

"Which a half sufferin', my good young sir!" said Mrs. Tester, as she pocketed the gold coin, "is more than I expected on. And will hease my spazzums like the Poor Man's Friend. Which my own son once'st gave me a bottle on. As had beautiful red whiskers with a tendency to drink. And was known to his friends by a strawbery mark in the small of his back. And was fine growed and the very moral of you, my good young sir, — which drink were his rewing and enlisted him for a soger, — when the yaller fever cut him off like a flower in the West Ingies, — which the remembrance brings on the spazzums, — to which I'm a hafflicted martyr, — and my grateful thanks to you, my good young sir, — and wishin' you a safe journey 'ome and 'ealth and 'appiness."

But we are somewhat anticipating events. It was not yet the next morning, nor was little Mr. Bouncer's breakfast at an end.

CHAPTER VII.

LITTLE MR. BOUNCER HEARS SOME THINGS FOR HIS ADVANTAGE, AND OTHERS FOR HIS AMUSEMENT.

ITTING and lounging after breakfast in little Mr. Bouncer's room, his friends were making themselves very happy, having the last day of Term before them, and no lectures to attend. As much enjoyment, therefore, and good fellowship as it was possible to cram into the next twenty-four hours, were now to be packed by them into that compass of time, so that they might carry away from Oxford a rich freightage of happy memories on which to dwell with satisfaction during the ensuing months of the Long Vacation.

"Did you hear of Warner of Exeter's Wine, last Monday night?" said Mr. Blades. "I was there; and he had asked two townsmen — tradesmen; perhaps he had ticks at their shops and wanted to be civil; any way they were very decent people and capital company. They seemed very much at home and not at all disposed to go; and, when they talked about doing so, Warner, like bold Turpin in Sam Weller's song 'perwailed' on them to stop."

Mr. Bouncer could not resist the opportunity of repeating the chorus from Sam Weller's song. " ' Chorus, sarcastically. But Dick put a couple of balls in his nob, and perwailed on him to stop.' Fire away, Billy."

" One of the townsmen," continued Mr. Blades, " was a very cheery bird, with a first-rate baritone voice ; and he sang no end of good songs, and was highly convivial. At two o'clock in the morning the two townsmen thought that it was time to go. Then came the difficulty; it was too late for the College gates; how were they to be got out? Warner's window opened on to the street, from the first floor; so we got a ladder and

placed it carefully. and the two townsmen made the descent. It was a brilliant moonlight night, and no sooner were they safely landed on the pavement than a policeman laid hold upon them. The one slipped a half-crown into the Peeler's hand, and the Peeler pocketed it; the other one imitated the pantaloon in a pantomime, and cried, ' I saw you do it ! if you split upon us, I shall split upon you for taking the money.' And while the Peeler was hesitating what to do, they made a clear bolt, and we hauled up the ladder. Then we chaffed the Peeler, but made it all right with him, and lowered to him, with a string, a goblet of gin-flip, and threw him some weeds. The two townsmen have since been in a mortal fright at being discovered; but they are quite safe so long as the Peeler holds his tongue. If he should peach, the townsmen will be discommoned, and Warner will probably be rusticated; but as nothing has yet been heard of it, and as to-day is the last day of Term, I should hope they are all safe."

" I heard a good thing of old Towzer," said Mr. Flexible Shanks, referring to the Senior Proctor, the Rev. Thomas Tozer, who was familiarly known by the name that Mr. Flexible Shanks gave to him. " He was in the Corn Market yesterday morning about twelve o'clock, when he met a University man with his gown over his arm. Old Towzer called to him, and pretending to take him for a scout, said, ' Here! you there! When next you carry your master's gown to the tailor's, I should advise you not to put on his cap.' With that, old Towzer walked off. That was not bad, I think."

" Not at all," said Charles Larkyns; " but did you hear of the Dean of St. Vitus's? Downton, of that College, has a twin brother, who came up to see him for the Commemoration week. The Dean met this twin walking by himself in the High Street, and, of course, without academicals. As you know, the Dean is very peppery unless he is duly capped; and the twin passed him without raising his hat. ' Stop, sir!' said the Dean; 'I am astonished that you should thus pass me without taking any notice of me.' ' I am not aware,' replied the twin, 'that I have the pleasure of knowing you.' ' Not know me!' cried the Dean; ' not know me! Why, is not your name Downton?' ' Yes; that is my name,' answered the twin. ' Then, sir,' fumed the Dean, ' what do you mean by passing me without capping me? And, how is it, sir, that you are walking

about here without your academicals?   Go to your College, at once, sir; and to-morrow' —— Here the twin
cut him short: 'I have no College.'   'No College,
sir!' cried the Dean; 'do you mean to deny that you
are Downton of St. Vitus's?'   'Indeed, I do,' said the
twin.   The Dean rubbed his eyes, and could bear
matters no longer.   'You shall be punished for your
impertinence, sir; you shall hear more of this!' and
then he walked off in high dudgeon.   The end of it was,
that the other brother was summoned to appear before
the Dean, where the matter might have been carried on
much further; but he thought it best to save himself
trouble by taking his twin brother with him, and explaining circumstances.   The Dean, who is a very jolly
fellow, laughed heartily at his mistake, and made them
stay and have a glass of wine with him."

"Talking of wine," said little Mr. Bouncer, "which of
you men are going to Effingham's Little-go Wine to-
night?   Don't all speak at once."

Two or three responded in the affirmative; and Mr.
Bouncer's question caused the conversation to turn upon
the recent "Little-go" and "Great-go."   The examinations of that day were not complicated by the introduction of "Mods."   Enough, for most men, were the
"Smalls" and "Greats;" some men, indeed, found
them to be more than enough; and it was of one of
these unfortunates that mention was now made.

"Poor Ellison has been plucked again," said Mr.
Flexible Shanks.   "Although the examiner blandly
asked him if he desired to maintain his opinion, yet
Ellison persisted that *etsi* was the perfect of a verb, of
which *etiam* was the subjunctive mood; and he further
hurt the examiner's feelings by rashly asserting that *clam*

was an adjective, accusative, feminine; and declined it
for him — *clus, cla, clam ;* after which the examiner declined to receive Ellison's further shots."

"I hear, too," said Charles Larkyns, as he puffed at
his long " Churchwarden " clay, "that Broughton, the

gentleman-commoner of Worcester College, has been
ploughed for his Greats.   You know his way of answering, in his hesitating way?   ' It is — aw — generally —
aw — thought — aw, that' so-and-so;   just as though he
had carefully digested all the known authorities on the
subject, and gave the result of their opinions to the

examiner. He had, as usual, fallen back on the stock answer, and had asserted that some city, of whose geographical position he was densely ignorant, was — aw — generally thought — aw — to be an — aw — island in the Ægean Sea; and he had also assured the examiner that it was — aw — generally thought — aw — that Troy was — aw — the capital of Italy; when the examiner, beginning to lose his temper, said — and, like the Verkus Boy of the song, he 'said it, and he said it with a sneer,' 'Perhaps, sir, you will be good enough to favour me with your opinion as to what country London is the capital of?' Upon which Broughton, as cool as a cucumber, hummed and hawed, and said, ' It is — aw — generally thought — aw — that it is — aw — the capital of England.' 'Generally thought, sir!' roared the examiner; 'why! was it ever doubted?' And then he plucked him. Alas, for Broughton! he was not like Adolphus Smalls, of Balliol, of whom — parodying the lines from ' Lars Porsenna' of Clusium,

> It was more than three stout oxen
> Could plough from morn to night —

it was said,

> He was more than three examiners
> Could plough from morn to night.

No! poor Broughton, if he had been in tune for it, could have sung with the Oxford Plough'd Boy —

> I am plough'd ! I am plough'd ! and the second time, too !
> I 've got no Testamur; what am I to do?
> Off, off, with my bands, and off, off, with my tie !
> I am plough'd, I am plough'd, and I cannot tell why.
> I read very hard the whole of last Term:
> I worked with a Coach — in vacation was firm;
> I went up to Town for a week, I confess,

To see a sick uncle — I could n't do less.
Short, short, were my slumbers, as paper-work near'd ;
My Logic was shady, my Latin I fear'd ;
Up, up in the morning — up, up late at night ;
And yet I am plough'd and my tutor is right.

Little Mr. Bouncer, with his love for a chorus, repeated the last line with great vigour, and would feign have volunteered an accompaniment on his post-horn; but (happily) that instrument was not just within his reach, and he was too comfortably ensconced in his easy-chair to rise up to get it; so he demanded an encore, and repeated the chorus to his great satisfaction.

Other specimens from the recent examinations were then quoted; but as they were for the most part replies to questions in the Divinity *vivâ voce*, the talk of them had better be left to the obscurity of the cigar-smoke in little Mr. Bouncer's room. It was very evident, however, that more than one Mr. Anser had failed to answer his examiners' questions, except in an outrageously absurd way; and that poor Mr. Goosey, in spite of his assumed look of wisdom, was in danger of being plucked. But, such is the goose's doom.

CHAPTER VIII.

LITTLE MR. BOUNCER BEGS CHARLES LARKYNS TO UNFOLD HIS TALE.

LITTLE Mr. Bouncer's guests were continuing their talk concerning the recent examinations, and the various unfortunates who had " come to grief" by the " ploughings " and " pluckings," that, in University parlance, signified rejection and failure. The plucking process seemed to be well-nigh as painful as the plucking of live geese for a few of their wing feathers and the soft down of their breasts — a scene afterwards witnessed by little Mr. Bouncer and Mr. Verdant Green when they were in the Cheviot country on a visit to the Honeywoods; and when they saw it, their lively imaginations converted the old woman into a real college Don, and the poor plucked geese into helpless undergraduates.

" At any rate," said Mr. Blades, commonly known as " Billy," the captain of the Brazenface Boat, " Broughton would not come to grief through too much cleverness, as they say Harwood, of Lincoln, did; for, when the examiners asked him some question on a frightfully abstruse subject, and said, ' What is your opinion on that point?' he replied, 'I should like to ask what is *your* opinion, gentlemen?' And it was generally thought — as Broughton would have phrased it —that the examiners could not have explained it to him half so clearly as he could to them. However, how it was I don't know; but it is certain that Harwood was recommended to wait for the next examination; and most people fancied that he was sent down for his bumptiousness."

"Some men," said Charles Larkyns, "get through by a fluke, and some men get plucked by a fluke."

"Charley, don't be personal!" groaned little Mr. Bouncer. "You hurts my feelings. I went to your rooms twice yesterday, and could n't find you. Where were you, and what were you doing with yourself? Tell us all about it."

"That 's a skilful way of diverting remarks from yourself, Bouncer, and carrying the war into the ene-my's country," said Mr. Flexible Shanks. "But by all means let us hear how Larkyns was improving the shining hours."

Charles Larkyns took a pull at his pipe and another at his pewter, and said, "So you want to know what I was doing with myself yesterday? Then, lend me your ears, and list, list, oh, list!"

"That's quite the recruiting sergeant," observed Mr. Bouncer. "Now Charley, unfold your tale, there's a good old doggie." And he patted Buz's head, who took the observation as intended for himself.

"You must know, then, my beloved friends, and all whom it may concern," said Charles Larkyns, "that I went down to Nuneham, with some men, in a house-boat. I daresay, altogether, there were about fifty of us, and Smirke, of Balliol, was there. He is a man who gets excited on a bottle of pop; and, as he had injudiciously mixed his liquors, although he had not taken much, yet the little he had imbibed had got into his head, and made him unusually hilarious. Just after we had started on our way home, I was sitting by him, and when some one offered him some claret-cup I advised him not to touch it, but to have a drink of water if he felt thirsty. 'Would the water be best for me, do you think?' said Smirke! 'because, if so, I had better have a good draught.' And, with that, before I could stop him, he jumped on to the side of the boat, and took a header into the river. We knew that he was a first-rate swim-mer; so we were not alarmed at his thus taking a bath with his clothes on; and he very soon appeared on the surface, puffing and blowing like a grampus. We quickly pulled him on board, and he was taken into the cabin, where he shook himself out of his wet clothes, and was rigged out in a new suit by subscription. One

man, who had a jersey on, lent him his shirt; another
man gave him a pair of boating-trousers that he had on
board; another, a boating-coat; another, a straw hat;
and so on. In order to prevent his catching cold,
indiscreet friends exhibited to him, as Doctors say, a
mixture of hot brandy-and-water, in which, I expect,
the spirit was in excess of the water. After this, Smirke
again grew hilarious; and one man after another kept
coming down into the cabin, and saying, 'Well done,
old fellow! you did that splendidly! you took to the
water like a Newfoundland dog!' and such like terms
of commendation.

"'You thought I did it well, did you?' said Smirke.
'Then I'll do it again!' and before any one could stop
him he jumped through the cabin window. As he did
so, the men who had rigged him out by subscription
thought it was high time to look after their property
and keep it dry. So the man who had lent him the
shirt rushed forward and managed to catch Smirke by
one leg, just as that leg was disappearing on the river-
side of the cabin window. But, Smirke being no
chicken, and, of course, being a dead-weight while he
was thus suspended in the air, it was too much for his
supporter, who, though he refused to let go his hold, was
gradually disappearing out of the cabin window. At
this critical juncture, the donor of the shirt was tightly
grasped by the donor of the trousers; and thus, for a
few seconds, the human chain was suspended, the donor
of the trousers exhorting the donor of the shirt not to
let go, and the donor of the shirt making a vigorous
but vain effort to keep both himself and Smirke out of
the river.

"Then there came the sound of a rent; Smirke's

trousers had given way, and yielded to the strain so unexpectedly put upon them; and their temporary wearer went headlong into the river, quickly followed by the owners of trousers and shirt; for the sudden jerk was too much for their equilibrium, and they top-

pled in after Smirke and after each other. All three could swim like fishes, and the only danger was that they might be lost through the convulsions of laughter into which those on board fell, and in which those who had fallen into the water heartily joined. Smirke paddled lazily to and fro, appearing to enjoy his ducking; and when the other two swam to him and endeavoured to convey him on board he declared that he was the Diver of the Adriatic, and that he was going in search of the ring with which the Doge of Venice had married the sea; and that the two others were base conspirators who wanted to get it from him: and a whole lot of bosh. Whereupon, they began a sort of duck-hunt in the water, which was no small fun, and which, from the jollity of its nature, seemed so infectious, that I confess

that I and a few others were very nearly tempted to join them in their worship of Isis."

"Oh! I say, Charley!" shouted Mr. Billy Blades, "don't do that again, or I shall vote that you are sconced. Your puns are ponderous."

"A pun' weight, I suppose?" laughed Charles Larkyns; for which further offence there was a yell of indignation. "But, to return to my muttons, who, in this instance, were like sheep being washed — except that it was warmer weather than that in which sheep are usually washed, and, consequently, the ducking was proportionately more enjoyable. At last we prevailed on them to cease their funning, and come on board; where Smirke trundled himself after the fashion of a Newfoundland dog when he comes out of the sea; and, of course, sent a showery spray over every one with whom he came in contact, while, like Mazeppa's horse, he urged on his wild career, until we locked him up in the cabin, safe out of harm's way. We were not long in getting back to Folly Bridge, where our three drowned men got themselves dry things at Hall's; and then, being dry without, must needs be wet within; and, so, adjourned to a tidy little shop close by, where we gave them some *callidum-cum* and got some *frigidum-sine* for ourselves; and so — as old Pepys would have said — back to College, and safe in before Gates. And there you have the full, true, and particular account of my doings yesterday." And Charles Larkyns filled the bowl of his long " Churchwarden " from a tobacco-box shaped like a nigger's head, and begged Mr. Bouncer also to fill his tankard.

CHAPTER IX.

LITTLE MR. BOUNCER TAKES PART IN A LITTLE-GO WINE.

CHARLES LARKYNS brought to an end the tale he had unfolded concerning Mr. Smirke, of Balliol, little Mr. Bouncer complied with his guest's request to fill his tankard, and said, "I shall meet Smirke to-night at Effingham's Little-go Wine. I hope he 'll be fun."

"What did you mean," whispered Verdant Green to his old friend, "by saying that you gave the wet men *callidum-cum*, and had *frigidum-sine* yourselves?"

"It's the short for hot-with and cold-without, my lad," replied Charles Larkyns. "Now that you 've come to Oxford, you 'll live and learn in a variety of ways."

"I have found that out already, have n't I?" said Verdant to little Mr. Bouncer, who knew that he referred to his Derby book and to Mr. Blucher Boots's dark horse.

"I believe you, my bo-oy," responded Mr. Bouncer, after the manner of Mr. Paul Bedford. "And, by the way, your friend The Knight has claimed maiden allowance, and is going to run The Great Mogul for a monkey."

"Oh, indeed!" said Verdant; which was a tolerably safe exclamation, as he had not the slightest idea what Mr. Bouncer meant; and the phrases "maiden allowance" and "running for a monkey" were quite as dark to him as was the horse in connection with which they were used.

Little Mr. Bouncer guessed as much, and said, "*Videsne puer?* d' ye twig, young un? Perhaps you 'd like to put a pot of money on him, eh?" But this was said *sotto voce*, and was not heard by the rest of the party; and, in the same tone, Verdant replied, "No, indeed; I've done with horse-racing. Many thanks to you for having taught me a good lesson."

"I say, you fellows," burst in Mr. Four-in-hand Fosbrooke, who was looking forward to the morrow, when he would be seated on the box of the Oxford and Birmingham coach, and would be permitted by the coachman to handle the ribbons, and temporarily to take the reins of government; "oh, I say, you fellows! have you heard a good thing that Hargrave, of Wadham, has done?"

"Paid his ticks?" suggested Mr. Flexible Shanks.

"No; I am afraid that that is not his particular form of good thing, and that his duns will still have to wait for the settlement of their little bills," replied Mr. Fosbrooke. "And it is odd how many of these little bills turn up just at the very end of Term; in order, I suppose, to prepare one's mind all the more to enjoy the pleasures of the Long Vacation."

"The little bill is made long for the Long," said Charles Larkyns. "But, what did Hargrave do?"

"Perhaps he screwed Big Ben in his Warden's room?" suggested little Mr. Bouncer, somewhat irreverently referring to the head of the college of which Mr. Hargrave was a member.

"No; he did nothing so dreadful," replied Mr. Fosbrooke. "I was reminded of what he did by Smalls's tale of old Peter, the cakeman. The baker's boy had paid a visit to Hargrave's rooms, when no one was there, and had bagged some wine from a bottle that was on the mantle-shelf, where, also, was another bottle containing medicine. The wine was Rosolio, and the physic was similar in colour. Hargrave found out what the boy had done, and laid a trap for him, in case he should repeat the experiment. He cleared out the medicine bottle, and clapped the Rosolio into it; and then put the physic into the wine bottle, and mixed it up with a stiff dose of jalap. The baker's boy duly came, when no one was about, and had his usual sip at the bottle; for, when Hargrave came back, he found that about half a pint of the true 'mixture-as-before' had disappeared, and that the Rosolio was untouched. The boy did n't appear again for two weeks. Q.E.D. Moral: he never, after that, touched Hargrave's wine, or his physic."

"I thought you were going to say he never smiled again," said Mr. Fosbrooke. "Well; my moral is that of Ingoldsby: Pitch Greek to a certain person, and stick to conundrums. We have done with the old Greeks for a time, and unless we are going in for a class we sha' n't want to meet with them all the Long. I must be off! I daresay I shall see some of you on the top of the Birmingham coach to-morrow. You 'll be there, won't you, Bouncer?"

"No; not this time; I have promised to spend a day or two with old Smalls," replied little Mr. Bouncer. "And then I shall wander home by way of the little village."

"I suppose you 'll be for the coach, Larkyns?" asked Mr. Fosbrooke.

"No; I too am wandering home by way of the little village, as Bouncer says," replied Charles Larkyns.

"London seems the shortest way to everywhere," said Mr. Fosbrooke; "but you 'll go back home by the coach, won't you, Green?"

And, on Verdant replying that he intended to do so, Mr. Fosbrooke said that he had better have breakfast with him before starting; an invitation which Verdant

accepted.   Little Mr. Bouncer also invited himself,
observing that it was his duty to see his friend, Giglamps, safely off the premises, for fear he should surrep-
titiously elope with old Mrs. Tester.   Then Mr. Bouncer's

breakfast party broke up, and the men went their various ways, in order to leave Oxford the next day.

In the evening, little Mr. Bouncer went to Effingham's Little-go Wine, given by that gentleman in celebration of his having " got through his smalls," or passed his first year's examination *in literis humanioribus*, also

called " Responsions."   " It was a very close shave, though," said Effingham, in acknowledging Mr. Bouncer's congratulations.   " I put on a tremendous spurt during the last month, or else I don't think I should have managed it, although I had the best ' coach ' in the 'Varsity.   If you will believe me, I never saw the inside of a billiard-room, or touched a cue, all through that month.   I can make up for it now, and I bless my stars that it is all over, and that I am well through."

That Little-go Wine was a far from quiet party; and the noise and confusion were not lessened by the songs that were sung, which, for the most part, were given in full chorus — a circumstance, however, which was not at all disagreeable to Mr. Bouncer's feelings; but when songs are shouted or yelled at the top of the voice, and without much attention to time or harmony, the result is anything but musical or soothing. Mr. Smirke was there, none the worse for his ducking of the previous day, but already anything but the better for an injudicious combination of coffee and punch. He had originally declared his intention of sticking to the former; but had gradually relaxed his resolve, and had glided into the punch-bowl. A couple of glasses were quite sufficient for Mr. Smirke, who was not, like the typical Englishman described by Iago " potent in potting," but rather resembled Cassio in having such " poor and unhappy brains for drinking " that he " could well wish courtesy would invent some other custom of entertainment." Like Cassio, too, Mr. Smirke, considering that this last night of Term was a " night of revels," had drunk " one cup that was craftily qualified," and yet had made " innovation," and was so " unfortunate in the infirmity," that he ought not to have dared to task his weakness with any more. Nevertheless, like Cassio, he drank more, and with the same result that befell Othello's lieutenant. After a third and fourth glass of punch, Mr. Smirke became obtrusively disagreeable and noisy.

To mild chaff ensued *epea pteroenta* and hot language. Supper was on the table, and a Mr. Bulpit, a " Skimmery " man, whom Smirke was addressing in language not borrowed from Chesterfield or Grandison, lost his temper, and flung a slice of tongue across the table into

Smirke's face. That gentleman, with the suddenness of movement that he had shown on the previous day, in leaping through the window of the house-boat, instantly returned the compliment with the whole of a cold duck, including the dish. Mr. Bulpit contrived to avoid the latter, which was dashed to pieces against the wall behind him; but he was not sufficiently quick to get out of the way of the cold duck, which struck him full on the nose.

Then ensued a scene of increased excitement and disturbance.

CHAPTER X.

LITTLE MR. BOUNCER IS ASKED TO ACT AS SECOND IN A DUEL.

IS not pleasant when you are at a supper party, and anxious to enjoy yourself, to be struck forcibly on the nose by the whole of a cold duck that has been hurled into your face by an individual sitting immediately opposite to you at the table. When, too, the dish is also sent with the duck, and only by your own quickness of movement escapes your head, to be smashed to pieces against the wall behind your chair, the clatter made by its broken fragments is not agreeable to sensitive feelings. Mr. Bulpit, of "Skimmery," felt this; and felt, moreover, the hurt of the blow and the indignity to which he had been publicly exposed. Being helped to duck in so rough and ready a way was decidedly an unpleasant episode in Mr. Effingham's Little-go Wine party.

To resent the insult was Mr. Bulpit's immediate resolve; and, to do so in the quickest way, he jumped upon his chair, and from thence on to the table, and was about to dash across it, regardless of plates and glasses, with the view of punching Mr. Smirke's head, and otherwise inflicting summary vengeance upon him, when Effingham caught him by the tails of his coat, and arrested him in his wild career. "Stop this, old fellow!" he said, as he endeavoured to drag him down from the table; "we can't have any fighting here. Bouncer, catch hold of Smirke!"

Little Mr. Bouncer promptly obeyed the summons, and at once seized Mr. Smirke by the arm, and tried to force him into his chair; for, when Mr. Bulpit had leapt upon the table, Mr. Smirke had also jumped up to defend himself from the threatened attack, and Mr. Bouncer, who had been sitting next to him, was on the alert to prevent the two quarrellers from coming to blows. "Let me go! let me get at him!" cried Mr. Bulpit; and "Let me go!" also cried Smirke.

"Not by any manner of means," said little Mr. Bouncer, as he tightened his grasp on the one side, and was assisted to hold the struggling Smirke by another of Effingham's guests. "You've shown one way of ducking a man's head, and you seem to be rather too fond of cold ducking. No, my beauty; you won't get away. It's only bears and lions that growl and fight, and your little hands were never made to tear out Bulpit's eyes; so you had better put your angry passions in your pocket. For the present, you must consider yourself my prisoner. I'm Detective Bouncer, of the A 1 Brazenface Division."

All the room was in a hubbub. It had not been by any means a quiet Wine from the first — Little-go Wines are usually noisy affairs; but now the confusion and racket were greatly increased. Mr. Bulpit was still forcibly striving to cross the Rubicon of the supper-table, and was wildly gesticulating, and uttering wilder threats as to what he would do to Mr. Smirke's head and various other portions of his body when he could get at him. At last, Effingham succeeded in pulling him from the table, and forcing him into his chair. Both the would-be combatants were in a pot-valiant state, and hot words were freely interchanged. More punch was also consumed by the two quarrellers; under the influence of which Mr. Smirke's speech became somewhat indistinct and incoherent.

"Shtrikes me," he said, as though the facts were just beginning to dawn upon him, "Bulpit 'tended to 'sult me. What you say, Bousher?"

"Strike you!" retorted Mr. Bulpit across the table,

as he caught the word that he now repeated; "why, you struck me with the duck!"

"You shied shlice o' tongue in my faish! hurt my feelings!" said Mr. Smirke, as he slapped the left side of his waistcoat. "My heart's in ri' plaish; feel for another, and all that sort-o-thing. Not to be shulted

with 'punity, I can tell you! then why shend shlice o' tongue in my faish? Thash what I wan' to know."

"There, old fellow! it was merely a slip of the tongue," said little Mr. Bouncer, endeavouring to pacify him. "Say no more about it."

But Mr. Smirke preferred to say more about it, and so also did Mr. Bulpit; and they noisily stated their individual grievances to those nearest to them, as well as to those remote. The clang and clatter were greater than in any rookery. A song, with the old chorus, "For he's a jolly good fellow," was vainly tried by little Mr. Bouncer; but, in every sense of the word, failed to produce harmony. Animal spirits were all very well up to a certain point; but, beyond it, degenerated to rude uproar. Throughout song and chorus, Mr. Bulpit and Mr. Smirke obtruded the wrongs they had individually sustained, and utterly refused to act as "jolly good fellows," and shake hands and end their quarrel.

"Now, do be quiet!" cried Effingham, addressing himself to Mr. Bulpit. "One would really imagine, to hear you two talk, that, after the manner of a melodramatic villain of a transpontine theatre, one of you will next say, 'This 'ere hinsult must be wiped out with bel-lood!'"

"Of course it must!" said little Mr. Bouncer, winking in a knowing manner at Effingham, and looking in a significant way to others at the table, in order that they might catch his meaning, and take the hint to carry out the joke; "of course it must! After what has occurred — after the gross personal altercation into which two invited guests of our esteemed host have permitted themselves to engage — I think, gentlemen all, that nothing less will satisfy the demands of the occasion than a duel."

Little Mr. Bouncer's hint was quickly taken, and a chorus of responsive voices was heard. "Of course! an affair of honour's the proper sort of thing!" "Pistols for two, and coffee to follow!" "A duel! a duel!" Mr. Bulpit's countenance fell.

"You'd wish for satisfaction, wouldn't you, Smirke?" asked little Mr. Bouncer.

"Shute me famoushly!" replied Mr. Smirke; meaning to say, that it would suit him.

But Mr. Bulpit heard the word, and understood it as it was pronounced. "Who 'll shoot you?" he said. "Not I, if I know it. You 're not worth powder and shot."

"Come, Bulpit," said Effingham; "you must n't back out of it."

"I shed shute me!" exclaimed Mr. Smirke, vainly striving at great deliberation of expression. "You shay that I shay shoot me. Never shed such a wor'! pononner! quia mishtake. I shed, shute me."

Little Mr. Bouncer and Mr. Effingham had taken the opportunity to interchange a few quiet words in the midst of the din and confusion. "It is quite evident, gentlemen," said the latter, "that there must be a duel. Nothing less will evidently satisfy Bulpit for his wounded honour, to say nothing of his wounded nose. Look at his poor dear nose, gentlemen, whereon still linger the greasy traces of cold duck; and then say what other reparation than an affair of honour can suffice to wipe out that gravied stain? Of course, Bulpit, you 'll fight! There 's no other course left open to you."

"Oh, yes, of course," reluctantly responded Mr. Bulpit, who failed to perceive that the whole affair was a jest, and that he and Mr. Smirke were to be made the victims of a hoax, and thus punished for their ungentlemanly conduct at the Little-go Wine; "of course I 'll fight, if it 's thought necessary."

"Nesheshary? courshe it is!" said Mr. Smirke. "You shulted me, and hurt my feelings! courshe it 's nesheshary."

" Then, gentlemen," said Effingham, " the two principals being agreed that a meeting with pistols is unavoidable, all that we have to do is to arrange the place and time, and make all other needful preparations — such as the attendance of a surgeon," he considerately added; an observation which did not tend to soothe Mr. Bulpit's feelings.

" Who 'll be my shecond? " said Mr. Smirke. " Bousher, old bird, you 'll shtick to me like a jolgood fellow, won't you? Never deshert a fren' while you 've got a fren' and a bottle to give him, as the shong says. I should like you to be my shecond."

" All right, my tulip; I 'll be your second," replied little Mr. Bouncer.

CHAPTER XI.

LITTLE MR. BOUNCER'S FRIEND PRELUDES THE DUEL WITH SOME TEA-TRAY AND POKER MUSIC.

"YES," said little Mr. Bouncer to Mr. Smirke, "I'll be your second; and I daresay, Effingham, that you will act as second to Bulpit?"

"Very happy, I'm sure; if you wish me, Bulpit?" said the host of the evening.

"Oh, yes; I should — like it of all things!" rejoined that individual; feeling, however, very much more disposed to ask Mr. Smirke to shake hands and be friends, and to forgive him for beginning the *fracas* by throwing the slice of tongue in his face. But Mr. Bulpit thought within himself, "If I do so, they'll all think I'm showing the white feather." So, out of the fear of being thought to possess and exhibit that most unpopular plume, Mr. Bulpit smothered his real feelings, being the more disposed to do so, as Mr.

Smirke appeared to be in a highly valorous state, and, like Bob Acres — before his duel — was ready to cry, "Odds flints, pans, and triggers! odds bullets and blades! odds balls and bullets!" so that Mr. Bouncer might have given him the advice of Sir Lucius in the comedy, and have urged him to decide the matter that evening; and then, "let the worst come of it, it will be off your mind to-morrow." In fact, Mr. Smirke became so very noisy and disagreeable, that his further presence at Effingham's Little-go Wine was unanimously voted to be undesirable; and he was summarily conveyed back to Balliol by two sympathising friends of his own college, who saw him safely to bed "in his room in the uppermost storey," where, like the hero of Dr. Maginn's parody, they "left him alone in his glory," prepared to give him the next morning,

A couple of red
Herrings and soda-water.

Little Mr. Bouncer had seen them safely out of the Brazenface gates, and had said to Mr. Smirke, "I shall be with you at six o'clock, sharp; and mind that I find you all ready for the duel. Effingham and I will arrange the place, and the time must not be later than seven."

"All ri'! all ri'!" was Mr. Smirke's response, as he once more essayed to explain to his friends what he considered to be the true state of the case. ".He shed that I shed shute me. Quia mishtake! I shed " ——

"There, old fellow, cut it short!" said Mr. Bouncer. "Never mind what he said, or what you said. Go to bed, and get to sleep, and don't get up with a shaky hand."

"Shaky," cried Mr. Smirke; "what d'ye mean by shultin' me? You're no great shakes."

"There! go off, and get to bed!" said Mr. Bouncer. "I don't want to insult you. I'm your second."

This sent off Mr. Smirke's thoughts in a fresh direction or train. "Shecond class! I always travel firsht. Tickets ready, gents! 'Timesh'! 'Shtandard'! 'Lustrated Noos'! 'Punsh'! — Yesh; just one more glash cold punsh. Thankee! Bousher old bird! fren' of my shoul, this goblet sip! Give me a lock of your hair, old fel'! I shall prishe it immenshcly!" On which Mr. Bouncer got rid of him, and the little wicket in the Brazenface gates was then closed upon him and his friends.

On returning to Effingham's rooms, Mr. Bouncer found that Mr. Bulpit had drunk to drown dull care, or to give himself fictitious courage for the morning's encounter — like the man in the song, who tried "to keep his spirits up by pouring spirits down;" and he also was taken away, and seen safely to his rooms in "Skimmery." Then a consultation was held as to the programme of the duel. Effingham proposed the Port Meadow as the place, and seven o'clock as the time. The two men were to be taken there by their respective seconds, with two others to watch the proceedings and to give the word to fire. The pistols were to be loaded with paper pellets. The seconds were to express to their principals their sorrow that no doctor was in attendance, and their assurance that no time should be lost in conveying the wounded to the nearest surgeon. The two combatants being thus primed for the duel, and placed in position, the word to fire would be given. The probability was that each of them would fire in the air; but even if they did not, no harm would ensue.

Then the seconds were to interfere, and declare that outraged honour was satisfied; and Messrs. Smirke and Bulpit were to be led away from the Port Meadow, to be thoroughly laughed at for having been victimised, and with a caution to behave themselves better for the future, especially in the matter of shying their supper in each other's faces.

Little Mr. Bouncer was in favour of Shotover Hill for the place of meeting, not only from its appropriate name, but also from its being a more retired spot; but, as they came to discuss the matter, they found that there were numerous obstacles in the way of successfully carrying out their plan, either at the Port Meadow or Shotover Hill, not only from the Police, and the Proctor and his "bull-dogs," but also from the circumstance that the morrow would be the last morning of the Term, and, consequently, that not many hours would be at their disposal. Very reluctantly, therefore, the programme of the duel was abandoned, and a milder form of bringing the two quarrellers to their senses was determined upon. This decision was ultimately arrived at very much to the sorrow of little Mr. Bouncer, who had anticipated much amusement from the mock duel, and, as he snatched a brief sleep on Effingham's sofa, he dreamed that he and Mr. Smirke were posted on the top of Shotover Hill, firing with a heavy piece of ordnance, at Mr. Bulpit and Effingham, who were posted far away on the towing-path on the other side of the river, just where the Isis makes the bend towards Ifley. In his dream, Mr. Bouncer saw the well-known spot where he had so often boated — the fringe of willows on the bank — the flat stretch of meadows, and the rising ground beyond, with its trees, hedgerows, and scattered houses.

It was all there, vividly and distinctly, and so were the combatants and their cannon; and little Mr. Bouncer awoke, to regret that the mock duel only took place in a dream. By that time, the hour had arrived when it

was necessary for the two seconds to go in quest of the would-be principals.

Mr. Smirke had not passed the night in sleep. When his friends had left him, as they thought, safely in bed, he remained there but a very short time; for, within the next hour, he suddenly made a reappearance outside his rooms, attired in the airy costume of a night-gown, but armed with a tea-tray and poker. With these he proceeded to a neighbour's bedside, and roused him up to inquire if he was "all ri';" but, being persuaded to

go away, he wandered to another staircase, where he encountered another Balliol man, the Hon. Felix Festoon, son of Lord Garland, ascending the stairs. Mr. Festoon had been at a wine party, and was humming a merry tune, when, with no small dismay, he suddenly came upon the strange apparition which arrested his progress. The light of the moon, streaming through the staircase-window, fell upon the white-dressed figure with ghostly effect; and Mr. Festoon might well be excused if, for a moment, he felt somewhat alarmed. That the ghost was brandishing a poker was also a circumstance that was not reassuring to Mr. Festoon's peace of mind.

"Shtop, sir!" cried Mr. Smirke. "You're making a mosht dishgusting noishe. You're toshicated, sir — beashly toshicated! 't will be my painful duty — mosht painful duty — to tell the Principal." Mr. Smirke had a considerable difficulty in pronouncing the last word; and it gave Mr. Festoon time to recover himself.

"You had better go to bed, Smirke," he said, "and let me pass to my bed. I'm tired, and I've a long journey in the morning."

"All ri', F'stoon! all ri'! Give my love to Garland — noble shwell, and ornament of Upper Houshe." And Mr. Smirke made a profound bow, and allowed Mr. Festoon to pass; but, instead of taking his advice, and going to bed, he wandered downstairs into the Quad, from whence tea-tray and poker music was presently heard, as though Balliol was hiving its bees.

Mr. Bulpit also distinguished himself on the same night. The friends who had taken him to his rooms at the "Skimmery," had not undressed him and put him to bed; and, after they had left him he wandered forth and amused himself in the donkey-like fashion of "kicking up his heels." Being shod with heavy boots, he tried their strength against the panels of various doors, and succeeded in smashing four, oaks. When afterwards asked why he had done so, he gave, by way of a reason, the answer that he had smashed two because he hated the owners of the rooms; and that he had smashed two others because he did not hate them, in order to make matters equal, and not create jealousy. This was an explanation which, probably, would not have been received with satisfaction by the authorities of St. Mary's Hall, who, in the interval of the Long Vacation, would have to see to the repair of the smashed oaks.

CHAPTER XII.

LITTLE MR. BOUNCER EATS TWO BREAKFASTS ON THE LAST MORNING OF TERM.

ISTURBING the solemn quietude that ought to dwell by night in the venerable quadrangle of a college, the tea-tray and poker music made by Mr. Smirke in the Balliol Quad was found to murder sleep in the most ruthless manner. At last, his discordant bee-hiving melody became so perfectly unendurable, that a summary stop was put to it by outraged hearers, who swooped down upon his night-gowned figure and forcibly bore him off to his own rooms, where they took measures to prevent a recurrence of the nuisance, by confiscating both the tea-tray and the poker.

Whether Mr. Smirke was put to bed by friend or foe, it is certain that when little Mr. Bouncer made his way to his bedside, at six o'clock on that sunny June morning, he found the bed to be duly tenanted by its owner, who was not only fast asleep, but was also snoring in a way that was almost as unmusical as the noise he had made down in the Quad, with his tea-tray and poker. Whoever had put Mr. Smirke to bed, had improved the occasion by artistically decorating his face with a large

pair of curled moustaches and threatening eye-brows,
executed with burnt cork. So far, therefore, as his face

went, he looked sufficiently valiant and warlike to be
prepared to fight any number of duels.

Little Mr. Bouncer drew up the blind and let the full
sunshine stream into the room and on the corked face

of the slumberer, who was sleeping so heavily that there was some difficulty in rousing him. "Smirke! awake, my beauty! my lady fair, arise, and, like the winking may-buds, 'gin to ope your eyes! You ought to be up and dressed."

"Oh, don't bother!" protested Mr. Smirke, not yet fully roused; "I want to go to sleep."

"Oh, indeed, you'll do no such thing," said Mr. Bouncer, as he gave him another vigorous shake and pulled the clothes off him. "It's all very well for Dr. Watts' sluggard to do the downy like the door on its hinges, so he on his bed; but I can't allow it."

"I wish you'd go away and not bother me," said Mr. Smirke, endeavouring to compose himself to sleep again.

"There, don't be offended! the only way to take a fence is to do it in that style," said little Mr. Bouncer, pointing to one of Alken's coloured hunting pictures that was nailed up on the wall over Mr. Smirke's head. "Come, rouse up, my beauty! not that you are a beauty without paint, as you'll see for yourself, when you come to look at yourself in the glass. If you don't get up at once, I shall give you cold pig. We've no time to lose; for, unless you are very quick, we shall not be there in time."

"Be where?" asked Mr. Smirke, rubbing his eyes.

"Where? why at the Port Meadow, to be sure," replied Mr. Bouncer, who was greatly tickled at the odd appearance of Mr. Smirke's elaborately-corked face.

"Port Meadow? What for?" asked that gentleman.

"Why, don't you remember? You were to be there at seven o'clock this morning — a duel, you know, with Bulpit, of Skimmery, whom you grossly insulted at Effingham's Little-go Wine, by shying a duck in his face."

At this brief mention of the scene of the previous evening, the wretched man's clouded brain was sufficiently cleared of some of its fogs and mists to recover a partial knowledge of what had occurred. "But Bulpit began it, with a slice of tongue. And — I have n't any pistols," pleaded Mr. Bob Acres.

"Oh! we'll manage all that. Look at yourself in the glass; you 've got your war-paint on already." And little Mr. Bouncer enjoyed Mr. Smirke's dismay when he surveyed the burnt-cork designs with which his face had been adorned. Then he made him wash his face and put on his clothes; and, during the time that he was thus getting himself dressed, frightened him by anticipations of the probable effects of the duel. At length the victim asked, "Is there no way of getting out of it? — of course, in an honourable manner." And Mr. Bouncer took pity on him by suggesting, "I fear that matters have gone too far. The only plan that I can think of, would be to write an apology to Bulpit; and, perhaps, you would n't like to do that."

"Oh, yes; I don't mind it at all," responded Mr. Smirke with alacrity. "If I shied the duck at him, as you say I did — and I confess that I don't remember very clearly about it — it would only be right in me, as a gentleman, to apologise to Bulpit: would n't it?"

"I quite agree with you. It is better to prevent bloodshed, if possible," replied little Mr. Bouncer, as he lighted a cigar, and threw his cap and gown on the floor. "But you must write the letter at once, if it is to be written at all; or Bulpit and Effingham will have started for the Port Meadow before we can stop them. You must pitch the letter very strong, and do the gentlemanly penitential in first-rate style; or it will be of no use to soothe Bulpit's savage breast."

So, while the little gentleman smoked and smilingly looked on, Mr. Smirke sat down and wrote a letter of

abject apology to his foe of the previous night. It was not a very easy letter to compose; but, by the aid of sundry hints from Mr. Bouncer's fertile imagination, it at last got itself written; and Mr. Bouncer hurried away with it to Effingham's rooms.

There, very shortly after, Effingham himself arrived, with a like letter of apology from Mr. Bulpit, with whom he had enacted a scene at St. Mary's Hall very similar to that which was being simultaneously performed, at Balliol College, with Messrs. Bouncer and Smirke for the *dramatis personæ.* It was agreed that the ends of justice could not be properly satisfied unless the two would-be combatants gave a breakfast at the Mitre to all who had witnessed their quarrel on the preceding evening; or, at any rate, to as many of them as would be able to accept the hasty invitation, and who would not be leaving Oxford till a later hour. This arrangement was heartily acceded to by Mr. Bulpit and Mr. Smirke, who greatly preferred the " breakfast to follow " instead of " the pistols for two."

As they were up and dressed, they at once sent out their invitations, and then went to the Mitre, where they shook hands, mutually apologised, and ordered the best breakfast that could be set upon the table. Thus, the proposed duel ended in a satisfactory and sensible way; and the two letters from the non-duellists formed a very fruitful theme for jokes at their expense, not only at that immediate time, but for many terms after.

Yet, when it was explained to them that they would have been made the victims of a hoax, and that, if they had met, their pistols would only have been loaded with paper pellets, Mr. Bulpit and Mr. Smirke were half inclined to regret that the programme of the duel had not been fully carried out, and that the Port Meadow had not been made the scene of their display of fictitious bravery. But, "all's well that ends well," and they joined in the laugh raised against them, and cheerfully shared the bill for the breakfast at the Mitre.

Of course, little Mr. Bouncer was there, though not for long; "for," said he, "I promised to look in at Fosbrooke's, and see him and Verdant Green off by the Brummagem coach; and, instead of feeling up to two breakfasts, I can't do justice to one. I must restrict myself to devil and Soda and B."

Either the soda and brandy, or the devilled turkey, prepared by the Mitre's *chef* in his best style, or the fresh morning air, gave little Mr. Bouncer an appetite; for, when he had left Messrs. Bulpit and Smirke, and had gone back to Brazenface, and had sat down at Fosbrooke's breakfast-table, he was able to take his due share of the good things placed before him. But, if he needed an excuse, he could plead that it was the last morning of Term, and that more than three months would pass before he would eat another breakfast in Oxford.

CHAPTER XIII.

LITTLE MR. BOUNCER BIDS FAREWELL TO MR. VERDANT GREEN FOR A BRIEF SEASON.

THE good things on Mr. Fosbrooke's breakfast table were done justice to by little Mr. Bouncer, notwithstanding the fact that he had already breakfasted at the Mitre, with Mr. Bulpit and Mr. Smirke. In the London season, "men may come and men may go," on the same evening, to two or three Balls, Receptions, At Homes, or whatever the entertainment may be called; and our hero may be excused if, on the last morning of Term, and under peculiar circumstances, he not only went from breakfast-party Number One to breakfast-party Number Two, but contrived to enjoy them both. And, in the matter of Brazenface College *versus* the Mitre Hotel, it would have puzzled a Lucullus to decide to which breakfast to award the palm. It must have been from a full knowledge of the powers of the College cook that Mr. Four-in-hand Fosbrooke, with an artful assumption of the capabilities of the Brazenface kitchen and buttery, said, "There's not much choice for you men; but I hope you'll find something to your liking. And if there's anything not here that you specially desire, Coquus will send it up in a twinkling." It was like to that fabulous host whose servant having, according to a prepared plan, fallen down as he entered the room with the turbot, cried out, "Bring another turbot!" and the other turbot, exquisitely cooked, was immediately brought. It was evident that a similar faith was reposed in Coquus, and that it was believed the Brazenface *chef* could produce any dish at a few moments' notice, even if the order were given for cassowary chops or roast ostrich.

"Coquus" was the name by which the head cook at Brazenface was familiarly known. He was a highly important personage, with an official salary larger than that of a resident tutor; moreover, he was believed to make, at the very least an extra two hundred a year by dripping and perquisites — things that were equal mysteries with the payments to the University chest. The eldest son of Mr. Coquus had distinguished himself at a grammar-school, and had been sent to a leading college in the rival University, where his birth and parentage were cleverly ignored, or only mentioned in a remote way that would not lead to detection. When pressed, Coquus, junior, asserted (with truth) that his father held a post in connection with the University of Oxford; further particulars were skilfully evaded. Coquus, senior, was not only a man who might be considered great, from his official position, but also from his personal dimensions. The warmth of his various ovens, fires, and stoves appeared to have developed

every particle of fatty substance in his body, and to
have bestowed upon him a rotundity of form that made

his figure most imposing to the spectator. The head
cook of Brazenface was not often visible to the outer

world in his professional costume; but occasional glimpses of him might be seen, as his portly figure filled up the doorway leading to the kitchens, the while he superintended the arrival of a whole cartload of meat, or received a smaller supply of sweetbreads from the basket of the butcher's boy. Dignity and diffidence were represented on such an occasion, when the great Mr. Coquus gave an audience to the small Cook's excursionist.

Mr. Fosbrooke's guests must have been hard to please if they could not find something to their liking in the various dishes which, under the superintendence of Mr. Coquus, were set before them; for there were beef-steaks, devilled kidneys, poached eggs and ham, curried chicken, veal cutlets, savoury omelettes with bacon, pigeon pie (or "dove-tart," to use the Oxford vernacular), and "spread eagle." Concerning this last-named dish, little Mr. Bouncer said to Verdant Green, "The Mum heard me talk about it, and made me promise to bring her a recipe for it; so I have got Coquus to write it down for me; and, when you come to us in the Long, and pay us your promised visit at my little shop in Herefordshire, I daresay the Mum will give you some for breakfast."

It may as well here be noted that the recipe for " An Oxford Spread-eagle," given by Mr. Coquus to little Mr. Bouncer, and by him handed to his mother, was as follows:— " Take a fine, tender fowl; split it down its back, and carefully press it flat. Grill it on a gridiron over a glede fire, from time to time rubbing it with butter, and sprinkling it with pepper. In about three-quarters of an hour it will be well cooked. Serve it up to table with mushroom sauce." When little Mr. Bouncer handed this recipe to his mother, he did not tell her that he had tipped the great Mr. Coquus with a sovereign. Perhaps such tips were a portion of the " perquisites " of the great cook of Brazenface.

" Pewter Potter promised to do some breakfast with us," said Mr. Fosbrooke.

" Pewter Potter? who is he? " asked Verdant Green.

" Oh! he is a New man," was the reply.

" A new man? Oh, I see! You mean a Freshman? " said Verdant Green.

" No; I mean that he is a New College man," replied Mr. Fosbrooke; and there was a laugh at Verdant Green's expense.

" Never mind, Giglamps," said little Mr. Bouncer; " this is the last day that you can properly be called a Freshman. When you come up next October, after the Long, you will no longer be a Freshman in name, and it will be your own fault if you are then a freshman by nature. Won't it, old fellow? "

" Either my fault or my misfortune," observed Verdant.

" You 're late! you must make up for lost time," said Mr. Fosbrooke to Mr. Pewter Potter, who just then entered the room.

" I had to see to the boats," explained that gentleman, as he seated himself at the table, and began vigorously to make up for the lost time. Mr. Pewter Potter took a great interest in his College crew, and had been recently coached in his trial eights.

" Your boat has done famously," said Mr. Fosbrooke.

" Yes," replied Mr. Pewter Potter; " though I hope we shall do still better next Term. But we had rather hard lines; for we had to pull in the wash of the Pembroke boat. Fortunately for us, Pembroke rowed in awfully bad form, and, at the last, had not a spurt left in them. We won by the skin of our teeth, and that was all. I suppose you are going down, as usual, on the box of the Birmingham coach?"

Mr. Four-in-hand Fosbrooke acknowledged that such was his intention, and that it was, even then, time for him to start. "So, I must leave you men to help yourselves. You and I must be off, Green, or we shall be too late for the coach."

Then, good-byes were said, and little Mr. Bouncer — who was presently followed by Mr. Smalls, Mr. Pewter Potter, and one or two others of the party — accompanied them to the Mitre, from whence the famous four-horse coach started to Birmingham. There also were other Oxford men, who preferred that old mode of conveyance to the newer railway; perhaps, because it carried them nearer to their various destinations. The breakfast-party given by Mr. Smirke and Mr. Bulpit was not yet over, for some of the guests appeared at the open windows on the first floor, from whence, as they smoked, they were looking on at the lading of the coach down below.

Little Mr. Bouncer and Verdant Green went into the coffee-room; and, as Verdant leant against one of the pillars near to the bow-window, and selected from his cigar-case a particularly mild Havannah, his friend said to him, "I'm like a parient to you, Giglamps! — coming here and seeing you safe off the premises, and keeping a sharp look-out, lest you should elope with old Mother Tester! Well, you 've said good-bye to Brazenface for a time; and now you 've got to say good-bye for a time

to yours, truly.   Don't forget your promise to come and
see me in the Long."

"I shall be sure not to forget that," said Verdant.

"Now, gentlemen, the coach is ready," said the
guard, looking into the room.

"Are you going to tool the tits?" asked little Mr.
Bouncer.

"No; I shall leave that and the box seat to Fosbrooke," replied Verdant.

" Well, good bye, Giglamps. Give my love to Sairey and the little uns," said Mr. Bouncer, with a kind remembrance of imaginary individuals.

Verdant Green clambered up to his seat behind the coachman; nodded another farewell to little Mr. Bouncer, who waved his cap as a parting salute ; the horses' heads were let go; and the coach clattered up the High.

CHAPTER XIV.

LITTLE MR. BOUNCER HAS HIS ATTENTION DIRECTED TO COACHES AND COACHMEN.

THE two friends, Mr. Verdant Green and little Mr. Bouncer, had bidden each other farewell for a brief season; and the former, mounted on the top of the Warwickshire coach, was quickly lost to the view of the latter, as the horses clattered up the High. In another ten minutes, the spires and towers of the beautiful City of Colleges, shining brightly in the full sunshine of a lovely day in June, were barely visible to the short-sighted gentleman whom Mr. Bouncer had called "Giglamps," although he turned round on the top of the coach, and peeped from behind its mountain of luggage, to get one other glimpse of the spot where he had passed his first happy and eventful term as an Oxford Freshman.

It was a very pleasant journey to Mr. Verdant Green. When they had got some distance on the road, the coachman gave up the reins to his box-seat passenger, who, from the workmanlike way in which he drove, showed that his *sobriquet* " Four-in-hand " Fosbrooke had been deservedly earned. When Mr. Fosbrooke had been put down at his destination, Verdant took his place on the box-seat, without, however, (as Mr. Bouncer had suggested), making any proposition to the coachman to allow him to " tool the tits," or " handle the ribbons; " which was quite as well, as the professional Jehu would have promptly, and, perhaps, curtly, refused his request. But Verdant made himself agreeable by supplying the coachman with cigars, and attending to his wants of " six of gin, hot," at the various inns where they stopped to change horses. Of course, Verdant smoked his weed as became an Oxford man and a box-seat passenger; and, although he could now perform this feat without a recurrence of those disagreeable sensations that he had experienced at his first wine-party at Mr. Smalls', yet it must be confessed that, on the present occasion, he somewhat exceeded his quantity even of the mildest Havannahs, and was not sorry when the coach pulled up at the cross-roads, where his father's carriage was in waiting to take him to the Manor Green. Having tipped the coachman, who had delighted him by observing that he " was a young gent as had much himproved hisself since he tooled him up to the 'Varsity with his guvnor," and having seen to the transference of his luggage (no longer encased in canvas after the manner of females) from the coach to the carriage, he saw the Warwickshire mail drive away along the dusty road towards Birmingham; and then, turning to the

Manor Green servant, was on the verge of saying, " I hope my mamma and papa are quite well," when he stopped himself just in time, with the thought that he was now an Oxford man, and altered his query to " All well at home, Jenkins? " They were all well, and how heartily they received him has been recorded by the faithful historian in other pages than these.

Turn we now, for a season, to a record of the sayings and doings of Verdant Green's friend, little Mr. Bouncer.

After the Warwickshire coach, with its freight of Oxford men, had driven away from the Mitre, Mr. Bouncer lingered there some little time longer in company with Mr. Smalls, Charles Larkyns, Pewter Potter, and one or two others who were gathered together in that favourite haunt, the coffee-room. They had considered that bitter beer would be an acceptable refreshment on a hot June morning; and they had, therefore, ordered the waiter to bring them a due supply. It was that same waiter, whose face resembled the interior half of a sliced muffin, who had attended upon Verdant Green and his father when they made their first appearance in Oxford, and had stayed at the Mitre. As he brought in the bitter beer, Charles Larkyns said, " I am somewhat of a connoisseur in art; but, after all, there is nothing that I admire more than this Bass' relief."

" Oh, Charley! " said little Mr. Bouncer, with a groan of anguish; " we will hope that you will do better if you are to do bitters."

The muffin-faced waiter opened the bottles of Bass, emptied their liquid amber into the various glasses, brushed some imaginary crumbs from the table, and vanished. The conversation turned upon Mr. Four-in-hand Fosbrooke and his friend the coachman.

"Like Jack Adams, of the Royal Defiance, that man is a bit of a character," said Charles Larkyns, "as are many of his race; more especially those who have

driven University coaches: like, for example, Smith of the Blue Boar, Trinity Street, Cambridge, who drove the Newmarket and Bury St. Edmunds coach that went by the name of the Slow and Dirty. Then, there was the Oxford coachman who had acquired a parrot-like facility for spouting scraps out of the Latin Grammar, for the use, and abuse, of which specimens of the dead language he was known as the Classical Coachman. Many of these old fellows are quaint characters."

"I was told, the other day," said Mr. Pewter Potter, "a story about old White, who used to drive the Oxford and Cambridge coach, and who, consequently, had many conversations with University men, who asked his opinions on a variety of subjects. He was once asked

by a Cambridge man whether he thought Oxford men more gentlemanly than Cambridge men; and he replied, 'Though you're going to Cambridge, sir, I'll tell you truly what I think. I drives an Oxford gent down, and, when he gets to the end of his journey, he says, "Mr. White," he says, "I shall be happy to see you to my rooms to wine this evening;" and then he hands me his card with his name printed upon it. Well, I goes at the proper time, and there I finds a many gents seated over various liquors; and Mr. So-and-so points to a chair, and says, "Here's a seat for you, Mr. White, alongside o' me. Glad to see you, Mr. White. What wine do you take? here's claret, if you prefer it." So then, perhaps, I has a glass or two o' claret, and helps myself to what I like; and Mr. So-and-so pushes towards me a box o' cigars and a jar o' baccy; and he says, "Take a weed, Mr. White; or, if you prefer it, have a pipe, Mr. White, and I'll join you." So, then we smoke a pipe or two, and drink perhaps more than a glass or two; and then comes in supper — some hot game, and wiands warious. And Mr. So-and-so insists on helping me first, and says, "What part do you take, Mr. White?" And I says, "Thankee, sir, I'm in noways pertickler." "They're all here," says he; so I fixes on the liver wing, and he sends it me. Then, after supper, we has a drop of grog, and smokes one or two more pipes; and then I gets up and makes my obeisance to them, and says, "I wish you all a very good night, gentlemen; and I'm much obleeged to you for your civility." Well, sir, that's Oxford. I drives a gent to Cambridge; and, perhaps, the gent asks me to look in at his rooms some time that evening, if I likes. So I goes, and I finds a many gents there, also with their liquors. And Mr. So-and-so says, "Well, old buck! I'm glad to see you. Clap yourself into a cheer somewhere." So I sets myself down, where I can. Then the wine comes round, and I looks at the bottles to see which is which. "Oh, I daresay, old buck, you'd rather have something hot!" says Mr. So-and-so, and he hands out the brandy. So, as I don't like to interfere with the arrangements, I says, "Thankee, sir;" and they has the wine, while I has the brandy. Then they ask me questions about the coaches that I have druv, and about the horses and passengers, and all that. Then says Mr. So-and-so, "You'd like to smoke a pipe, old buck, I daresay." So I smokes a pipe. Then comes in supper, and hot game and wiands, also warious; and Mr. So-and-so helps 'em all round; and, when he has finished them he says, "Old buck, would you like to pick a bit of pheasant?" Well, sir, that's Cambridge — at least, according to my experience.' So," said Mr. Pewter Potter, as he ended his anecdote, "old White evidently gave the preference to Oxford."

"Old White was a wise man," said little Mr. Bouncer, with a pardonable preference for his own Alma Mater.

Here they were joined by some of the stragglers from the breakfast party that had been given in the room above by Messrs. Bulpit and Smirke; and then they dispersed to their various Colleges, from which, ere the evening had come, they would have gone forth in quest of the pleasures of the Long Vacation.

CHAPTER XV.

LITTLE MR. BOUNCER LEAVES OXFORD IN COMPANY WITH MR. SMALLS.

ITTLE Mr. Bouncer and Mr. Smalls, having no very tedious railway journey before them, did not leave Oxford until the afternoon of the day on which Verdant Green and Mr. Four-in-hand Fosbrooke had quitted the City of Colleges on the top of the Warwickshire coach. By luncheon time, the University had lost the larger portion of its members ; and Oxford tradesmen would be compelled to wait three months for the return of their best customers. This is a serious item in connection with the much-abused credit system, that must be considered whenever any so-called overcharges of Oxford tradesmen are questioned by a Paterfamilias. People must needs make hay while the sun shines; and if the sun is under a cloud for a quarter of the year, it is clear that no hay can be made during that space of time. And, indeed Oxford tradesmen might make a pithy proverb to suit their own case : —

> With sons away,
> We can't make hay,

and, therefore, it behoves them to turn the sons to as much account as possible during Term time, with the hope that the sons' parents and governors will not, in the Long Vacation, or whenever the bills are presented, repudiate their liabilities, and set up the preposterous plea of infancy.

In accepting the invitation to go down with Mr. Smalls for a day or two in the country, little Mr. Bouncer experienced a difficulty with regard to the disposal of Huz and Buz. He scarcely liked to leave them in the coal-cellar outside his room-door at Brazenface, there to be fitfully attended to, or wholly neglected, by Mrs. Tester and Mr. Robert Filcher; and he did not wish to be temporarily separated from them, even if they were placed in Tollitt's stables, or confided to the care of Mr. Charley Symonds. But when he mentioned his hesitation to Mr. Smalls, that gentleman at once solved the difficulty by extending his invitation to Huz and Buz, and promising that they should be heartily welcomed at his father's house during the time of their master's visit. Mr. Bouncer was, therefore, made easy in his mind on this, to him, important subject. Not that Huz and Buz were personages to be dealt with easily in their transit from place to place; and at the Oxford railway station they rendered themselves especially obnoxious and disagreeable — now, frightening timid ladies by their loud barkings and profuse display of teeth; and then making wild rushes at the tempting calves of little children and old gentlemen. They were far too noisy and obtrusive to enable Mr. Bouncer to smuggle them into his own carriage; and the guard, being proof against bribes, insisted on their being placed in a locker in the luggage van. Then followed an agitating scene with a large but loose-limbed porter, who essayed to gain the confidence of the two bull-terriers, and failed to find them reciprocate his attentions. After all, their master had to summarily and roughly thrust them into the locker at the very last moment before the starting of the train; for Huz and Buz set at defiance and kept at bay both porters and guards.

In that dark age, a smoking compartment was an unknown luxury on railway lines; but as there were several Oxford men who were going down by that train, they secured a carriage to themselves, where they could blow a cloud to their hearts' content; and, of course, Mr. Smalls and little Mr. Bouncer were two of the passengers in that particular carriage. In the train, too, were several young ladies with their mothers and chaperones, who were on their way back home from the Commemoration, in company with elderly dons, younger tutors and fellows, and brotherly or cousinly undergraduates. Thus the University was largely represented, and contributed an unusual number of passengers to the train. It slid out of the station; and in another half-hour Oxford had been lost to sight, and its familiar aspect and well-known spires and towers could only be viewed in dreams or memory.

The railway journey of little Mr. Bouncer and Mr. Smalls was terminated at the Poynton Station, where they bade adieu to their undergraduate companions, and released Huz and Buz from their temporary impris-

onment in the locker.   The two travellers had between
them an abundance of luggage; for their *impedimenta* —
exclusive of Huz and Buz — included a weighty box of

books, which Mr. Smalls made it a point of honour to
carry down with him at the end of the June Term, alleg-
ing that he intended " to read hard for his Little-go
during the Long; " though it is to be feared that his

virtuous intentions in this respect were not destined to be carried into effect, and that the box of books would remain unopened until it was taken back to Oxford in the ensuing October. There was a horse and cart for the luggage; and there was a mail phaeton and pair for the two travellers. Mr. Smalls lighted a fresh cigar, and took the reins; Mr. Bouncer occupied the place beside him with Huz and Buz on the driving-apron at his feet; the coachman jumped up behind; and away they drove from the Poynton Station.

It was six miles to the Woodlands — which was the name of the house where lived Mr. Smalls' father; and it was a very pleasant drive through a richly timbered country, whose wealth of greenery was irradiated by a June sun that was flooding the western sky with a sea of gold. The quick-stepping horses took them along at a rapid pace, along dusty turnpike roads, and down shady tree-arched lanes, until they brought them to a little village, with a scattered group of cottages and farm-houses, a smithy, a public-house, a rectory, a new school, an old church, and a large house in a small park, with a tiny lodge at the gate near to the village school.

"Here we are at the Woodlands!" said Mr. Smalls, as he reined up the horses at this little lodge, and re-turned the greeting of the woman who opened the gate.

"What a pity that I put my post-horn in my port-manteau!" said little Mr. Bouncer. "I generally carry it loose with walking-sticks, umbrellas, fishing-rods, and that sort of gear. If I had it out I could have given a tantivity to signal our approach. 'Hark! 'tis the twang-ing horn from yonder bridge! he comes, the herald of a noisy world!' and all that sort of thing. Perhaps if I pinched Huz and Buz's tails and made them bark that would help us a bit. Or, as your shop is called the Woodlands, we might sing in chorus, 'Haste to the

woodlands, haste away! Lads and lasses, all so gay!' Whichever you choose, my little dears; we are in noways pertickler, especially when you pays your money, wipes your innocent noses, and don't breathe on the glasses."

But although Mr. Smalls did not, like the Irish postilion, reserve a canter for the avenue, but drove up it at a moderate pace, they had arrived at the hall door of the Woodlands before little Mr. Bouncer had decided to carry into effect any of the propositions that he had just made to his friend.   Yet he realized the fact that he had left Oxford and Brazenface behind him, and that he had entered upon the three months' enjoyments of the Long Vacation.   During the pleasant time of that long summer holiday, he hoped to be able to entertain his friend Verdant Green at his own home in Herefordshire.

CHAPTER XVI.

LITTLE MR. BOUNCER FORMS THE ACQUAINTANCE OF DR. DUSTACRE.

ON THEIR way from the Poynton Station to the Woodlands, Mr. Smalls had given some particulars of his family to the friend who was going to be his father's guest, but who, as yet, had only known him at Brazenface as a College friend. His mother was dead; his elder brother was in the army; a younger one was in the merchant service; his eldest sister was married; his younger sister and two younger brothers were at school, and would not be at home for some weeks to come. Except his father and the servants, the only other inmate of the house, at that time, was a cousin — a son of the Squire's sister — Thomas Winstanley by name, who had been early left an orphan, and had been adopted by his uncle, who had

educated him with his own children.   Young Winstanley
was now eighteen years of age.

"It is a very sad case," said Mr. Smalls to Mr. Bouncer, as he drove him from the Poynton Station to the

Woodlands; "he used to be the nicest lad possible;
bright and intelligent.   But he had a fever; and, since
then, softening of the brain, or something of that sort,
has come on.   He is quite harmless, though he is not
quite right in his head.   He fancies all sorts of things;
forgets his own name; thinks that he has not been at my

governor's for years, and all that sort of thing. He is very shy at meeting strangers ; and, perhaps, will avoid you, or not speak to you, if you meet him. It is but right to tell you this, in order to put you on your guard ; but you will now understand how matters are, if you should meet poor Tom and he should seem queer."

"Poor fellow!" said Mr. Bouncer. "I understand ; and I will try not to annoy him."

Then they reached the Woodlands and had a hearty welcome from Mr. Smalls, the Squire. ·"You must kindly take us just as we are, Mr. Bouncer," he said. "Circumstances, unfortunately, have prevented my asking friends to meet you. We dine in an hour. Perhaps you would like to see your room?" So, Mr. Bouncer went upstairs, under the escort of a man-servant.

"How 's poor Tom?" asked young Mr. Smalls of his father when they were left alone.

"Your cousin is much worse," replied the Squire. "During the last week he has developed fresh symptoms, and seems inclined to be unruly. I think it will be needful to put him under restraint for a time, and remove him to some place where he can be properly attended to. Johnson "—this was their surgeon's name —"is quite of that opinion. He says that in these mental diseases the very kindest and wisest course to pursue is to place the patient at once under the strictest medical *surveillance;* and that, in nine cases out of ten, the disease, when thus taken in time, can be very greatly alleviated, if not wholly cured. As poor Tom's guardian, I, of course, stand to him *in loco parentis;* and I am bound to care for him, as I would do for one of my own children."

"Of course; Tom is one of us, and we all look upon him as a brother. What does Johnson advise?"

" He agreed with me that it would be better to refer poor Tom's case to Dr. Dustacre; and I did so," replied the Squire.

"Who is Dr. Dustacre? I don't remember his name."

"No; you don't know him," said the Squire. " But he is a medical man of very much experience and skill in mental diseases. I used to know him, some years ago, when, as a magistrate, I had to visit the County Lunatic Asylum, of which he had then the management. Since that time he has had a private establishment at Fairford, which is very well spoken of, and where poor Tom, if it were needful for him to go there, would find 'all the home-comforts that he has been used to. I have interchanged one or two letters with Dr. Dustacre on this painful subject, and have suggested that he should come here and see poor Tom. I daresay there will be a letter from him in the morning, to make an appointment. I am sorry that this should occur at the time of your friend's visit; but I hope that Mr. Bouncer will not allow it to interfere with any little amusement that he may be able to find at the Woodlands. Does he know about poor Tom? "

"Yes; as we came along from Poynton, I told him all that it was needful for him to know."

" Then, nothing more need be said on the subject in his presence. It is useless to obtrude upon him a painful family business in which he can have no personal interest, and in which he cannot render any aid."

As Mr. Smalls quite agreed with his father on this point no mention was made, that evening, to Mr. Bouncer, of young Tom Winstanley, who failed to put in an appearance at dinner, preferring to take that meal in his own room, where he could not be watched by the eyes of a stranger.

The letter-bag was not delivered at the Woodlands until after breakfast-time. It brought, the next morning, the expected letter from Dr. Dustacre to Mr. Smalls; and stated that he would pay a visit to the Woodlands on that day, and would take a conveyance from the Poynton Station, which he presumed would be his nearest point.

"So it is," said the Squire, to his son, as they talked together in the study, little Mr. Bouncer not being present. "Geographically speaking, Poynton is certainly our nearest station; but Dr. Dustacre is not aware that no vehicle of any description can be obtained there. Barham Station is the point that he ought to make for. There is nothing for it but to meet him at Poynton. I should think he would be there by the twelve-thirty-five train. You had better drive me; and then we can talk over matters with the Doctor without a servant listening to what we say. I daresay your friend, Mr. Bouncer, will excuse our absence, and we shall not be away long."

Mr. Smalls the younger therefore sought out his college friend and said, "My father wants me to drive him over to the Poynton Station on a matter connected with poor Tom. I hope you won't mind me leaving you for two or three hours. We shall be back to luncheon."

"Pray don't mind me. I 'll make myself happy, and poke about, and have a look over the premises," replied Mr. Bouncer.

So the two Mr. Smalls, father and son, drove off to the Poynton Station; and Mr. Bouncer lighted his pipe, and paid a visit to Huz and Buz, who were delighted to see him, and were still further pleased when he released them from the stable in which they had been penned, and took them with him for a stroll round the gardens and little park, which, from its fine and plentiful timber, justified the name of " The Woodlands " that had been given to the house.   It was a fine summer's morning, and a quiet walk and meditative pipe under the shade of the wide-spreading trees was very agreeable to Mr. Bouncer and his canine pets.   When he had brought his stroll to an end, and was passing by the house, he saw that he was furtively watched, from the window of the study, by a young man, whom he judged, and rightly so, to be Mr. Winstanley.   Little Mr. Bouncer thought to himself, " I will go in and try to make friends with him."   But when he had put Huz and Buz in their stable, and had returned to the house, he found the study deserted.   Winstanley had seen him coming, and had crept out of doors into the garden through the open window.

The morning newspapers were on the table; so Mr. Bouncer concluded that he would have a look at them, and that, while he was doing so, young Winstanley would probably return.   The atmosphere was warm, the chair was comfortable, the pipe that he had been smoking had exercised a soothing influence, and Mr. Bouncer found that the " Times " leader on the political crisis in Moldavia failed to convey to his mind any other feelings than those that invited slumber.   He read dreamily through the well-phrased lines of exquisite English, and had just succeeded in dismissing Moldavia and its crisis to the realms of forgetfulness, when he was roused from his forty winks of sleep by some one entering the room.

This some one was no other person than Dr. Dust-acre, who shut the door behind him, and made a low bow to. little Mr. Bouncer.

CHAPTER XVII.

LITTLE MR. BOUNCER IS SOMEWHAT SURPRISED AT DR. DUSTACRE.

DUSTACRE had the aspect of a bird; perhaps a raven, after its metempsychosis, would have presented much the same appearance. Pythagoras might have credited him to have belonged, at some previous stage of his existence, to a member of the corvine tribe; and even those who did not adopt the old Samian creed may, in looking at his strange face and the general solemnity of his countenance, have gazed upon him with a certain superstitious awe, as though he were a bird of ill omen. Physiologists and phrenologists, from Theophrastus to Gall, Spurzheim, and Lavater, would have been delighted to make their observations on the head and face of Dr. Dustacre, and to have propounded their pet theories from a superficial examination of his nose and forehead.

The latter was very high and bald, coming almost to a point at the summit where the skilled phrenologist would place the organ of veneration, which is termed, by the unlearned and vulgar, " the bump of benevolence." If, therefore, the disciples of Gall were correct in their theories, it was indubitable that Dr. Dustacre was a kind and good man; but the peculiar form of his bald head made it resemble the polished egg of an ostrich, rather than the customary white billiard ball. Over his ears was a fringe of black hair; so that it was not until he took his hat from off his head that any portion of its baldness was disclosed to view; and, when he put on his hat again, it was as though he had covered the ostrich's egg with a *chapeau* for the performance of some trick of jugglery. A smaller fringe of black hair, in the shape of whiskers, was carried straight down his cheeks and continued under his chin, which retreated sharply from his mouth and nose. This was unusually prominent; and, in conjunction with the facial angle, greatly helped to give the peculiar raven-like aspect to his face. It might be said of Dr. Dustacre's nose and face, as Wordsworth wrote of Paulinus: —

> Black hair, and vivid eye, and meagre cheek,
> His prominent feature like an eagle's beak ;
> A Man whose aspect doth at once appal
> And strike with reverence.

His eyebrows were dark and shaggy: his eyes bright and piercing, even when seen through the gold-rimmed glasses that he wore; and his face was spectral and colourless. He was dressed in an entire suit of black; wore a starched white neckcloth, and carried an ebony cane that was tipped with gold.

Dr. Dustacre walked up to the Woodlands, past the tiny lodge, and through the little, well-timbered park;

and when he came to the front door of Mr. Smalls' large
house, there was the footman standing on the steps,
surveying the beauties of nature. Hence it happened
that Dr. Dustacre had no occasion to ring the hall-bell.

To his inquiry, " Is Mr. Smalls at home? " the servant
replied that his master and young master had driven
over to the Poynton Station, to meet a gentleman
who was expected to arrive by the twelve-thirty-five
train.

"Dear me!" exclaimed the Doctor; "this is particularly unfortunate; for I am the gentleman whom they were expecting to meet there. My business here is of a very urgent nature, and, as I have other important engagements to fulfil, I am anxious to get back to the train with as little loss of time as possible."

"Would you oblige me with your name, sir?" said the servant. The Doctor handed him his card. "Dr. Dustacre is the name of the gentleman that my master has gone to meet," said the servant.

"I had intended to have gone to the Poynton Station," said the Doctor, by way of explanation; "but, at the last moment, a friend told me that I should not be able to get any carriage there; so, I got out at the Barham Station, and have driven over from there. For a particular reason, I have left the car at the turn of the road a short distance beyond the lodge. I have to see young Mr. Winstanley, and to inquire professionally into his case. It is important that I should see him at once, and alone. Is he in the house?"

"Yes, sir; he is in the study. Shall I show you in to him?" asked the servant.

"No," replied the Doctor; "I would rather go in by myself. It will be better not to announce me, or to give my name. Which is the study?"

The servant pointed it out. Dr. Dustacre crossed the hall, opened the study door, shut it carefully behind him, made a bow to a youthful-looking gentleman who was seated in a comfortable chair and nodding over the "Times," and, for the first time in his life, found himself face to face with little Mr. Bouncer. If either of them had gone to the open window and looked out, they might have discovered young Winstanley, crouched behind a thick laurel, ready prepared to lend an attentive ear to their conversation.

Dr. Dustacre gave a keen look through his gold mounted spectacles, and made a rapid, but careful, survey of Mr. Bouncer's face and expression. It was such

a look as Van Amburgh may have bestowed upon the lions when he leaped into their den, and stood among them in that picturesque dress which, at the great Duke of Wellington's desire, was represented in a famous picture by Sir Edwin Landseer. But the celebrated lion-tamer had a cast in his eye, which, as was alleged, was a part of the secret of his success, as it enabled him to gaze upon two beasts at the same time.   Dr. Dustacre had no such obliquity of vision, but looked straightly and fixedly at the object before him.

Mr. Bouncer rose from his easy-chair, and silently returned the silent bow of the other.   The Doctor took a chair and brought it to the writing-table, near to Mr. Bouncer, all the while making an eye-study of his appearance and manners.   It was such a skilled, professional study, that it might have been called eye art. Mr. Bouncer had again settled himself in his chair, and began to experience the sort of sensation which a bird is supposed to feel when it is being fascinated by a serpent.

Thought the little gentleman to himself, "This is a very rummy-looking cove!   I wonder who he is, and why he came into this room, without being shown in by the servant.   I don't remember hearing the front-door bell ring; but I half suspect that I was having forty winks.   What a peculiar-looking old gentleman! who can he be?   By his togs he looks like a parson; white choker, black coat and sit-upons.   I daresay he is the rector of the parish, and a great friend of the Squire's. By the way, I remember Smalls telling me he used to read with the rector two hours a day.   This is the identical individual, no doubt.   I daresay he is like a tame cat, and comes in and out as he likes.   What a skull the old bald-pate has got! and how he stares at me!   ' He fix'd me with his glitt'ring eye.'   ' He came, I could not move, for his eye was upon me.'   I wonder, by the way, why coves have only one eye in poetry, like Polyphemus and those monoptical parties.   This old fellow has two eyes under his gig-lamps, and knows how to use them.

I wonder when the parson's going to open his lips and begin to preach?"

It was at this point in Mr. Bouncer's reverie that Dr. Dustacre cleared his throat, opened his lips, and began to speak; while young Winstanley, outside the window, listened to what was said.

CHAPTER XVIII.

LITTLE MR. BOUNCER IS STILL MORE SURPRISED AT DR. DUSTACRE.

OINTING with his gold-headed ebony cane to the copy of the "Times" over which Mr. Bouncer had been nodding, Dr. Dustacre said, interrogatively, "Fond of reading?"

"That all depends upon the sort of reading that I get hold of," replied Mr. Bouncer, as he thought of the leading article that he had just been dozing over, when the sonorous sentences on the political crisis in Moldavia had failed to excite or amuse him. "A good murder or a daring burglary is interesting, so is a prize-fight, for the matter of that."

"Do you prefer the perusal of works of modern fiction to the study of classical authors?" asked Dr. Dustacre.

"I should rather think I did," answered Mr. Bouncer, heartily, as he thought to himself — This old bald-pate is the parson of the parish who coached Smalls. I hope he 's not going to put me through an examination, and thinks that, as I 'm fresh from college, I ought to be well up in the classics.

" Yet the study of classical authors is a most improving and healthy pursuit," observed the Doctor, who, from the sententiousness of his remark might have been Dr. Johnson himself.

" I don't know about that — at least, in my case," replied Mr. Bouncer. " Pickwick 's more in my line than Plautus; and I prefer Bulwer to Virgil any day. But, I suppose I have n't the brains for Greek and Latin."

" Do you find that the study of dead languages affects your brain in any particular way?" asked Dr. Dustacre.

" Makes it like pap!" replied Mr. Bouncer, frankly, " or else they gave me too much pap when I was a baby, and softened my brains."

" You were not here when you were a baby, I think?" inquired the Doctor.

" Oh dear, no; at that uninteresting period of my existence I was in another part of England," was Mr. Bouncer's reply.

" Though you have been here, residing in this house, many years?"

" Oh, no; I have not."

" Not for the last two years?"

" Not for the last two weeks."

" You were not here, for example, last week?" asked Dr. Dustacre, continuing his examination of the supposed Mr. Winstanley, while the real Simon Pure, crouched behind the laurel outside the open window of the study, listened to every word of the conversation.

"Most decidedly I was not here last week," replied Mr. Bouncer.

"Then you have not been in the house for some time past?"

"Never set foot in it till last night!" said Mr. Bouncer, as he thought — This old bald-pate is a very queer party; he can't be, as I imagined, the parson of the parish, or he would not ask such questions. Perhaps he's some parson who is on a visit to the Rectory.

Dr. Dustacre nodded his head in a Burleigh-like way, as though his examination had satisfactorily determined one point in the case on which his professional opinion had been requested. "It is as Mr. Smalls wrote to me," he said to himself. "One of the mental delusions of this Mr. Winstanley is, that he imagines that he has not been at the Woodlands for many years." Dr. Dustacre then, as sailors say, went on another tack. Meanwhile, the Simon Pure, who was crouched behind the laurel, had a significant smile upon his face as he attentively listened to the conversation in the study.

"What a nice man Mr. Smalls is — I mean the Squire!" said the Doctor.

"So he seems," replied Mr. Bouncer.

"You must be very much attached to him?" pursued the Doctor, interrogatively.

"Me? Why?" asked Mr. Bouncer, with some surprise.

"For all that he has done for you," said the Doctor.

"He has done nothing for me, that I am aware of," said Mr. Bouncer, "beyond giving me a good dinner last night and a capital glass of port, and allowing his son to invite me here."

Thought the Doctor — This confirms what Mr. Smalls told me. This unfortunate young man imagines that his uncle has done nothing for him. This corroborates what was reported to me concerning the second point in

his mental delusions. "Let me see," he added, aloud, "your name is — bless me, what a bad memory I have; your name is — what is your name?"

Thought Mr. Bouncer — He'll next ask me who gave me that name, and what did my godfathers and god-mothers then for me. "I might reply," answered Mr.

Bouncer, "if I wished to evade the question, that my name is Norval, on the Grampian hills; which, perhaps, it might be, if I had ever been there. But, as I don't care to provide myself with an *alias*, I may as well confess that my Christian name is Henry, and my surname is Bouncer."

"You think it's Bouncer, eh?" inquired Dr. Dustacre, looking at him with a searching gaze, through his gold-mounted spectacles, and tapping his chair with his gold-headed ebony cane.

"Think?" echoed Mr. Bouncer. "Well! I've been known by that name as long as I can remember anything." And he thought to himself—Whatever is the old bald-pate driving at? he's a very rummy looking cove, and he entered the room very mysteriously. I hope he's not an escaped lunatic! if so, what shall I do? he's between me and the door, so I can't get away in that direction. Here's the window open behind me; perhaps I can jump through that, like a clown in a pantomime, if he should get wild and attack me. He's got a formidable-looking stick; and I've nothing to defend myself with, unless it's an ivory paper-knife. He's evidently very eccentric; and I should n't wonder at his being a lunatic. I suppose it will be my best policy to humour him. Yes; I'll humour him.

Meanwhile, Dr. Dustacre was thinking—Mr. Smalls was quite right. It is another evidence of mental delusion on the part of this unfortunate young man that he cannot remember his own name.

And so the conversation went on. Dr. Dustacre started two or three subjects; but, to Mr. Bouncer, they appeared as disconnected as though they were consecutive readings from Johnson's Dictionary, or the medley news column from a provincial newspaper. But the conversation, such as it was, was sufficient to confirm the two speakers in the opinions that they had mutually formed of each other.

Old bald-pate, thought Mr. Bouncer, is certainly a most eccentric party, both in his looks and ways. He has evidently got a tile off. By which phrase the little gentleman meant that his temporary companion was, to a certain degree, *non compos mentis*. Though Mr. Bouncer would have been greatly astounded could he have known that the bald-headed individual with a skull like the egg of an ostrich, who was seated before him, had arrived at a like conclusion regarding himself; and he would have been even more surprised if he had been told that the mysterious visitor to the Woodlands was about to act upon that conclusion.

" Perhaps you would not mind walking with me to the gate? " asked Dr. Dustacre, as he rose from his seat, and gave evidence that he had brought the interview to an end, and was about to quit the house, and imitate the juggling trick of covering the ostrich's egg with his hat.

" Oh dear, no! I shall be grattered and flatified — that is to say, flattered and gratified," replied Mr. Bouncer. And he thought to himself — It will be quite as well for me to see old bald-pate off the premises. If poor Tom Winstanley should meet him, and get into conversation with such an eccentricity, it might make him as mad as a hatter, and do poor Tom a great deal of harm. So it will be best for me to take charge of bald-pate, and see him safe to the Rectory, or wherever he may be hanging out.

As Dr. Dustacre and Mr. Bouncer passed through the hall, the latter, while getting his hat, might have been observed to select from the umbrella-stand the thickest walking-stick that was in Mr. Smalls' collection. Armed with this cudgel, he walked forth boldly with his companion, and accompanied him down the drive that led from the house to the lodge. There was no fear of young Winstanley meeting them; though he curiously watched their movements from behind a safe covert of shrubs and trees.

CHAPTER XIX.

LITTLE MR. BOUNCER IS TAKEN CAPTIVE BY DR. DUSTACRE.

WATCHING them from behind the safe concealment of dense laurels and tree-stems, young Winstanley saw Dr. Dustacre and little Mr. Bouncer walking from the house down the carriage-drive that led to the lodge; and he chuckled to himself at the thought how very much those two persons were deceived with each other. They had turned their backs on the real Simon Pure and were the mutual victims of a mistake, which, however ludicrous in its elements, was becoming a very serious matter to each of them.

Mr. Bouncer was still firm to his purpose of keeping his eccentric friend in good humour until he had seen him safe off the premises or housed at the Rectory, from whence he thought it highly probable that he had come to call at the Woodlands. By way, therefore, of starting a conversation that would be agreeable to the gentleman — whom, from his costume, he presumed to be a clergyman — he asked him if there were many fine churches in that neighbourhood?

" I really don't know," replied his companion. "You ought to be better acquainted with this part of the country than I am."

" But I never saw it till yesterday; and, from what you say, I suppose this is your first visit to these parts? " said Mr. Bouncer in his turn being the interrogator.

" To this particular parish it is; though I know other parts of the county at no great distance from here," was the answer.

" Are you staying at the Rectory?" asked Mr. Bouncer, boldly.

" No; why do you ask? "

" Curiosity, I suppose. Excuse my impertinence."

" Oh, I don't think it impertinent. On the contrary, I think it pertinent," said Dr. Dustacre with a laugh. Though he thought to himself — This poor young Winstanley is very shrewd; although his hallucination as to his not having been here for many years would appear to be firmly fixed in his mind.

At the same moment these thoughts were chasing each other through Mr. Bouncer's brain — I hope the old bald-pate is not going to cut up rough. I wonder where he 's hanging out? Perhaps he 's a parson, from some neighbouring parish, come to solicit a subscription from the Squire. Or he may be a deputation from some Parent Society, out on the loose, and wanting to hold a missionary meeting, or something of that sort. Having this impression on his mind, he firmly grasped his thick walking-stick as he thought — I must humour the old bald-pate and keep him civil: it is lucky that I have taken him out of Winstanley's way, for he might have alarmed the poor fellow and done mischief. Mr. Bouncer said, " Are you fond of missionary meetings, sir? "

Thought the Doctor to himself — How his mind wanders! I must humour him by answering his questions. " Well, I don't profess to any overweening attachment for them. I think that we ought to be able to do without them; but I suppose they are necessary in our imperfect state of existence."

Little Mr. Bouncer thought to himself — Sold again! If he's a parson, he's not a deputation.

By this time they had reached the tiny lodge. Mr. Bouncer held open the drive-gate, and signified by his action that he would there take leave of his companion; who, however, said to him, " Do you mind giving me the pleasure of your company just a little way along the road? "

Mr. Bouncer replied, " Certainly, if you wish it." But he thought — The woman at the lodge would not be of much use, except for screaming; and I don't know what excuse I could make for calling her. I only wish I'd time to let Huz and Buz loose; they would have been some protection in case of accident, and would have worried the old bald-pate's pantaloons if he took it in his head to turn obstreperous. He's the rummiest parson that I've met for many a day.

So Dr. Dustacre and Mr. Bouncer, turning their backs on the tiny lodge, walked along the road by the skirts of a plantation that marked the boundary of Mr. Smalls' picturesque little park. In the plantation was a thick undergrowth of evergreens — laurel, box, and berberis — specially planted for the encouragement of the Squire's pheasants; and, stealing through these shrubs, young Winstanley might have been seen curiously watching the movements of Mr. Bouncer and his companion, while the dense thicket and its umbrage prevented him from being observed from the road. At the end of the plantation the road from the lodge came at right angles into another road; and, when the two temporary companions had turned the sharp corner, they saw a one-horse car pulled up by the side of the road with the horse's head in the direction that led to Poynton and Barham. The driver was in his place on the box, and a commonly dressed and powerfully built man was standing in the road, waiting by the side of the car. The road was much shaded by some tall trees, whose thick foliage made a screen on either side; and there was no farm-house or cottage to be seen.

"This is my conveyance," said Dr. Dustacre. "Perhaps you'll take a little drive with me?"

"Well, if it's the same to you, I'd rather not," replied Mr. Bouncer. "You see I'm expecting my friend and pitcher — I mean my friend and host — back to luncheon."

"Oh," said the Doctor, with a winning smile, bright as his own gold-mounted spectacles, "I am sure that Mr. Smalls, who is also a friend of mine, will readily excuse you, especially when he knows that you are in my company. So pray oblige me by getting into this car."

But little Mr. Bouncer could not see why the elder Mr. Smalls should be pleased at this act of elopement from the luncheon at which he had promised to be present; nor could he imagine what motive should constrain the mysterious individual in clerical dress, and with the bald head and hooked nose and gold-rimmed spectacles, to desire his company. , And, for his own part, as he entertained very strong suspicions that, as he mentally expressed it — The old bald-pate had a tile off or a screw loose somewhere — he had considerable scruples for not desiring to take a country drive with him, immured in the narrowed limits of a car. The presence of a third person would not be altogether re-assuring, even though he should prove to be a keeper from a lunatic asylum. For Mr. Bouncer thought — Is it possible that this old bald-pate had got away from this square-shouldered resolute looking party? If so, perhaps I had better humour him a little to prevent an outbreak.

These thoughts coursed rapidly through Mr. Bouncer's mind as the Doctor said, " Pray oblige me by accompanying me for a short drive! allow me to help you! " and, taking him by the arm and using some little strength, he forced, rather than guided, Mr. Bouncer to the car, the door of which was held open by the broad-shouldered man. Cabby, on the box, was regarding the scene with an unconcealed grin. Young Winstan-ley was also looking on from his covert of shrubs and trees, with a cunning smile on his face.

" After you! you get in first! " said Mr. Bouncer, taking the opportunity to tip an expressive wink to the broad-shouldered man, as though to say — If he can be got safely in, then you can see to him, and I can go about my business.

" Oh, no! " said the Doctor politely; " I could not think of it. You get in first, and I will follow you."

It struck Mr. Bouncer that the broad-shouldered individual had neither reciprocated his wink, nor made any movement towards assisting the old bald-pate into the car. He began to be suspicious. " Now, what do you

want me to be up to?" he added, as he grasped his stick; " and where do you want me to go, and why? I 'm generally game for anything, from pitch-and-toss to manslaughter; but I like to know the programme."

" It is a pleasant day for a country drive," said the

Doctor in his blandest tones; "and I only want you to be good enough to take an agreeable little excursion with me. Pray be calm!"

"Calm!" echoed Mr. Bouncer. "I'm as calm as a duck-pond. It's you that are putting yourself about. I don't want to take a drive, because I've other fish to fry; so I wish you good morning."

"Oh, don't go!" pleaded the Doctor, but in a very polite way; "do oblige me by getting into the car."

"Flatly, I won't!" said Mr. Bouncer; and he meant what he said, and he looked as though he meant it. That was quite enough for Dr. Dustacre.

"Brand!" said the Doctor quietly to the broad-shouldered man, "don't use more force than is necessary."

Little Mr. Bouncer could never exactly tell how it was done, for it was done so quickly and expertly; but, by a rapid flank movement, just as Mr. Bouncer was turning away, he was seized from behind by the individual addressed as Brand, who held him by his arms in such a way that the little gentleman was powerless, either to use his stick, or to show fight. He struggled and kicked; but it was all in vain; and, in another moment, he felt himself hoisted into the car.

CHAPTER XX.

LITTLE MR. BOUNCER IS GRATIFIED TO FIND THAT DR. DUSTACRE HAS MADE A SLIGHT MISTAKE.

STRUGGLING and kicking, and with his hat knocked off, little Mr. Bouncer, uttering a few powerful Saxon expletives, was forced into the car. By compulsion he was hoisted there-into by the burly, broad-shouldered individual who had been addressed by the name of Brand, and who quickly followed Mr. Bouncer, and took a seat opposite to him. The clerical-looking gentleman, with the raven-beaked nose and gold-mounted spectacles, nimbly jumped in after them, shut to the door, popped his head through the window, cried " All right! drive on! lose no time!" and then, turning to Mr. Bouncer, by the side of whom he had seated him-self, said, in the most affable manner, "Excuse my apparent rudeness; but I am so very anxious to have the pleasure of your company; and this is a lovely day for a drive. How beautiful the play of light and shade is on the side of that wood!"

But Mr. Bouncer sulkily replied, "Bother the play of light and shade! I want to know what's the meaning of all this, and what game you chaps are up to."

" Pray don't agitate yourself," said the gentleman in spectacles; " it is only a drive to do you good."

But Mr. Bouncer could not see the transaction in this light, and did not approve of being rapidly whirled away, a captive in the old bald-pate's car, sitting knee to knee with a burly individual who appeared to be prepared to pounce upon him if he gave the slightest evidence of attempting resistance or escape. What would the three inmates of the car have felt, or said, had they known that young Mr. Winstanley had watched the whole scene of Mr. Bouncer's abduction, and, from his covert of shrubs in the plantation, was, even then, chuckling with joy as he gazed upon the lessening shape of the four-wheeled chaise as it grew smaller in the distance, until a bend in the road removed it out of sight! When he had witnessed this, young Winstanley executed a species of wild fandango, as a *pas d'extase*, expressive of his unbounded satisfaction at what he had seen; and then leaving the covert of the box and berberis and laurels that composed the undergrowth of the plantation, calmed his outward deportment to its ordinary seeming, and returned, placidly, across the small park to the Woodlands.

When he got there, he said to the footman, " Has the gentleman gone?"

" Dr. Dustacre, sir? "

Young Winstanley nodded an affirmative.

" Yes, sir; he let himself out, sir. Leastways, I suppose Mr. Bouncer let him out; for I saw them walking towards the lodge together. That was more than a quarter of an hour ago."

"Then Mr. Bouncer is not in the house now?"

"No, sir; he has not yet returned."

"I think I should like to see him when he comes in: I shall be in the study. Perhaps you will send him to me?"

"Yes, sir."

Whereupon young Winstanley, who had looked quite grave during the brief colloquy, walked into the study, shut the door, and then, throwing himself into the easy chair in which Mr. Bouncer had sat during his interview with Dr. Dustacre, burst into laughter, which was none the less hearty because it was noiseless.

While Simon Pure was thus enjoying his brief time of victory, his innocent victim was being whirled on in the four-wheeled chaise to the Barham Station, sitting in uncomfortable proximity to the burly, broad-shouldered individual who had hoisted him, by main force, into the vehicle. When Mr. Bouncer was enabled to look at this person more closely, it struck him that, both in appearance and costume, he was very like a bailiff. Now, the only bailiff with whom the little gentleman had any sort of an acquaintance, was Dibbs, his own farm-bailiff in Herefordshire. But Dibbs, although he was burly, and had broad shoulders, conveyed to the spectator's mind a very different impression to that left upon it by a survey of the individual who was now Mr. Bouncer's *vis-à-vis*. This person seemed to belong to the class of obnoxious people who tap impecunious gentlemen on their shoulders, and show them slips of paper in which the name of her Majesty is brought forward in an unpleasant manner. Mr. Bouncer had a general idea of this particular kind of bailiff, whose official duty it is to arrest debtors; but, happily, he had not hitherto formed their acquaintance. Perhaps that uncomfortable experience (so it struck him) was now to be his.

It is said that drowning men can review the deeds of a lifetime in a minute, and that, in a few moments of acute danger, the actions of many years pass swiftly through the brain, as though made visible in a rapidly rolled out panorama. Certainly little Mr. Bouncer, in less time than it would have taken to utter the words, thought to himself — or, as he phrased it, "deeply pondering, like those old classical Greek parties," — that certain events in his college career might be turned against him in an unpleasant manner. Glancing mentally at these, as he looked into the face of the burly, broad-shouldered individual, he said to himself — I know that I have a great amount of ticks — a fearful lot I'm afraid; but I've never been pressed for them, and I had no fear of running a horrid mucker. Yet I seem to be in Queer Street. Is this old bald-pate some species of attorney? They often wear black togs and white chokers. If so, he has got his bailiff in attendance, and has, perhaps, come to arrest me, and carry me off to the limbo of a debtor's prison. If that's their game, although they are two to one, I must show fight, and demand an explanation. I am not going to be pulled up without a struggle.

These thoughts rapidly coursed through Mr. Bouncer's brain; and, acting upon the idea that they conveyed to him, that he was being arrested for unpaid debts, and was being clandestinely conveyed to a sponging-house, of which his two companions were, respectively, the proprietor and gaoler, he turned to the bald-pated gentleman, and asked, "Do I owe you any money?"

"Owe me money?" repeated Dr. Dustacre.

"Yes," replied Mr. Bouncer; "owe money. You know what owing money means, don't you? Have you any ticks in my name; because, if so, you had better say so at once. I can refer you to Stump and Rowdy, my bankers; and, I daresay, they'll soon make it all square with you."

Thought the Doctor — Poor young man! his head wanders sadly! But he replied, "Pray do not agitate yourself, my dear young friend."

"Oh," said Mr. Bouncer, with scorn, "you need n't come the dear young friend dodge with me! I daresay you get your fifty per cent.; and, no doubt, you propose to take half of it out in bad pictures and worse claret! If you want me to fork out for anything that you 've got against me, I daresay Stump and Rowdy can find the cash, without my having to go to the Jews for it." Little Mr. Bouncer put in this home-thrust, because, in connection with the ideas to which he was giving expression, it suddenly occurred to him that his unknown bald-pated companion, with the very prominent nose, had something of the Hebrew in his countenance.

Dr. Dustacre was about to reply, as best he might, to Mr. Bouncer's observation, when there clattered past them a mail-phaeton and pair, driven by a young gentleman, beside whom an older gentleman was seated. Mr. Bouncer spied them at once, and quickly thrusting his head out of the window, before the broad-shouldered man could prevent the act, shouted, lustily, "Hoi! Smalls! stop! pull up! Bouncer! prisoner!" He was unable to say more that was audible to the occupants of the mail-phaeton, as the burly individual who had been addressed as Brand forcibly pulled him back to his seat.

But both the Mr. Smalls had recognized his voice,
and the mail-phaeton had been at once pulled up; while
Mr. Smalls, in his turn, stood up, and shouted to the
cab-driver, "Stop! there is some mistake!"

At the same moment, Dr. Dustacre had put his head
out of the window of the chaise, and, with his gold-
headed ebony cane, had tapped the driver on his
arm, and told him to pull up. "I fear," said the Doctor, turning to Mr. Bouncer, "that there is a slight
mistake."

"I have not the slightest doubt of it, old cock," replied the little gentleman.

As soon as Dr. Dustacre had arrived at the conclusion that there must be a slight mistake, the end had virtually arrived of what Peter Quince would have called "the most lamentable comedy," or of what old Polonius would have termed the "tragical-comical" piece, that had been unconsciously enacted, with little Mr. Bouncer and the Doctor for the two chief performers. Mr. Smalls was the *deus ex machinâ*, whose arrival on the scene released the hero of the piece from the predicament in which he had so unexpectedly been placed, and the *dénouement* had now been reached when the principal characters must say a few words before they are hidden by the fall of the curtain.

The younger Mr. Smalls had pulled up, wheeled round his pair of horses, and reined them in by the side of the chaise. He was the first to speak, and his words broke the spell that had held Dr. Dustacre enthralled. "Hallo, Bouncer! who'd have thought of seeing you? Where are you off to?"

"That's just what I want to know! These two people seem to have taken a fancy to me. Whether it's kidnapping or imprisonment I shall be glad to be told."

While these words were being uttered by little Mr. Bouncer, whose head appeared at that window of the chaise which was nearest to the mail-phaeton, Dr. Dustacre had let himself out at the opposite door, and had gone round to the elder Mr. Smalls, with whom he exchanged a few words that were abundantly sufficient to clear up the mistake under which he lay. He advanced to the side of the chaise at which Mr. Bouncer's head appeared, made the little gentleman a most profound bow, opened the chaise door for him to step out, and said, " Mr. Bouncer, I ought to have believed you when you told me your name; but I construed your words to mean what, in vulgar parlance, is called ' a bouncer;' and I thought that you were purposely deceiving me. I owe you more apologies than I can express, and I know not how sufficiently to ask your pardon. Through a series of misconceptions, I arrived at the conclusion that you were the young Mr. Winstanley whom Mr. Smalls is entrusting, for a time, to my care as a patient; and, in point of fact, I was escorting you to my house for that purpose. I beg you ten thousand pardons for the mistake I have so stupidly made, and also for any inconvenience to which I may have put you. Any reparation that I can make, or any apology that you think fit to require, shall be most cheerfully proffered to you."

Little Mr. Bouncer cut short the Doctor's speech by laughter that could not be controlled. He was not only the essence of good-nature, but was also keenly alive to a joke; and the absurdity of the scene through which he had passed was too much for his feelings, as he thought how he and the Doctor had been mutually deceived. The sight of the Doctor standing bowing to him and revealing glimpses of his bald ostrich-egg-looking head, and then covering it up again with his hat, as though he were performing a juggling trick, moved Mr. Bouncer's risible faculties. " It's as good as a play," he managed to say, between his bursts of laughter; " the richest thing I've known for a long time! Forgive you? Of course I do, sir! You've got the worst of the joke, I think; for you've had all your trouble for nothing. I'm quite right, and have no need to be your patient. Though, perhaps, I 'm not quite as wise as a judge, yet I 'm thankful to say that I 've my wits about me, and have not got a tile off; or, as they say down in my part of the country — I 've got all my buttons on, and they 're all shanked."

Mr. Bouncer's laughter was infectious. Mr. Smalls and his son joined in it; the cabman grinned; the broad-shouldered Brand chuckled; and even the solemn bird-like face of Dr. Dustacre was transiently lit up by a wan smile. He murmured profuse thanks, and then conferred with the Squire. His going on to Barham to meet the train by which he had desired to return, was now out of the question. He must go back to the Woodlands and there see the real Simon Pure; and, if it should be found needful, take him to Barham by a later train. This plan was, therefore, adopted. The broad-shouldered Brand mounted the driving-seat of the chaise, into which the Squire and Dr. Dustacre entered, in order to talk over young Winstanley's case; while little Mr. Bouncer and his friend Mr. Smalls drove back in the mail-phaeton, Mr. Bouncer giving his friend a graphic description of the scene that had occurred, and the impressions he had received during his interview and walk and drive with "the old bald-pate." "I think," added Mr. Bouncer, "that he began to be afraid I should pull him up for assault and battery. If so, the old cove has had a greater fright from me than I had from him. So, it 's about square between us."

Luncheon followed their arrival at the Woodlands, and the Squire contrived that his nephew, Tom Winstanley, should not escape from an interview with the Doctor. The result of that interview was, that it was deemed expedient to place the Squire's nephew, for a period, under the Doctor's care; and, by four o'clock, the chaise was again at the door, and Winstanley was the companion of Dr. Dustacre and Brand, to meet the five o'clock train at Barham. He went quite willingly; and, as we shall not again meet with him in this history, it may here be said, that, under the Doctor's skilful care and judicious treatment, he returned to the Woodlands, perfectly restored to health, in time to see his cousin before he went back to Oxford at the end of the Long Vacation.

The Squire was very pleased with Mr. Bouncer. As they sat together, after dinner, he said, " You let the Doctor off lightly. You might, as you say, have had him up for assault and battery; though it would have been rather awkward for me, if you had asked me, as a magistrate, to grant the warrant."

" I 'll warrant you would n't have granted it, if I had asked for it," said Mr. Bouncer.

So this episode in Mr. Bouncer's life ended with a laugh, and was treated as a joke.

CHAPTER XXI.

LITTLE MR. BOUNCER JOINS IN A VERY PECULIAR PIC–NIC.

WAKING up the next morning, and reviewing the events of the preceding day, little Mr. Bouncer was gratified to find that the bright June sun was shining down upon him at the Woodlands, and was not streaming into a bedroom occupied by him in Dr. Dustacre's house. During the day, he and his friend Mr. Smalls had a gallop over the Squire's estate, accompanied by Huz and Buz, who enjoyed themselves with a famous rat-hunt in the farmyard of one of the Squire's tenants, where Mr. Smalls and Mr. Bouncer put up their horses, stopped to have a glass of ale and a smoke, and to make a critical survey of certain fat oxen and pigs that were expected to cover themselves with glory and prize medals at the next meeting of the County Agricultural Society. Then they cantered back again to the Woodlands, across fields and through woods and plantations, where Huz and Buz were temporarily demoralised by the sudden up-springing of hares and the scuttling of rabbits in and out of their holes. The rector of the parish dined at the Woodlands that evening, and little thought how he had been taken by Mr. Bouncer for Dr. Dustacre.

From that gentleman there arrived, on the following morning, a most elaborate letter of mingled apologies and thanks, addressed to Mr. Bouncer; and also another letter to the Squire, saying that Mr. Winstanley had accompanied him in a quiet way, and seemed happy and contented in his temporary home. He was commissioned, he added, by his friend Dr. Plimmer (who was his successor at the County Lunatic Asylum, and was well known to Mr. Smalls), to invite the party from the Woodlands to the first annual pic-nic for the season to be given to the patients of the Asylum, on the Tuesday in the ensuing week, at Firs Hill, a spot about seven miles distant from the Woodlands. Dr. Dustacre expressed a hope that, if Mr. Bouncer had not then left, he would also join the party, and thus permit Dr. Dustacre to have the pleasure of renewing an acquaintance so singularly and inauspiciously commenced.

Said the Squire to his son's friend, " I hope you will go with us. Such a pic-nic will be a novel scene to you, and also an interesting one. I, as a visitor to the asylum, have attended more than one of their pic-nics, and also their Christmas gatherings, balls, and theatricals. Of course, only such patients are allowed to take part in the pic-nics who are sufficiently well to do so; and Dr. Plimmer is as careful and judicious on this point as was Dr. Dustacre, who originated these entertainments at our asylum. Several visitors are always invited to be present at these pic-nics, and they freely join in the dances and amusements. This helps to give a social character to the gathering, that appears to exercise a

salutary influence on the afflicted inmates of the institution, whose unvarying demeanour on such occasions is a
sufficient evidence of the beneficial results that have
been accomplished in laying aside the terrors of chains,
and whips, and darkened cells, for cheerful rooms, kind
words, and humane treatment. The patients always
seem glad for lady and gentleman friends to join their
pic-nics, and I think you would be pleased to go with us
on Tuesday. It will be a novelty for you, if nothing
more."

As Mr. Bouncer had promised to stay at the Woodlands beyond the day mentioned, he, together with his
host and friend, accepted Dr. Dustacre's invitation; and,
when the Tuesday came, they drove over to the spot
appointed for the rendezvous.

Firs Hill — or, as it was sometimes written, Furze
Hill — might have received its etymology either from
its firs or furze; the furze spreading in golden patches
over many portions of the slope of the hill, and a small
plantation of Scotch firs crowning its summit. When
the trio from the Woodlands reached the spot, soon
after noon, the pic-nic party had already arrived from
the asylum, which was five miles distant in an opposite
direction. They had come in carriages, and waggons,
and a break; and, of the patients, there were about forty
females and twenty males, with the matron and steward,
and a staff of nurses and attendants. Dr. Dustacre and
Dr. Plimmer were with them, with a few ladies and gentlemen who had received special invitations to be present.
The weather was all that could be wished for such an
occasion, and the party appeared to be a very happy
one, the patients enjoying themselves in an orderly way.
Luncheon had been laid out in *al fresco* style, upon the

grass, within the shade of the group of Scotch firs; and, after luncheon, the party dispersed, and wandered over the hill-sides and the neighbouring meadows, enjoying the beautiful prospect, under careful, though not obtrusive, *surveillance*.

The spot had been admirably chosen for the purpose. At the base of the hill was a narrow, willow-girted river, winding its devious course amid rich pastures, in some of which the mowers were at work sweeping down the swathes of long grass, or sharpening their scythes, with a pleasant tinkling sound that was quite audible to the pic-nic people on the hill. A little way off was a stately mansion, of which a bird's-eye view was seen from Firs Hill, with its park and mile-long avenue of elms; then came undulating ground, with hanging coppices and a long stretch of well-wooded landscape, over which shot up the spires and towers of the county town. In the other direction was a noble range of hills, of which Firs Hill was one of many spurs, with a valley dotted with farmsteads and hamlets, and traversed at one point by a lengthy railway viaduct. Just below the hill was an old and well-cared-for church, with its trimly-kept church-yard screened by a row of chestnuts and limes, whose bright foliage contrasted with the dark solemnity of three ancient yew trees. A landscape such as this, bathed in the glories of one of the brightest and latest days of sunny June, could not fail to awaken pleasurable feelings in the breasts of those whose faculties, though obscured on certain points, seemed to be more keenly susceptible of the delights of sight and sound.

Many of the patients had wandered down the hill to the churchyard, where the rector, who was among Dr. Plimmer's visitors, showed them the old cross, and a curiously carved Norman doorway, and took them over the church, wherein were many stately monuments of members of the family who had lived at the mansion hard by.   Mr. Bouncer, to whom Dr. Dustacre was making himself very agreeable, had joined this party, and was requested by one of the female patients to show her the tomb of Abel.   In answer to an expressive look of the Doctor's, Mr. Bouncer pointed out a small tomb-stone in a corner of the south aisle; with which informa-tion the patient appeared perfectly satisfied, merely saying, "Poor Abel! he was a keeper of sheep.   My father was a shepherd; but he kept out of wicked Cain's way."   One of the male patients appeared to be quite an archæologist, and gave a very correct description both of the church and the dates of the various styles in which it was built.   "I perfectly remember," he said to Dr. Dustacre, " that Early English capital being carved." The Doctor quietly explained to Mr. Bouncer that this patient's fancy was that he was a son of Methusaleh, and that he had already lived through a thousand years. Another patient, who had appeared to be perfectly rational while walking through the church, became some-, what excited, as they returned to the hill, at hearing some one speak of a field of turnips near to which they passed.   It appeared that he was under the delusion that his head was a turnip, and that it would, some day, be appropriated for culinary purposes.   But the peculiar fancies of many of the patients were not evidenced throughout the day.

When they had returned to the summit of Firs Hill, the brass band of the institution began to play a lively air.   This band was not only a significant feature in the government of a lunatic asylum conducted on humane and enlightened principles, but it was also an evidence of what might be done by perseverance and instruction. It was composed of the warders of the institution, who, notwithstanding that their hours of practice were necessarily limited, had, under the judicious tuition of their bandmaster, become most efficient performers. The band played at the Asylum on certain evenings in each week; and, on Friday evenings, the patients had a dance. Dr. Plimmer assured Mr. Smalls that the introduction of music and dancing into the institution had been marked with the most beneficial results. The drummer was one of the patients; while another stood near, and with perfect gravity, held his hands up to his face, and, with voice and action, imitated the sound and playing of a trumpet.

"He is one of our most harmless and quiet people," said Dr. Plimmer; "but, one of his notions is, that his nose is a trumpet."

"It is to be feared," observed the Squire, "that many of those who are accounted sane, while they certainly blow their own noses, yet do not blow their own trumpet in such a harmless fashion."

The band struck up a country dance; and, to the lively measure of its music, the majority of the patients were soon tripping, their nurses and attendants mixing with them. The females appeared to prefer dancing with each other; and so, for the matter of that, did the males, unless they danced by themselves, as some eccentric persons preferred to do. So much had the pleasure of the day been anticipated, said Dr. Plimmer, that the patients had devoted the previous evening to unceasing "ball practice" and the preparation of polkas for the next day's performance; and they certainly proved themselves to be as admirably proficient in the mazy steps as if they had studied under a Coulon or a D'Egville.

Mr. Bouncer had particularly noticed one female patient, who was past middle age, and whose dress, although much faded and worn, betokened, together with her manner and appearance, that she had once moved in a class of society superior to that of the generality of her companions. At luncheon, she sat apart from them, by the side of the matron; and, when the dancing began, she withdrew to a lower part of the hill, where, turning her back on the gaiety, she sat down on the grassy slope, and, screening herself from the sun with a large, old-fashioned parasol, looked sadly over the landscape spread beneath her. Mr. Bouncer pointed her out to Dr. Dustacre, and asked who she was.

"She is a widow; Mrs. Flabby by name," replied the Doctor. "She came to the asylum some years ago, when I was in charge of it. She has seen better days, and been in a superior position; but a series of reverses that befel her family and fortune unsettled her reason. I fancy that she had no great strength of mind, even in her best and earliest days; but she is perfectly quiet and calm, and has never exhibited the least violence. She can be controlled by a word, or even by a threat to deprive her of her parasol; and, as you may have noticed, she keeps up her dignity, and does not mix much with her companions, although she is always polite to them. She usually sits apart, and rarely converses, except with the matron or nurses, or with the medical staff."

"I don't like to see her moping alone, and not enjoying herself like the others," said Mr. Bouncer. "Would there be any impropriety in my going and talking with her a little?"

"Certainly not," replied Dr. Dustacre. "It would be very kind of you. She is always pleased when what she calls a real gentleman or lady will converse with her. She accepts the attention as a recognition of her former social position. Of course you must be prepared to hear her talk a great deal of unconnected nonsense."

"Oh, of course! Perhaps I shall enjoy her conversation more than if she were a thoroughgoing bluestocking, who could talk like a dictionary on all sorts of subjects, from præ-Adamite formations to Shakspeare and the musical glasses."

So little Mr. Bouncer went down the hill with the benevolent intention of cheering poor Mrs. Flabby by having a chat with her.

CHAPTER XXII.

LITTLE MR. BOUNCER LEAVES THE WOODLANDS FOR "THE LITTLE VILLAGE."

RECLINING on the grassy slope of Firs Hill were other patients of the Institution, who were not joining in the dance to the music of the band; but poor Mrs. Flabby sat apart from these, and sheltering herself from the hot sun with a large parasol, looked sadly towards the fair stretch of landscape that was spread before her. In accordance with the sanction that he had received from Dr. Dustacre, little Mr. Bouncer went to her and introduced himself, in true English fashion, by a remark upon the weather.

"How highly favoured we are, ma'am; it is just the very day for a pic-nic, is it not? I hope that you have enjoyed it."

Mrs. Flabby graciously bent her head, evidently pleased that she should be addressed by one of the gentlemen visitors. She accepted it as a recognition

of her former rank in society, and, therefore, felt much flattered.

"I," said Mr. Bouncer, "have enjoyed coming here very much indeed; and I should be glad to light a cigar, if smoking will not be any annoyance to you, ma'am?"

"Oh, dear no!" replied Mrs. Flabby; "pray smoke! it will remind me of my poor dear husband. He always smoked, night and day. In my happier hours, I called him my limekiln; but, it was not his fault, poor dear soul! it was his misfortune. He was compelled to smoke, you know, in consequence of that bond with the Great Mogul."

"With the Great Mogul?" echoed Mr. Bouncer, who was busily engaged in lighting a cigar from his fusee-box, as he sat on the grassy slope near to Mrs. Flabby: "dear me! I never heard of that."

"No, perhaps not; it was tried to be hushed up," replied Mrs. Flabby, in the most serious, matter-of-fact way; "but, murder will out. Yes, the Great Mogul was his particular friend. They had formed an early intimacy when searching for the North Pole, and the recollection of that terrible incident with the Great Bear was never effaced from his memory, and cemented a friendship which resulted in an impediment of the speech, from which my poor husband suffered most acutely, more particularly when he put on a clean shirt, with which I always kept him well supplied, and he had never to complain of the want of a button."

"That is a very unusual circumstance," said Mr. Bouncer, as he puffed away at his cigar, while the strains of the dance-music floated merrily in the summer air. "But what did he do about the smoking and the Great Mogul?"

"Ah, that was very sad!" said poor Mrs. Flabby, with a sigh; "I grieve to speak ill of any one; but, I am sorry to say that the Great Mogul was no gentleman, and that I was quite deceived in him."

"Why, what did he do?" asked Mr. Bouncer.

"What did he do?" echoed Mrs. Flabby, most solemnly, "why, he poisoned Victoria's mind, and led her to act towards me in the way that she did."

"What Victoria? You don't mean her gracious Majesty, do you?"

"Hush! not for worlds!" hoarsely whispered Mrs. Flabby, "people are hung for high treason! I should not like to see your head cut off for any indiscretion."

"I shouldn't like to see it myself, as Paddy would say," replied Mr. Bouncer. "So the Great Mogul poisoned Victoria's mind, did he?"

"Yes! he told her lies — base calumnies, as I can prove. It all arose from jealousy. I had written a poem, called 'The Plaintive Periwinkle: A lay of the Affections.' It taught an excellent moral, my young friend! Buy it for your children, if you can meet with a copy; but, I fear that Victoria has suppressed the edition."

"Why should she do so?"

"She was so jealous of me — of my fame as a writer, you will understand. But I was resolved to persevere, and to surmount all obstacles. A voice within told me that I should be ultimately rewarded by a nation's gratitude, and that generations yet unborn would grow up to bless the author of 'The Plaintive Periwinkle,' and to drop a silent tear over her gorgeous tomb in the Poets' Corner. As a beginning I had twenty millions of copies printed for immediate distribution. They were to be sown broadcast; thrown into cabs and omnibuses, and dropped down areas. Victoria heard of it!"

"Do you think," asked Mr. Bouncer, as though deeply interested in the narrative, "do you think that the Great Mogul could have told her?"

"Of course! who else could have told her?" replied Mrs. Flabby.

"Of course! no one!" observed Mr. Bouncer, as though that matter were now sufficiently self-evident.

"He never forgot the North Pole!" said Mrs. Flabby, solemnly. "I had warned my poor husband against him from the first; but he would not take my advice. It was entirely through him that he lost half his fortune in that unfortunate speculation in Train Oil and Whales' Blubber. And yet, I told him how it would be."

"I should like to hear what Victoria did about your book — 'The Plaintive Periwinkle,'" said Mr. Bouncer, anxious to divert Mrs. Flabby from her reminiscences of the Great Mogul.

"She at once come down from — But, no! high treason!" whispered the poor lady. "She took lodgings over a pastry-cook's, just opposite to my window. Could you have believed it?"

"Not unless you had told me!" replied Mr. Bouncer, politely.

"Alas, it is too true!" said Mrs. Flabby. "There she sat and watched me, all the day long. My poems were seized by her spies and myrmidons. They waylaid my messengers, and robbed them of the precious packets that were intended to do so much good. And this, after all my years of labour, and after having ruined myself to get the work printed. Oh, what an effect it had upon me! I have had no such blow until now! My poor, poor cat!"

"Your cat?" asked Mr. Bouncer.

"She died yesterday; she breathed her last in these arms. Oh, that I could recall her! she was my only solace. But how could it be otherwise, when my dear daughter's spirit was in her?"   Here the poor demented lady burst into convulsive sobs.   Mr. Bouncer, with kindly words, endeavoured to soothe her; but in vain. "My poor cat!" she sobbed; "she was all that was left to me.   I shall never have another daughter.   Oh, she was so good and loving!"

The conversation had taken an unexpected turn, and Mr. Bouncer began to fear he should be doing harm if he continued the interview with Mrs. Flabby; so, with a few more cheering and reassuring words, he got up from the grass, and said, "I will go and see how the dancers are getting on.   They seem to be enjoying themselves. Won't you come nearer to them, ma'am?"

"Not just yet! soon.   Oh, how kind you have been to me!" said poor Mrs. Flabby.

After Mr. Bouncer had rejoined the party on the summit of Firs Hill, he mentioned to Dr. Dustacre a portion of Mrs. Flabby's conversation, and asked if there were any foundation for her statements.

"For her poem, I know there is," answered the Doctor.   "She published some little book for children, of which she thought highly, and from which she expected to gain both money and reputation.   She was deceived, as other authors have been; and, I daresay, it preyed upon her mind.   As to her cat, that is, unfortunately, true.   When a kitten, it belonged to the master of the institution.   Mrs. Flabby begged to have it, and her request was granted.   I think she must have had it nearly five years.   Unfortunately, it died about a fortnight ago; and Mrs. Flabby has felt its death the more keenly as she believed that it was animated by the spirit of a deceased daughter.   Such a belief is by no means rare.   A similar fancy, you may remember, is mentioned in Byron's 'Bride of Abydos,' where, in the notes to the poem, mention is made of a wealthy lady at Worcester, who believed that her deceased daughter existed in the shape of a singing-bird; and who, in consequence, was allowed to furnish her pew in the Cathedral with cages of birds, whose songs must have somewhat interfered with the service."

Poor Mrs. Flabby had dried her tears and recovered her composure by dinner-time, though Mr. Bouncer did not attempt to renew his conversation with her concerning either her cat or the Great Mogul. The pic-nic dinner was laid out, as the luncheon had been, on the summit of the hill, in the shade of the group of Scotch firs. Three o'clock was the hour fixed for it; and by that time, as everyone's appetite was sharpened by air and exercise, full justice could be done to the beefsteak pies, and the joints of cold meat, and the pastry, and other good things provided for the occasion. Even poor Mrs. Flabby, seated between the matron and Dr. Plimmer, appeared, for a time, to forget her sorrow; and one and all, patients and visitors, enjoyed the social gathering. After dinner, music and dancing alternated for the remainder of the evening; and little Mr. Bouncer not only persuaded Mrs. Flabby to be his partner in a country dance, but also covered himself with glory by singing Dibdin's " Tight Little Island," which he had often sung at wine-parties at Brazenface, where, however, the chorus to that patriotic song had never been so enthusiastically rendered as it was by the pic-nic company assembled on Firs Hill. It did Mr. Bouncer's heart good to hear the full chorus of voices proclaiming —

For, oh ! she 's a right little island,
A tight little, right little island ;
Search the world round,
There ne'er will be found,
Such another sweet, beautiful island.

There was quite an *al fresco* concert. One of the female patients sang "Auld Robin Gray," in a manner to bring tears to many eyes; though these tears were soon chased away by that male patient, who had acted as drummer of the band, singing, with admirable humour, two comic songs, one of which was " Villikins and his Dinah," then in the height of its Robsonian fame. And so, with music, song, and dance, the happy day drew to its close; and they, for whose healthy amusement this pic-nic had been designed, took back with them, it is to be hoped, many sunny fancies wherewith to cheer less happy moments. The party from the Woodlands had bidden adieu to Dr. Dustacre and Dr. Plimmer an hour or so before poor Mrs. Flabby and her companions were driven away from Firs Hill — a spot which Mr. Bouncer long remembered.

After spending a few more pleasant days at the Woodlands, it was time for him to get home, which he sought to do by way of what he termed " The Little Village ; " so he said good-bye to the Squire and to his college friend, whom he would not meet again until they had got back to Oxford at the end of the Long Vacation. A groom drove him to the station in a dog-cart, which was somewhat heavily weighted with luggage, and, to the back seat of which, Huz and Buz were securely chained. Mr. Smalls' late guest pulled up at the tiny lodge to give a tip to the woman who opened the gate; then they drove along the road where he had walked with Dr. Dustacre; past the plantation, with its under-growth of evergreens; then, round the corner, by the cross-roads, where had stood the chaise into which he had been forcibly hoisted by the broad-shouldered Brand; and, so on, past the point where he had been opportunely rescued by the Squire in his mail-phaeton. Little Mr. Bouncer laughed to himself as he recalled the scene.

He was in good time at the Barham Station. Dismissing the groom and dog-cart, he saw to his luggage, and took Huz and Buz, tethered by a chain, on to the platform. It was a hot July day, and it struck Mr. Bouncer that it would be advisable to refresh himself with a glass of bitter beer. He, therefore, went in search of the refreshment-room; but, he sought for it in vain; the small Barham Station could not boast of so valuable an addition to its provision for the public wants. At the same moment, there walked on to the platform a seedy and battered-looking man, who carried on his arm a large basket, the contents of which made it self-evident that it was, in fact, the peripatetic refreshment-room of the Barham Station. Any doubt on this subject would have been removed from Mr. Bouncer's mind, by the man approaching him with the query, " Refreshments, sir? " and holding out to him, as the most tempting sample of the contents of his basket, a greasy mutton-pie, the sight and smell of which delicacy were not so agreeable to Mr. Bouncer as to Huz and Buz, who tugged and tore at their chain, in the vain endeavour to possess themselves of so choice a dainty.

CHAPTER XXIII.

LITTLE MR. BOUNCER IS UNAVOIDABLY DETAINED AT BARHAM.

S the mutton-pie was held forth by its owner and vendor for little Mr. Bouncer's approval and purchase, an aroma stole from it that altogether overpowered the sweet scent of the newly-mown grass by which the July air was exquisitely perfumed. Loose-shirted rustics, sweltering in the heat of a noon-day sun, were tossing up and turning over the fragrant shocks of tedded hay in the fields that lay around the Barham Station, doing their best to practically carry out the proverb that directs us to make hay while the sun shines; and although his calling was different and less poetical than that of the haymaker, yet the seller of mutton-pies, who had appeared before Mr. Bouncer in the character of the peripatetic refreshment-room of the Barham

Station, was, in effect, endeavouring to make his hay while the sun shone, by trying to procure a sale from the beneficent patronage of Mr. Bouncer.

Now, to purchase mutton-pies — and that, too, under a hot July sun — from a gentleman whom you have casually met, and the antecedents of whom (and his pies) are altogether hidden from your knowledge, must be a daring experiment under any circumstances and to any person. And as, in the present instance, the outward appearance of the vendor did not offer a sufficient guarantee for the inward excellence of the proffered pie, the proposed transaction did not by any means recommend itself to Mr. Bouncer, who, therefore, promptly and curtly declined the proposal of the individual who represented the peripatetic refreshment-room of the Barham Station. Nevertheless, that greasy-looking personage continued to hold out the specimen of his wares, and to beg the little gentleman to purchase it.

"Do try one, sir! it 's only tuppence; and it 's cheap and nourishin' for the money. The finest mutton-pies in Barham or hanywares; made by myself out o' the very primest and juiciest cuts. Just try one, sir! you can do so, free, gracious, and for nothin'; and if you don't like it, you need n't pay for it, and no questions shall be ever axed. You can wash it down with some o' this first-rate pop — only a penny a bottle, and likewise made by myself. The best pop, remember! recommended by the faculty as the primest and wholesomest drink in 'ot weather. Warranted to cure the colic and the gout, pains within and pains without; and all for the small charge of a penny a bottle. One bottle taken with one mutton-pie 'as been known to make the face shine like the best bear's grease; and two bottles, swallered in conjunction with two mutton-pies, 'as produced effects upon the curlin' of the 'uman 'air and whiskers, which must be seen to be believed."

But Mr. Bouncer remained proof against the temptation of the mutton-pie, even with the addition of the ginger-beer; and, as he gazed on the delicacy that was held out to him from the man's basket, he wondered how much dyspepsia — to call it by its mildest name — was compressed within the narrow limits of that two-pennyworth of paste and meat. And he thought of Dr. Wm. Brinton's clever *Frazer* parody of Campbell's "Hohenlinden," where the railway passengers took their hurried meal at Swindon —

> When the train came at dead of night,
> Commanding oil and gas to light
> Much stale confectionery.

·After which occurred the pangs —

> Where curious tart and heavy bun
> Lie in dyspeptic sympathy.
> Few, few digest where many eat,
> The nightmare shall wind up their feat,
> Each carpet-bag beneath their feet
> Shall seem a yawning sepulchre.

But, although Mr. Bouncer considered it highly probable that a like result would ensue on his patronage of the contents of the man's basket, yet, with Huz and Buz, it was a very different matter. Those intelligent animals struggled hard at the chain by which their master held them and made every outward demonstration of their desire to obtain possession of the dainty, the very whiff of which was to them so appetising. Mr. Bouncer, being tender-hearted and fond of his pets, and being, moreover, amused with the man's quaint and persistent recommendation of his viands, patronised the peripatetic refreshment-room by expending the sum of fourpence in the purchase of two mutton-pies for the express delectation of Huz and Buz; and, as he watched them greedily devouring their pasties, he hummed a fragment of a popular song —

> They gave me mutton pies
> In which I did recognise
> The flavour of my old Dog Tray.

At any rate, Mr. Bouncer had spared himself from any similar recognition; and he was quite satisfied with witnessing the enjoyment of Huz and Buz, who, however, did not appear to be equally well satisfied, but, like Oliver, asked for more. "No, no," said their master; "it won't do, my doggies. A little of that sort of thing goes a long way on a railway journey; and, if you were to eat more of them, they might interfere with your digestive apparatus, and then you'd get the mulligrubs in your collywobbles." So, he removed Huz and Buz out of the sight of the unwholesome dainties, and was glad when the vendor of the mutton-pies had taken himself from off the platform.

Except when trains came in, there was not much life to be seen at the Barham Station; and, as it was situated in a deep cutting, there was but little view from the platform. There was a coal *dépôt*, and there was a spasmodic engine, vaguely wandering up and down, with the ultimate object of getting some trucks out of a siding. The entire staff of the station (two men and a boy) was so fully engaged in this noisy duty, that, on Mr. Bouncer's arrival, Mr. Small's coachman had taken the luggage on to the platform while Mr. Bouncer held the horse. Of course, as there was no refreshment for the body — except the mutton-pie man — so, there was no refreshment for the mind, in the shape of a bookstall or newspaper stand; and, if Mr. Bouncer desired to purchase the latest copy of the " Barham Mercury and Poynton Gazette," he must do so elsewhere than at the Barham Station.   His train was already due; and, while he was debating whether he should have time to make his way to an inn that he had passed, not far from the station — the same inn that had supplied Dr. Dustacre with the chaise — and there have a glass of beer, the ticket-taker told him, in answer to his inquiry, that the up-train would not be in for at least an hour; for, the line was blocked further up.

" Not a serious accident, I hope?" inquired Mr. Bouncer.

" Oh, no," was the prompt reply; " only a coal run into a cattle."   Experience had taught him to look on these events with official calm.

Now, it would be wearisome to pass at least an hour of unavoidable delay at so uninteresting a place as the Barham Station.   There were the usual notices and time-tables hanging in frames on the wall; but, the mind would soon be fatigued with attempting to unravel the wild enigmas of " Bradshaw," or spelling out the large-lettered advertisements of somebody's Cocoa and some one else's Tea.   There was a waiting-room, it was true; but, it was not inviting, with its hard benches and its haggard and dirty aspect, as though it had sat up ever so many nights, and had not washed itself in the morning. There was nothing else, except the impenetrable wooden screen that concealed from view the form of the ticket-taker; but, as he was a youth of fourteen, with an un-wholesome face, and an appearance of having lived chiefly on pickles, the screen was a merciful interposition, more especially at such times as the ticket-taker's wooden window was tightly closed.   There was nothing, in short, in the aspect of the Barham Station to induce any sane person to try the experiment of wiling away a long hour in its precincts. So, Mr. Bouncer made friends with a porter, who was temporarily disengaged from his shunting duties, and Huz and Buz were shut up in a lamp-and-grease room until the time was come when the line should be cleared and his train in readiness to take him to " the little village."

Then he went to the inn and had a glass of beer; but did not care to remain there, as he saw the driver of Dr. Dustacre's chaise, who recognised him with a familiar grin, and pointed him out to an ostler and chambermaid as " the party who was took for a loonattic." As Mr. Bouncer did not care for this particular kind of notoriety, he thought that he would consume the hour of his detention by walking through the little market-town of Barham; but, as the town was not very large, and did not contain many greater objects of attraction than the old market-place, the town-hall, and town-pump, his survey of it was soon exhausted. Then he beguiled himself by looking in at the shop-windows, and thereby raising hopes in the breasts of several shopkeepers that were doomed to be disappointed.

But, there was one exception. In one of the windows were two wax busts of a very pink-cheeked gentleman and a very large-eyed lady, who were attired in nothing to speak of except a little fancy satin and their own luxuriant heads of hair. The contemplation of these florid works of art suggested to Mr. Bouncer the notion that he might as well consume the time profitably by having his hair cut. Over the door was the name of Quickfall, with the further information that Mr. Quickfall was a hairdresser and perfumer, and that, in Quickfall's spacious hair-cutting saloons, ladies and gentlemen would be waited upon by the proprietor and competent assistants from London and Paris. So, Mr. Bouncer went into the shop.

CHAPTER XXIV.

LITTLE MR. BOUNCER MAKES HIS ESCAPE FROM MR. QUICKFALL.

PENING Mr. Quickfall's shop-door, Mr. Bouncer set off a small shrill-tongued bell into a screaming summons for the immediate appearance of the proprietor and his competent assistants from London and Paris. Perhaps the latter were mythical persons; or, they may have been engaged at their dinners; any way, Mr. Bouncer's head was not confided to their tonsorial care; and it was the proprietor of the establishment who waited upon him, and ushered him, through the shop, into one of the advertised "spacious hair-cutting saloons."

Perhaps, when Mr. Quickfall had thus described his premises, he had contemplated vast alterations which he had never carried out; for the small apartment into which Mr. Bouncer was shown had all the cheerlessness of the desert, without its limitless prospect. In fact, the view through the solitary window was restricted to a water-butt of bloated dimensions, and a dead wall of uncompromising brickiness. On the floor was an attenuated piece of oilcloth, the pattern of which had long since been starved out; and on a table by the window were arranged the unguents, soaps, brushes, combs, hair-oil, cigars, and other commodities in which Mr. Quickfall dealt. He was a tall, largely made man, who, in years, had passed what is usually called " the prime of life " — a most uncertain and indefinite expression, especially when we call to mind such examples of youthful, hard-working septuagenarians as Lord Palmerston and many of our Judges and Lord Chancellors. Mr. Quickfall had a slow, ponderous manner, in keeping with his dimensions, and suggesting the notion of an amiable elephant who had taken to hair-cutting from mere philanthropy. He was in his shirt-sleeves and carpet slippers, and was girt about with a white apron, furnished with pockets for the implements of his trade.

Mr. Bouncer took his seat on the operating chair, where Mr. Quickfall, by the aid of a cotton wrapper, folded him into the semblance of a parcel, as though he were to be forthwith ticketed and sent away by the next train from the Barham Station. Such a journey had, in fact, to be taken by Mr. Bouncer, who began to fear that his progress to " the little village " would be somewhat delayed, if this Barham barber did not hurry himself a little more than, at the present, he seemed inclined to do. For it very quickly was made evident that, although Mr. Quickfall was slow in action, yet he was quick in speech, and was a most communicative person. He had no sooner got Mr. Bouncer well tucked up into a parcel, and had brushed his hair all over his eyes, than he solemnly paused at the very initiation of his work to commence a highly uninteresting narrative concerning the election of a new member of the Town Council. It appeared, from the statements to which Mr. Bouncer, in his helpless and packed-up state, was compelled to listen, that Mr. Quickfall was a member of that august body, and that the present contest was tearing Barham to pieces, and wounding it in its very tenderest points; and that, if the obnoxious person — whose name was Tarver — should succeed in his election, the doom of Barham was virtually settled, and its position in the eyes of Europe irretrievably compromised. But Mr. Quickfall entertained the hope that he himself might be the humble instrument of opening the eyes of Barham to a proper sense of its true position, and of ridding the Town Council of the dreadful incubus of a Tarver.

While he uttered these patriotic sentiments, Mr. Quickfall was far too engrossed with his subject to continue his hair-dressing duties; and, with comb and scissors in his outstretched hands, he stood in front of his customer, as though time were no object with him, and that the business of hair-cutting could be continued at convenient intervals during the progress of his address. Little Mr. Bouncer, who was utterly indifferent not only to the success of Tarver, but to the doom of Barham, thought of Crowquill's sketch of the talkative parrot of a hairdresser, who says to the bear, upon whose head he is engaged, " Do you think we shall have a war with

Roosher, sir?" To which the old bear sulkily replies, "Don't chatter, sir; but dress my hair." And, further, he called to mind the old anecdote how a person in his position had repeatedly said to the loquacious barber, "Do cut it short!" until the barber, accepting the adjuration as applied not to his own narrative, but to his customer's hair, replied, "I don't think it can be cut shorter, sir; for there is no more hair to cut." Pondering on this anecdote, Mr. Bouncer thought it wiser to hold his tongue, and to sit, like Patience on the oilcloth, while Mr. Quickfall harangued him.

It seemed as though the barber of Barham might have said, "Bid me discourse; I will enchant thine ear;" for he, evidently, must have entertained a strong impression of his own capability for a monologue entertainment. Something that he had said in reference to an anonymous letter that had been forwarded to him in connection with that terrible Tarver business, and which letter Mr. Quickfall denounced as an impudent forgery, reminded him of an episode in his younger years, which, as a matter of course, Mr. Quickfall very leisurely narrated, the while he made a full pause in the operations on Mr. Bouncer's head.

"It was while I was apprentice to Hopkins, late Nicholson, in London, that I was sent for to cut a party at his own private house. A very pleasant and respectable party he was, with a handsome face, bold features and a fine physic." By which Mr. Quickfall meant *physique*. "Most affable he was in his conversation, and he asked me what I had heard about the reports that were afloat concerning Marsh and Stracey's bank in Berners Street. I told him all that I knew, which was not of the best; but, he seemed to think that it would blow over, and that all would come right. Well, sir, I finished cutting that party; and it was n't till three days after that I found out who he was. He was Fauntleroy,

the banker and forger; Marsh and Stracey's had broke, and he was in prison. Nothing could save him; the Bank of England lost three hundred and sixty thousand pounds by him; and he was condemned to die. I well remember the day; it was November the thirtieth, 1824. Having been the last person to cut that party, my governor gave me leave to go and see the execution at Newgate. Such a crowd I have never seen before or since; but, Mr. Fauntleroy bore himself like a man, and passed away quite quietly. Yes, sir; you see before you the very same individual who was the last person to cut a party who was hung for forgeries that cost the Bank of England three hundred and sixty thousand pounds." Mr. Quickfall mentioned this sum very slowly and with great unction, as though the extent of the crime in some way reflected credit upon himself.

"I, also, must cut a party, for I must cut away from you," said little Mr. Bouncer, as he rose to his feet, and endeavoured to shake himself free from the semblance of a parcel. "I 'm not a wedding guest, and you 're not an ancient mariner; and, if I stop to hear any more of your rummy nuisances — that is to say, reminiscences — I shall miss my train."

"But, I 've only cut your hair on one side, sir!" remonstrated Mr. Quickfall.

"All the same, I can't wait to have the other side cut; so, I must journey up to Town half shorn." And Mr. Bouncer meant what he said; for, he freed himself from the cotton wrapper, and, despite the entreaties of Mr. Quickfall, quitted that person's spacious hair-cutting saloon, its proprietor being "left lamenting," like Lord Ullin in Campbell's ballad, but firmly refusing to take his customer's sixpence, on the ground that, if he were paid for an incompleted job, it might provide his implacable foe, Tarver, with a stinging taunt against him as a member of the Town Council of Barham.

CHAPTER XXV.

LITTLE MR. BOUNCER IS LANDED AT THE " LITTLE VILLAGE."

ASTENING from the shop of the too communicative hair dresser, and leaving to future customers the task of discovering the exact dimensions of the spacious hair-cutting saloons of Mr. Quickfall, and also to identify the competent staff of assistants from London and Paris, who, together with the spacious saloons, had not been visible to the naked eye of Mr. Bouncer — that gentleman made the best of his way through the little market-town to the Barham Railway Station. As he did so, and thought of his half-cropped head of hair, the following scene was vividly recalled to his memory.

One morning, after lectures for the day were over, he had gone into Verdant Green's rooms, and, after consoling himself with a pipe, had said, " Giglamps, old fellow! I vote we do the pretty gee-gees this afternoon ! "

"What do you mean?" asked Verdant, who had not yet become fully acquainted with his friend's peculiar phraseology.

"Why, have a ride instead of taking a constitutional," explained Mr. Bouncer.

"Oh, certainly; all right! I shall be delighted," said Verdant.

"Then, if you 're delighted, and if I 'm delighted also," observed Mr. Bouncer, "we shall be like Ingoldsby's ' Babes in the Wood ' —

> ' The two little dears were delighted
> To think they a cock-horse should ride,
>   And were not in the least degree frighted.'

You won't be frighted to ride a cock-horse now, shall you? now that you have got that easy-going old screw — no! we won't call him a screw! we 'll say, that noble steed of Charley Symonds. He 's warranted not to toss you up without catching you again, is n't he? and he carries you as though you were sitting in an easy-chair without any stuffing in the cushions, does n't he? If you keep your seat as well as you contrived to do when we went to Woodstock the other day, I expect you 'll be bursting into verse, like Eliza Cook in breeches, with something of this sort —

> I love it, I love it, and who can tear
> My seat from C. Symonds's old bay mare !

Singing 's thirsty work, Giglamps. Why don't you order some beer, you ungrateful wretch? Shall I holloa for Robert?"

Mr. Verdant Green gave the required permission; and Mr. Filcher, after much shouting, eventually brought the desired refreshment.

" Well," said Mr. Bouncer, when he had quenched his thirst and ended his smoke, " I 'll get my usual hack at Tollitt's, and join you at Symonds's after lunch, and we 'll have a canter somewhere, and, perhaps, a decanter afterwards. There 's a fine old crusted joke for you! We can supply them to you at thirteen to the dozen; country orders executed with promptitude and despatch. Well, ta-ta, Giglamps! you 'll be on the look-out for me at the gateway in Holywell Street, won't you, my precious? "

So it was agreed upon. But, when Mr. Bouncer went to Tollitt's, he could not get a hack. For some reason, there was a great demand for them that day.

" It 's what we may call a haccident, Mr. Bouncer!" said the stable-man.

" A hack-sident, did you say? Why, you 're setting up quite for a wit, Joe! we must call you Joe Miller, if this sort of thing goes on. You 'll be saying next that, instead of the horses running, there 's a run upon the horses." The stable-man grinned. Mr. Bouncer was a favourite, and was generally good for a glass.

The little gentleman went on to Pigg's; but, every horse in those stables was engaged, except one that was being clipped. The operator had just finished one side of the animal, and was about to begin work on the other side, when Mr. Bouncer cried, " Hold hard, my man! I must have that horse."

" But, he 's only half-clipped, sir ! "

" Never mind ! a sweater will do him good."

".But, he 'll look so queer ! "

" Oh, never mind that. I 'll manage to present his broad-side view to the public, and they 'll never see that one side 's different from the other." So, despite further protestations on the part of Mr. Pigg's man, who was jealous for the honour of his master's stables, Mr. Bouncer had the horse saddled, and rode him to Holywell Street.   He found Mr. Verdant Green in front of Symonds's gateway, waiting there on foot, being fearful to mount his steed before his friend's arrival, lest the horse should become fidgety with waiting, and bring him to grief, untimely.   But, the easy-chair bay mare was quickly produced, and the two friends went for their ride; nor did Verdant notice the state of Mr. Bouncer's half-clipped horse; but, then, the eyesight of Mr. Verdant Green was not particularly good.

They had turned their horses' heads in the direction of Oxford, on their way back home, when Charles Larkyns cantered up and joined them.   He was mounted on that very hack of Tollitt's that was usually hired by Mr. Bouncer; and, after a few moments' scrutiny, as he reined in his horse by his friend's side, he said, "Why, you 've changed your horse since you started!"

"Indeed, I have n't," replied Mr. Bouncer.   "Giglamps will tell you it 's the werry identical.   There is no deception, my little dear."

"But," said Charles Larkyns, " though you did n't see me, I chanced to see you, just as you and Verdant had turned out of Holywell Street; and I'm perfectly sure that you were then on a mouse-colour; and this is a bay."

"A bay!" echoed Mr. Bouncer; "why where are your eyes, old boy? there must be some defect of vision.   This is the mouse-coloured hack.   What'll you bet? a bottle of blacking?"

"I could lay you any odds that this is certainly a bay," said Charles Larkyns.

"Now, Giglamps, you shall decide!" said Mr. Bouncer, who was riding between the other two.   "Is this a bay or a mouse-colour?"

"Oh, it is undoubtedly a mouse-colour!" said Verdant, judicially; as though he was an authority on all that related to horses.

"Well!" cried Charles Larkyns, "then all I can say is, I never saw a mouse-coloured before!"

"But, did you ever see one behind?" asked little Mr. Bouncer, as he took his hack a few paces in advance, and then slowly turned him round, in such a way that the clipped and unclipped sides were distinctly seen, and the subject of the dispute was at once made clear. Charles Larkyns declared that he would write a parody on the fables of "The Chameleon" and "The Knights and the Shield."   It was evident that there could be two sides to every question, including that of a horse's colour.

Turning over this circumstance in his mind, little Mr. Bouncer rapidly made his way to the Barham Station. Intelligence had been received that the line was now cleared, and the train for London was expected every minute.   He went to the sliding panel in the wooden screen, where, as in a frame, he saw the head and shoulders of the youthful and unwholesome-looking ticket-taker, whose aspect had suggested his living upon pickles. Then he released Huz and Buz from their detention in the lamp-and-grease room, and refused, on their, and his own, behalf, the proffer of more mutton-pies and ginger-beer from the peripatetic refreshment-room. Then the delayed train came, screaming through the deep cutting, and pulled up at the Barham platform, where Huz and Buz were hastily thrust into the guard's van, and Mr. Bouncer was, as speedily, hurried into a carriage, half filled with ladies and children, in whose company he was, of course, deprived of the solace of a smoke. This, however, did not affect his safe arrival in London; and, in due course, he found himself landed at " the little village," and, as he held Huz and Buz by their chain, replying to the porter's question, " 'Ansom or four-wheel, sir? "

CHAPTER XXVI.

LITTLE MR. BOUNCER IS TAKEN CAPTIVE BY THE FRENCH.

CAB No. 7542, a four-wheeler, rattled through the London streets, and passing Covent Garden Market, set down Mr. Bouncer and Huz and Buz at the Old Hummums. The little gentleman always patronised this hotel when he visited town unaccompanied by his mother and sister; but, when they were with him, they all stayed at Morley's — the Old Hummums, for some reason, declining to lodge ladies within its comfortable walls, and, therefore, necessitating the taking of Mr. Bouncer's women-kind to other quarters. Huz and Buz were far more troublesome fellow-travellers than were Mrs. and Miss Bouncer, for they demanded a great deal of thought and attention as to their board and lodging; and, when in strange quarters, they howled so pertinaciously and dismally, that they constituted themselves into a gigantic nuisance that could not be tolerated over a second night's stay, without a demand being made from the sufferers for the intervention of the police. Mr. Bouncer, however, was enabled to make such arrangements for the lodgment of his dogs that there seemed a reasonable hope that the sleep of the sojourners in the Old Hummums would not, on that night, be disturbed by the discordant howlings of Huz and Buz.

After luncheon, Mr. Bouncer thought that he would make a call upon Messrs. Stump and Rowdy. They were the individuals who, according to the little gentleman's own language, had got all his tin or property until he came of age, and only let him have money at certain times, because it was tied up, as they facetiously termed it; though, why they had tied it up, and where they had tied it up, Mr. Bouncer had no more idea than had the two dogs that he had left tied up in the little yard at the rear of the Old Hummums. But, he now desired to extract some " tin " from these gentlemen — his purse, at the end of the Oxford summer term, having shrunk to the smallest dimensions; a circumstance by no means peculiar to Mr. Bouncer. It, therefore, became necessary for him to work the tin-mine, and to extract the highest possible sum from his purse-bearers.

When he had started on his way to Stump and Rowdy's, it occurred to him that his half-cropped head of hair might present an appearance that would be, to say the least, peculiar. In fact, he wondered what effect it had already produced upon the waiters at the Old Hummums, and upon the stately old lady who presided over the bar. He, therefore, decided to turn into the nearest hairdresser's shop, and there to obtain the completion of that tonsorial process that had been commenced by Mr. Quickfall at Barham. When he came to this resolution, he was in the near neighbourhood of Leicester Square; and, if he had troubled himself to think twice on the subject, he might have concluded that he should infallibly enter the shop of a foreigner. Such was the case. Passing into a hairdresser's shop, bright with gilding and mirrors — neat, clean, and polished, tasteful and elegant in all its appointments, and, in a word, an utter contrast to the poky and dirty "spacious hair-cutting saloon" of the Barham barber, Mr. Bouncer found himself in the presence of the proprietor of the establishment, who was so decidedly French, that, as was soon apparent, he had not picked up sufficient English to enable him to converse with such a true-born Briton as was Mr. Bouncer.

It was that little gentleman's misfortune, rather than his fault, that, although he had been taught Greek and Latin, both at school and college, he had never been instructed in the tongue spoken on the other side of the Channel. Perhaps, the knowledge of French was expected to be developed spontaneously, and to come in the course of nature, like the growth of whiskers; but, as yet, Nature had neither favoured Mr. Bouncer with whiskers nor the capacity to speak French. Therefore, he was only able to make signs to this second of the brace of barbers who chanced to be his tonsors on that day, and to take a seat and point to his hair, and say, in pigeon-English that he fancied would be intelligible to the Frenchman — "De hair — cut — *sivoo play?*" Little Mr. Bouncer was rather pleased at being able to produce this genuine fragment of French.

Probably (very probably!) he did not give it the

genuine Parisian accent, and the proprietor of the establishment may have at once discerned that he was an insular personage who was not conversant with the language of grace and civilisation; for, he replied, in the very best English that he could produce for the occasion, "De har? var goot!" Then he tucked him up in a wrapper, and, as he briskly combed out his hair, said, "From de contree? ha, ha! jusso!" Mr. Bouncer felt inclined to further air his little stock of French by answering, "We, Mossoo!" but he timely reflected that this display of knowledge might plunge him into colloquial difficulties out of which the mossoo would alone rise triumphant; and, therefore, as he felt that he would be unable to frame a reply to further remarks, he thought it best to grunt out a monosyllabic "Yes!" and to wonder within himself — whatever will the Mossoo think of Mr. Quickfall's haircutting?

Mossoo had relapsed into silence, and, perhaps as a token that he had no desire to force his customer into an unwished-for conversation, had politely placed in his hands a newspaper, wherewith he might beguile himself during the tedium of the haircutting. It was a copy of the "Journal des Débats" and, to Mr. Bouncer, it might as well have been a page of Chinese, or a sheet of cuneiform inscriptions.

If, before entering the shop, he could but have glanced at a book of French and English conversation, he might, by its aid, have been able to say to the hairdresser, with an approximate imitation of his own language —

"I wish my hair cut. I wish it cut short. I wish it cut not too short. I wish it left long behind. I wish it left short behind. I wish the curls over the ears to be preserved. I wish it to be parted on the left side. I wish it to be parted on the right side. I wish it to be parted at the back. I wish it not to be parted at the back. I wish the whiskers to be trimmed. I wish the whiskers not to be touched. I wish you to shampoo me. I do not wish you to shampoo me. You may put some grease to my hair. I desire that you do not put any wash to my head. I hope your brushes are clean. Have you a clean comb? Can you supply me with cosmetics, fancy-soaps, tooth-brushes, bandoline, pomades, hair-oil, combs, hair-pins, curling-tongs, hair-brushes, shaving-cream, razors, scent, and articles for the toilette?"

But, Mr. Bouncer was not provided with a copy of such a work as this — which, it may be presumed, would be published by the Society for the Confusion of Useless Knowledge, and, therefore, he was cut off from the possibility of chattering to the hairdresser in his native French — as pronounced at Stratford-at-Bowe — which, perhaps, was not of much consequence; for, unless the hairdresser had replied in the words, and with the accent, set down for him in the Guide, Mr. Bouncer would have been left all abroad in the conversation.

As it was, both he and Mossoo kept silence; and, as he held the "Journal" of an unknown tongue in his hands, he could not but reflect how very unlike this Parisian hairdresser of "the little village" was to the barber of Barham.

French taste reigned around him, and French sights and sounds met his ears and eyes.

A few hours since he was in Mr. Quickfall's unmistakably English shop at Barham, and now he might have been in the heart of Paris for all that he could see or hear to the contrary.

A young and fashionably dressed woman was standing

on the other side of the brightly polished counter, who
was evidently Mossoo's wife; at any rate, he called her
" Thérèse," and she addressed him as " Auguste."

To this elegant lady there entered a sprucely attired
gentleman, who, with much gesticulation and shoulder-
shrugging, engaged her, over the counter, in a lively

conversation in French, the while he purchased something " pour la toilette."

To all this " jabber " — as he was disposed linguistically to pronounce it — Mr. Bouncer listened as in a dream, and as though he were in a foreign land, and not in the midst of the great roaring Babel that he had figuratively termed " the little village."

He sat, tucked up in his wrapper, with the French unreadable newspaper spread out over his knees, while the silent perruquier worked vigorously at his hair, with a couple of brushes, almost dancing round him, in a rapid movement, very different to the slow, ponderous motion and tedious loquacity of Mr. Quickfall, of Barham.

" Of the brace of barbers that I have bagged to-day," thought Mr. Bouncer, " give me Mossoo."

Then he heard Madame calling " Alphonse! Alphonse!" and Mr. Bouncer thought to himself, " this Alphonse is, doubtless, an assistant, who will enter all grimace and smirk."

But a patter of little feet upon the floor soon showed him that "Alphonse" was a small, white, quaintly cropped poodle, who at once trotted up to Mr. Bouncer, and looked knowingly in his face, apparently seeing, with an intelligent glance, that his master's customer was a friend to dogs.

CHAPTER XXVII.

LITTLE MR. BOUNCER DEPARTS FROM MOSSOO'S IN COMPANY WITH ALPHONSE.

URIOUSLY regarding the quaint-looking poodle, who answered to the name of " Alphonse," and who had trotted up to him with so much confident friendliness, Mr. Bouncer thought that, if he only knew enough of the French language, he would venture to make a bid for this funny specimen of the canine species —whose nature was so improved (?) by art— and would take it home with him as a present to his sister, and as a possible companion to Huz and Buz during the months of the Long Vacation.

He wondered what his own two dogs, with their sturdy English breed and manners, would have to say to such a funny little foreigner; and he thought that it might prove a great joke to introduce Alphonse to Huz and Buz. It appeared, moreover, that Alphonse was a poodle of intelligence as well as friendliness; for he sat up on his hind legs before Mr. Bouncer, wagged his tail, cocked his head knowingly on one side, and was evidently prepared, on the slightest invitation, to display all the tricks that he had acquired. But a few words from his master, informing Alphonse that he was a nuisance, a pig, and a camel for thus intruding himself upon a strange gentleman, had the immediate effect of depressing that sagacious animal's spirits, and bringing him once again to his normal position. So, Alphonse, resuming the use of his four legs, trotted round the counter to Madame, who talked to him in her native tongue.

Mr. Bouncer was very much struck with this circumstance. The poodle knew French; and he himself, was ignorant of that language! Was this to be accepted as a sarcasm on the curriculum of education that obtained at the schools and colleges of his native land? Mr. Bouncer merely gave this question a fleeting thought, and then dismissed it from his mind. Yet, the fact of the canine intelligence of Alphonse appeared to him to surpass the case of Sterne's Sentimental Traveller, who, on first landing on French ground, was so much astonished to find that even little common children could speak French. Albert Smith, too, in his "Overland Mail" entertainment, confessed that the same thought had passed through his own mind; and that he was unable to repress a feeling of surprise at hearing the peasant children fluently conversing in a language that we, in England, commonly associated with ideas of refinement and education. Such a circumstance is, indeed, a continued source of wonderment to the average British tourist.

But, to Mr. Bouncer's mind, the present instance was far more striking than the case of the travelled Briton who, for the first time, hears French prattled by illiterate children.

Here was a dog who could understand the language spoken by a Parisian, and who, in that respect, was in advance of Mr. Bouncer in intelligence. If he made a bid for Alphonse, should he be able to instruct that quaint-looking poodle in the English tongue, and to talk to him much in the same way that he spoke his mind, and gave his orders to Huz and Buz? Then it occurred to him, that his sister Fanny could speak French, and that she would be able, if needful, to address Alphonse in his native tongue. He determined, if it were possible, to purchase the poodle, and to take it home with him, as a present to his sister.

Monsieur Auguste removed the wrapper from Mr. Bouncer, and, by significant gestures, explained to him that the operation of haircutting was at an end, and bade him regard himself in the mirror that surmounted a small marble, set upon a gilt bracket. Mr. Bouncer, accordingly, laid down the unperused "Journal des Débats," and advanced to the mirror. There he was confronted by a reflection in which he had some little difficulty in recognizing himself. His hair had been cropped quite short all over the head, and parted, severely, in the middle, from the nape of his neck, straight over the crown, to the forehead. Monsieur stood behind him, evidently regarding his work with considerable satisfaction, and accepting it as a triumph of his art. He had transformed the appearance of the young gentleman "from de contree" to that of the civilised dweller in the gayest city in Europe. Monsieur was an artist, and not a barbarian like the barber of Barham.

The first thought of Mr. Bouncer, as he gazed upon the mirrored reflection, was, "Well! Mossoo has been and gone and done it, and no mistake! it is a regular Newgate crop!"—an idea that would have scandalised the professor of the scissors. It was, therefore, quite as well that the little gentleman kept his thoughts to himself. The deed was done, and he could not undo it. His hair was cropped; and not all the hair restoratives in Mossoo's shop could make it grow again, with a mustard-and-cress celerity, so that it might resume its usual length and appearance before he presented himself to the admiring gaze of his mother and sister. He must make the best of a bad bargain; so, by panto-mimic action, he signified to Mossoo that he approved of his work, and he held out to him half a crown, in order that he might give him what change he thought proper.

Then he proceeded to the dog-dealing business that he had in view; and, in order to make himself more intelligible, framed his question in broken English— "How much you sell little dog, eh?" while Alphonse frisked about, and stood on his hind legs, and went through all his little performances, as though he would say—See what a clever dog I am, and don't insult my feelings by offering a small sum for a poodle of intellect.

It is not, by any means, an easy matter to negotiate a transaction, when the terms of the bargain have to be debated in broken English, greatly assisted, it is true, by expressive pantomime, but damped in intelligibility by a strong infusion of a language that is utterly unknown to one of the contracting parties. It was evident to Mr. Bouncer, that Madame was protesting to Auguste that she should be desolated by the loss of her cherished Alphonse; and it was equally evident to him — more, however, by gesture than by words — that Monsieur was expostulating with his charming Thérèse, and de-monstrating to her, with voluble eloquence, that the young man from the country would amply compensate them for the loss of a troublesome pig of a dog. Eventually, Mossoo gained the day; gold triumphed over affection; and Mr. Bouncer was made aware that the small French poodle could become his property, in exchange for the sovereigns that he had laid upon the counter. Madame caught up Alphonse, and embraced him with effusion, while Mr. Bouncer discreetly turned his head and placed his hat upon it; whereupon, in con-sequence of the close cropping that he had undergone, it slipped down to his eyes.

Hallo! thought the little gentleman; Mossoo's mowed me so short that my tile's too big for my head. It's a regular case of Box and Cox; and I might exclaim with Mr. Cox, the journeyman hatter — " I 've half a mind to register an oath that I 'll never have my hair cut again! I look as if I had just been cropped for the militia; and I was particularly emphatic in my instructions to the hairdresser only to cut the ends off. He must have thought I meant the other ends! " Mossoo has evidently cut the other ends; and, like Mr. Cox, my hat that fitted me quite tight before, now slips over my eyes; but, unlike Mr. Cox, I have not got two or three other hats; so, I shall have to buy a new one.

This incident diverted Madame's attention, and she released Alphonse in order to stuff some cotton-wool inside the lining of Mr. Bouncer's hat, who thought, as he put it on, " As Cox said, it wabbles about rather less, and I can manage to keep it on my head." Then he called a cab, and bade adieu to Madame, who delicately wiped away a tear, as she bestowed a parting kiss on the little white poodle. Mossoo politely handed Alphonse into the cab, and Mr. Bouncer drove back to the Old Hummums, to place his new purchase in safe quarters, apart from Huz and Buz.

CHAPTER THE LAST.

LITTLE MR. BOUNCER RETURNS TO THE HOME OF HIS ANCESTORS.

OONLIGHT shed its silvery lustre over the fair landscape in the midst of which s t o o d the large and c o m f o r table o l d h o u s e, k n o w n a s Gay's Court, the home of Mr. Bouncer and his ancestors for many generations. The cold beams fell upon the village church, softening its hoar austerity, and,

Leaving that beautiful which still was so ;

though this Byronic quotation could scarcely be continued,

And making that which was not,

as regarded the grotesque gurgoyles; for, no natural or artificial light could ever make such stony monsters beautiful; and a bewildered owl, coming suddenly upon one of them, might have dropped its prey out of its claws, from sheer alarm.

The moonbeams also penetrated the little yard at the rear of the Old Hummums, where Huz and Buz had been housed for the night, and where Alphonse was bewailing his separation from Madame in a lugubrious French recitative, to which Huz and Buz added an English chorus, by way of sympathy.

If their united voices — and, as Mrs. Gamp said, " their howls was organs " — kept any one awake, it was certainly not their master, who slept in the front of the hotel, and whose sound slumbers were not even disturbed by the rumble of the early market-carts that brought the treasures of the garden and orchard to Covent Garden Market.

Mr. Bouncer bought a new hat, that fitted his cropped head somewhat better than did his old one; he also restored the parting of his hair to its usual place, and, as much as was possible under impossible circumstances, brushed his hair to make it assume its ordinary appearance. He also called upon Messrs. Stump and Rowdy on that important matter which he designated as "forking out tin:" and, from the little gentleman's pleased appearance at the end of the interview, there was reason to believe that the " tin " had been forked out in a highly satisfactory manner.

He set out for home the next day, accompanied by Alphonse and Huz and Buz, to whom he had explained that the queer-looking little French poodle was intended as a present to his sister, and would not in any way supplant them in his own affections.

The Great Western carried him quickly by Reading and on to Swindon; and, as he journeyed, and thought of the brace of barbers under whose hands he had placed himself, Mr. Bouncer was not only reminded of the incident of his half-clipped horse, but also of another circumstance that had recently come within his knowledge.   It was this:

One of the Brazenfacemen, Kelly by name, but usually known either by the sobriquet of " The Wild Irishman " or the shorter name of " Paddy," had driven over to Woodstock, and had there met with a " Maudlin " Hall man named Blatherwyck, who was in a very maudlin state, and far from sober.   Now, this Blatherwyck was not a very popular man in his College, being far from agreeable in his manners and distinguished for nothing in particular, unless it was for a pair of large bushy whiskers of which he was exceedingly vain, and to the curling of which he was believed to devote much of his mind and leisure hours.   His whiskers, moreover, had earned for him the cognomen of " Esau."   When Paddy found that Esau was not able to take due care of himself, he put him in his own cart, and drove him back to Oxford.   With the assistance of men of his own College, Blatherwyck was put to bed; when it suddenly occurred to one of the party that it would be a great lark to shave off one of Esau's pet whiskers.   This was accordingly done, and the slumberer was left to sleep off the effect of his potations.

Meanwhile, his father, who was a country rector, had come up to Oxford for the Commemoration, and had called, late in the evening, at his son's rooms; but, not finding him in, had gone back to the Star. The first thing in the morning the elder Mr. Blatherwyck returned to his son's rooms, with the intention of having breakfast with him.

He found the breakfast already laid in the sitting-room, and, hearing a snore from the bed-room, walked in and saw his son asleep in the bed, with his whiskerless cheek uppermost.

Now, as he knew that his son possessed a remarkably fine pair of whiskers, it was at once evident to him that the individual who was snoring in bed in the dimly-lighted room was not his first-born, and that he, Mr. Blatherwyck, must have made a mistake, and had entered the rooms of a stranger.

He, therefore, at once beat a retreat, and went down into the Quad, where he met a scout, to whom he politely said, "Will you be good enough to direct me to Mr. Blatherwyck's rooms?" "The first pair to the left, sir," replied the scout, pointing to the staircase. "But I have just come from there," said the other, "and they are not my son's rooms." "They are Mr. Blatherwyck's rooms, sir," replied the scout, "and I took his breakfast there not a quarter of an hour ago. He was in bed. I think he had been making hisself pleasant last night. You'll find them all right, sir — first pair to the left."

"Very odd!" thought the country rector, as he walked back to the rooms, and again heard the snoring of the slumberer. He picked up several books, and, in each of them, saw his son's name. In various parts of the room he also recognized articles that he knew belonged to his son. But the gentleman who was snoring in bed could not be his son, for there was no whisker on his upturned cheek. Some other man must have got into his son's bed! He would go and wake up the intruder, and ask him if Mr. Blatherwyck was coming to breakfast.

With this intent he went to the bed, and gave its occupant a hearty shake. To his great surprise, the roused slumberer turned round his head, and displayed one well known whisker, and the features of his son. The son's question, " Hallo, Governor! where did you spring from?" was answered by the father's question, " Why, Tom! where's your other whisker?" " My other what?" "Whisker!"

The unhappy undergraduate placed his hand to his cheek, and felt, with a bitter pang, that it was denuded of its hirsute attraction. Then he sprang from his bed, and rushed to the looking-glass, and there saw the peculiar figure that was presented to his view.

"It's that wild Irishman!" he cried, as he vowed vengeance on the perpetrator of the deed.

"Make a clean breast of it, Tom, and tell me how it all happened," said his father.

So, poor Esau made a clean breast of it, and told his father everything — what he had done at Woodstock, and how Kelly had driven him back to College, and put him to bed.

" Let it be a warning to you, Tom, never to get tipsy again," said his father. " If you acquire tippling habits, you will lose what will be worth more to you than a whisker." The son promised amendment, and they sat down to breakfast; after which, Blatherwyck shaved off his other pet whisker, and appeared at the Commemoration festivities, looking so altered that his friends scarcely recognized him. It was but a sorry consolation to assure him that, before the end of the Long

Vacation, his whiskers would have grown again, and would be as fascinating as ever. As for Paddy, he disowned the deed, and it never could be proved against him.

Little Mr. Bouncer thought of this incident as he was whirled towards his home, and wondered whether his own cropped head of hair would grow as quickly as Blatherwyck's whiskers.

On from Swindon, the train hurried him to Glouces-
ter; then Ross was reached, and at Hereford he had
come to the termination of his railway journey.

There, according to his instructions, his groom was
in waiting, with a saddle-horse and the Whitechapel cart.
The luggage and three dogs were placed in the latter;
Mr. Bouncer mounted the former, and galloped away to
Gay's Court, where his mother and sister were delighted
to see him, and where he once again found himself in
the home of his ancestors.

Under what more favourable circumstances could we
leave the little gentleman?

Ladies and gentlemen! Mr. Bouncer makes his best
bow to you, and thanks you for having tolerated his
society. He has been well pleased to meet you, and
hopes that you also may have experienced some little
pleasure in meeting him. And now he must say "Good
bye!" having got to

THE END.

TALES OF COLLEGE LIFE.

PREFACE.

THESE " TALES OF COLLEGE LIFE" were written at various times during the last six years, and were published, piece-meal, in various serials. They have been revised and collected, and are here brought before the public in a cheap form, with the hope that they will not prove an unacceptable addition to that light and pleasant food which abler hands than mine have prepared for the mental banquet of those countless guests, who daily sit down at the well-supplied table of Literature.

May, 1856.

THE

FOLLOWING PAGES

Are Affectionately Inscribed

TO

MY BROTHER,

T. W. B.

ÆGER; OR, MISTAKEN IDENTITY.

It 's a wise father that knows his own son.
WALKER'S APOTHEGMS.

CHAPTER I.

THE SICK MAN IN OXFORD.

"ARE you *æger* this morning, Sir?" asked the Scout.

"*Æger?* why, of course I am! Don't I look *æger?*" answered his master.

"Well——"

"Well? but it is n't well! it 's *æger!*"

"Well — I don't know, Sir," replied the Scout, who (like Truth) was not to be driven from his *well;* "at least, I *did n't* know; but, in course, I knows now that you *is æger.*"

"In course you does," replied his master. "So, post the *æger* till further notice. And — here, Thomas! tell the cook, if he can't devil kidneys better than this, he'd better give up his profession, and go to the d—, that is to say, diggins."

"Yessir!" said the Scout, who would have made the same answer, if his master — or rather, *one* of his masters, for Mr. Percival Wylde had but a share in the ownership of the faithful Thomas — had directed him to convey his compliments to the Vice-Chancellor, and would feel obliged by the information whether his maternal relative had yet disposed of her mangle : — " yessir ! " *Exit* Scout, leaving his master *solus*.

Mr. Percival Wylde was seated in his easiest easy-chair, in his comfortable rooms in the fine old College of St. Boniface, Oxford, over a well-garnished breakfast-table, to which an Apicius, or even an Alderman, might not have disdained to sit down. And Mr. Percival Wylde was making the viands disappear in a way which seemed to demonstrate that Mr. P. W. was in the enjoyment of the rudest health ; and this, notwithstanding the fact above alluded to, that, on that very morning, there would be sent in to the proper authorities an " Æger," or document to the effect that Mr. Percival Wylde was prevented attending Chapels, Lectures, and other University duties, in consequence of severe indisposition. A shrewd observer, on contemplating Mr. Percival Wylde's healthy countenance, and vigorous assaults on the breakfast fare, might, from these trifling· circumstances, have drawn the deduction, that the young gentleman's " indisposition " was nothing more nor less than an indisposition, or unwillingness, to subject himself to the fatiguing routine of collegiate duties; and that he was in the enjoyment of a *mens sana in corpore sano*. Nevertheless, he was *æger* in the sight of Dons and Tutors; and his mantelpiece was furnished with three half-emptied physic bottles in support of the assertion that he was on the sick list.

As Mr. Percival Wylde concluded his breakfast with a draught of Buttery ale (they are famed for their beer at St. Boniface), and proceeded to fill a short clay pipe from a tobacco-box that stood beside a bottle labelled " Two tablespoonsful to be taken every three hours until the fever abates," he cast his eyes upon the reflection in the mirror placed over the mantelpiece; and, half-vocally, half-mentally, addressed the following observations to the individual before him: " You are looking your best, this morning, Sir! I never saw you look brighter or handsomer. You will spoil your complexion if you keep to your rooms all day: you will expire with *ennui* before night comes; your own society ain't particularly captivating; you had better give the Dons the slip, and take a run into the country — Or, why should n't you run up to town, and steal a look at Fanny Douglas? She has been in Wilton Crescent these three days, and, of course, is dying to see you. What if, as Dick Swiveller says, the old min is not friendly, and your governor wants you to marry Wilhelmina? are there not *two* people to be consulted on this point; and don't you and Fanny love one another all the more because your engagement is opposed? It will do you good, Sir, to get away and see her: there are heaps of time, and you can be back before Gates. What is the good of posting an *æger*, if you are not to make use of it? What, indeed! "

.And here, Mr. Percival Wylde, having filled his pipe, sat himself down to smoke it, and digest his thoughts; the which proceeding was complacently regarded by his Skye-terrier " Mac," who, seated upon the rug, alternately winked at his master, and blinked at the fire, from under his shaggy eyebrows.

By the time that the pipe was smoked out, the smoker's mind appeared to be fully made up; for Mr. Percival Wylde sprang from his chair, and exclaimed,

"Fanny! you have gained the day. What, ho! my kingdom for a ' Bradshaw ' !" And hunting about among a *débris* of newspapers, railway-books, puffing tradesmen's circulars, odd numbers of magazines, and other specimens of that miscellaneous literature which spreads, nettle-fashion, in all the available corners of a bachelor's apartment, Mr. Percival Wylde at length lighted upon the desired periodical, and, by this, put a stop to the premature expectations and groundless excitement of "Mac," who, with eyes of the keenest speculation, had been following his master's search, evidently anticipating that it would terminate in rats — if not cats.

But it ended in a less lively subject; to wit — (not that there was any wit in it) — " Bradshaw." "Now, let me see ! " murmured the undergraduate, as he turned over the leaves of the bewildering book, and consulted its still more bewildering index:

"Oxford, W. S. 10; Gt. W. 53·57; L. and N. W. 75; O. W. and W. — the Old Worse and Worse, — 77; Shr. and Ches. 86. Mid.   Remarkably explicit and clear, certainly.   Oh, here it is!   Down-train — London. Express leaves at five fifteen; Bletchley, six twenty-five; all right so far! only, this blackguard Junction — Oh, I see! departs from Bletchley at six-twenty-five; arrives at Oxford — why, confound it! it never arrives at Oxford at all!   Oh! here's another train at seven fifteen; reaches Oxford at eight thirty.   That's the ticket! that will just land me in time for Gates.   So, to Town I go, and have a chat with Fanny.   When a man's *æger*, there's nothing like going to London in search of first-rate advice.   After all, Love's the best physician ! "

Having arrived at this comforting decision, Mr. Percival Wylde was not long in putting it in execution.

Watching his opportunity, he ran across Quad., and sped out of the College gates unseen by other than friendly eyes. Then, stealing down the lane which runs at the back of St. Boniface — in which lane many a hack had been waiting to convey him to the cover side, — by divers paths he reached the Railway Station, and ascertained, to his great satisfaction, that no hostile Tutor was bound by the same train to London.

When the Great Metropolis — or " the little village," as Mr. Wylde and his companions facetiously termed it — had been duly reached, and Mr. Percival Wylde's inner man had been duly refreshed, that young gentleman forthwith took his way, on foot, to Wilton Crescent, anticipating the pleasure which Miss Fanny Douglas would doubtless feel at his unexpected visit, and already experiencing some of the delight which he himself would (of course!) entertain at his forthcoming interview with *her*—the adorable one! Filled with these agreeable expectations, he walked, " as upon air," to the Victoria Gate, and crossed the Park in the direction of the two towers of Babel that flank the bestagged pillars of the Albert Gate. But, as he was trampling the rough gravel of Rotten Row, the sight of a female equestrian, the *tournure* of whose form and face resembled that of the incomparable Fanny, carried him on further than he had purposed; and he had followed the horsewoman as far as the Achilles Statue before he discovered that he had been in pursuit of a perfect stranger.

Upon what trifles do the hinges of our life turn! If Mr. Percival Wylde had not caught sight of this young lady equestrian whom he had never seen before, and never wished to see again, he would have gone through the Albert Gate to Wilton Crescent, would have had an

interview with the beloved Fanny, and would altogether
have avoided that impending fate into the threatening
jaws of which he was now thrusting himself.

If he had not done so and so, then so and so *might*
have happened, and so and so would *not* have happened.
Exactly! And so it might be argued of all the great
events of ancient and modern times. *If* Cleopatra had
squinted, the fortunes of the world would have been
changed; *if* Helen had been otherwise than beautiful, the fate of nations would have been different.
" Verily," as honest Touchstone saith, " there is much
virtue in *If*."

Mr. Percival Wylde, then, to make up for the lost
time, walked briskly by Apsley House, and turned down
Hyde Park Corner towards Wilton Crescent — the goal
of his expectations. " How surprised dear Fanny will
be to see me!" he thought; " but an interview is
doubly valued when it has been least expected." And
here, the young gentleman's thoughts were compelled
to flow in a very different channel, and to acknowledge
that there must be an exception to every rule, whether
it prove that rule, or no; for, to his amazement, his
roving eye lighted upon the portly figure of a middle-
aged gentleman, who was slowly toiling up the slight
ascent opposite the St. George's Hospital, and was
advancing towards him with an ill-boding look of mingled surprise and indignation.

CHAPTER II.

THE SICK MAN AT HYDE PARK CORNER.

MR. PERCIVAL WYLDE'S first impulse upon perceiving the advancing foe, was to wheel round, and dart through Mr. Burton's screen to screen himself, as best he might, in the mazes of Hyde Park. His second impulse was to hail a passing cab, leap into it, and bid the cabby drive to Jericho. His third impulse was to meet the difficulty in the face, — take the bull by the horns — beard the lion in his den, and the Douglas in his hall, — and trust to his own boldness and readiness to bring him off the victor.

Mr. Percival Wylde decided to act upon impulse the third.

He did this almost instantaneously; and, without altering his pace, or betraying by his features his sense of the disagreeable nature of the approaching *rencontre*, he advanced to meet the adversary. As he did so, he rapidly delivered this mental soliloquy: " The Governor, by all that's blue! What on earth can have brought him to town? I thought the old bird was safe in Shropshire. He looks uncommonly black at seeing me. By Jove! I *have* done it now, and no mistake! I remember now! there was that letter I sent him the day before yesterday, — through being so beastly hard up, — telling him that I was very bad, and all the rest of it; and asking him to send me a cheque for medical fees, and all those sort of things. If he's got that letter, what will he say to meeting me here! He 's rather corky at the best of times; what will he be now? He 'll see directly that I 'm on my road to Fanny, whom he hates like the bad; and that won't improve the old boy's temper. He expects one to stick so particularly close to College, that he 'll be no end riled at seeing his hopeful play truant in this fashion. I must deny myself to the old boy, and stick out that I 'm somebody else. There 's nothing like impudence! and I flatter myself that I can be as cool as a Covent-garden full of cucumbers. Now for it!"

By this time "the Old Boy" had advanced with quickened steps and eyes of wonder, and had pulled himself up full in the face of his unfilial son. The Old Boy had a highly-coloured, port-and-claret countenance, the radiant hues of which were shown off to the greatest advantage by the snowy colour (that is to say, if white is a colour) of his white neck-handkerchief, which appeared to have been.wrapped round his neck a countless number of times, after an antique fashion. The Old Boy, being of a puffy, apoplectic habit of body, was not accustomed to ascend gradients, however easy, without a certain amount of stertorous breathing, that, for a time, proved a slight impediment to the freedom of conversation; and thus, when he encountered his son, he could only gasp, "Why — why! Percie!" and was then compelled to stop short, and to lay his hand upon his son's arm to arrest his farther progress.

Mr. Percival Wylde paused, and slightly lifted his eyebrows with an air of well-bred surprise.

"Why, Percie!" at length said Mr. Wylde, senior, as he regained his breath, without losing his astonishment; "why, Percie! what in the name of fortune brings *you* here?"

Mr. Percival Wylde gazed calmly on his interrogator, and, without betraying himself by the slightest show of confusion, said, in a careless, drawling tone, " You have the advantage of me, Sir."

" The what ! the advantage ! the doose, Sir ! " cried the Old Boy, exploding at the first onset. " What the doose do you mean, Sir, about the advantage ? "

" Really, Sir," replied the younger one, with a well-affected air of astonishment, " I can only repeat that you have the advantage of me."

" What ! " cried the Old Boy, waxing even redder in the face, and hitting his stick upon the pavement after the manner of irate parents and guardians on the stage ; " what ! deny your own father ! mean to say you don't know your own father ! "

" Father ! " said the other, with a slight shadow of polite astonishment in his tone ; " Father ! really, Sir, I —— "

" What ! " cried the Old Boy, " not own your own father ? I suppose you 'll say next that you are not my son ? "

" You flatter me, Sir, by the supposition that I could be the offspring of so remarkable an old gentleman," was the cool reply ; " but, really, I must confess my inability to lay claim to so singular a parent."

" Why ! you — you — " stammered the Old Boy, whose rage was now at boiling point ; " but, come, Sir ! no more nonsense ! Just turn your steps, and come with me to Morley's."   Mr. Wylde, it must be remarked, *en passant*, patronised this Trafalgar-square Hotel, as it was in convenient neighbourhood to his Club, which was at the opposite corner of the square.

" Excuse me, old gentleman ! " replied his son, with

undisturbed nonchalance; "but I have no wish to go to Morley's, although you hold out to me the tempting offer of your agreeable company. My way lies in the opposite direction."

"I know it does, Sir!" cried the Old Boy, as choleric as Mr. Wigan in "The Bengal Tiger": "I know it does! I knew it, Sir — knew it from the first! From the very first moment that I set eyes on you, I said, That rascal's on his way to Wilton Crescent."

"You must be gifted with the spirit of prophecy, though not of politeness; for I *am* on my way to Wilton Crescent," was the reply.

The Old Boy was furious at this frank confession. "I knew you were!" he cried; "I knew it! and did n't I forbid you making love to her? did n't I tell you that I would never sanction any tomfoolery of love-making with a girl that won't have as much as will keep her in — in hair-oil, by Jove!" continued the Old Boy, anxious for a striking example in his statement of the presumptive fortune of Miss Fanny Douglas. "Perhaps you are not aware where I am just come from, Mr. Percie?"

"In the first place, Sir," replied the son, "as I am personally unknown to you, I cannot see why you should address a perfect stranger as 'Mr. Percie,' although that name might, perhaps, do as well as any other. But, in the second place, Sir, I think I can give a very shrewd conjecture as to the place from which you have just come, — namely, the Lunatic Asylum; to which place I should advise your speedy return. You are not fit to be trusted without a keeper."

Mr. Percival Wylde said this with perfect gravity, and with the air of pity which any one might be supposed to feel towards an unfortunate gentleman ; but his words angered the Old Boy above all bounds. His loud tone of voice, his thumpings of his stick upon the pavement, and the highly dramatic action that he threw into the dialogue, had already attracted the notice of many of the passers by, and had drawn to the spot more than one of those London street-boys, who rise up, by a species of magic, wherever there is an exhibition of any-thing for which no payment is demanded ; and, it must be confessed, that Mr. Wylde *was* making a gratuitous exhibition of himself. These small boys, moreover, after the habits of their species, indulged in a running commentary on the passing scene, expressed in the common vernacular, and modelled on the Chorus of the ancient Greek drama. As may be imagined, their varied sallies of wit, and cutting sarcasms, were not without their effect ; and their observations of " Draw it mild, old un ! " " Don't bust yourself ! " " You 'll split yer veskit, guv'nor ! " were, to Mr. Wylde, as the lash-ings of the tail that excite the lion to fury.

" Asylum ! keeper ! " gasped the Old Boy, who would have roared, if his shortness of breath had permitted him to make so much noise ; " by George, Sir ! you 'll make me cut you off with a shilling ! "

" He says," explained one small boy to another, who had just arrived upon the scene ; " he says that he cut off with a bob. The old gent 's vun o' the swell mob." An explanation which was by no means satisfactory to Mr. Wylde.

" Cut me off with a shilling ! " echoed the son ; " really, Sir, your language is most extraordinary. But you must excuse my giving my attention to more of it, as I have my engagement to keep. Allow me to wish you good morning, and, at the same time, to thank you for your diverting society."

This was more than Mr. Wylde could bear. Catching his son tightly by the arm, he exclaimed, "Not so fast, Percie! you are not going to escape me in this way, without giving an account of yourself; and explaining why you are here in London, going to see a person you ought not to see, when you ought to be ill in bed in Oxford, running up doctors' bills, which you expect me to pay, and send you cheques for! and then to disown your own father, and — and — by George, Sir —" Mr. Wylde paused for lack of breath, not for lack of words.

"Hit him while he's down!" cried a small boy, probably as a suggestion to Percie to take an unfair advantage of his parent, the while he was in his gasping state of speechlessness.

"Pray let me call a cab for you; you are getting outrageous. This is probably the time for one of your fits," said Percie; and with an air of kind protection, he put his arm within his father's, and sought to lead him to the neighbouring cab-stand.

"By George!" cried the Old Boy, as he recovered his breath, and broke from his son's hold, "this is more than I can bear! to be disowned, and called a madman by my own son — my own son, Sir!" he added to a passer-by who had tarried a moment, impelled by curiosity to listen to what was going on: "my own son, Sir! who ought to be at Oxford, and ill in bed."

"My eyes! ain't that a whopper, neither!" remarked one of the Chorus.

"Ill in bed, Sir!" continued Mr. Wylde, "and writing to me for cheques for doctors' bills, Sir! and then denies himself, Sir; and talks about me having the advantage,

— although he confesses to being on his way to Wilton Crescent. What do you think of that, Sir?"

The gentleman to whom Mr. Wylde addressed himself appeared to be unable or unwilling to commit himself to a reply, not having seen much connexion or probability in Mr. Wylde's far-from-lucid *resumé;* and his suspicions of that individual's sanity were strengthened, by the explanation which Percie gave to him and the other bystanders, in the abbreviated style of Mr. Alfred Jingle: " Poor man — touched here — very sad — sees a likeness — thinks I 'm his son — distressing case — very ! "

" I 'll tell you what, Percie !" cried the Old Boy; "I 'll make you suffer for this ! Disown me, and call me a lunatic ! by Jove, Sir, I 'll cut you off with *less* than a shilling ! Come with me directly, Sir; or never expect me to own you again."

" This," said a small boy, in the didactic manner of Mr. Robson, in the pathetic ballad of "Villikins and his Dinah," " this is vot that brute of a parient hobserved to the hoffspring of his haffections."

" Really, Sir," said Mr. Percival Wylde, "I have endured your eccentricities quite long enough, and it is now time to put a stop to them. You may, perhaps, be a very fine fellow down in your own part of the country, and accustomed to bully labourers and swear at tramps; but you 'll find, Sir, that this conduct won't do in London, where no man is suffered to publicly insult or annoy another with impunity. If every eccentric old gentleman was to take it into his head to claim any one he fancied as his own son, and was permitted to indulge in such absurd paternal cravings, young men, like myself, would not be able to walk the streets in safety, so long as old gentlemen like you were left at large. If you annoy me any further, I shall have no other course left than to give you in charge to this policeman." And Percie pointed to a blue-coated official who had strolled (by accident) to the spot.

"It's all stuff and nonsense!" cried the Old Boy, keeping a tight hold of his son's arm: "I'm not going to be cheated out of my own eyesight in this way, and told to my face that I'm a madman, and not the father of my own son — a son who deceives me, and imposes upon me with his sham sickness and his doctors' bills! But I'm not the man to be tricked in this way; so, come along with me, Sir! I insist upon it! and you know very well that I keep my word, and am not to be trifled with."

"Vot a huncompromising old trump!" observed one of the Chorus.

"Since you compel me to adopt so disagreeable an expedient, I have no other alternative than to give you in charge:" and Mr. Percival Wylde beckoned to the blue-coated official.

"Hook it, old 'un!" cried a kindly-disposed small boy; "hook it! the Peeler's a-coming!"

"Come, Sir!" said the *Peeler:* "I think you'd best not trouble this gent., but move on: becos, if so be as he hinsists upon it, in course it'll be my dooty to take you in charge."

"But," expostulated Mr. Wylde, "he's my own son — who ought to be at Oxford, ill in bed — my own son!"

"Ah, Sir!" said the philosophic Peeler, "you see, there is *has*tonishing likenesses to be met with in the world. Sometimes it takes a wise child to know its own father, and sometimes a wise father ain't able to know his own son.   *We* sees such things every day, bless you.   But you *must* move on, Sir; or else I must take you in charge for annoying this gent.   As it is, you're a *h*obstructin' of the pavement."

"Ho, Soosanner!" sang one of the Chorus, as a consolation for the sufferer; "Ho, Soosanner, don't you cry for me! yer a goin' to Hallerbarmer, with yer banjo on yer knee!"

"I have no more time to lose, Sir!" said Mr. Percival Wylde, referring to his watch: "it is already past the time when I ought to have been in Wilton Crescent," — (the Old Boy flinched at the mention of this locality), — "and I must again repeat, that if you persist in annoying or *following* me" (for I had better be on the safe side, thought Percie), "I must give you in charge.   Having given you this final notice, I must leave you to pursue your own way."

"Very well, Sir!" roared the Old Boy, at the culminating point of his fury; "you shall suffer for this, Sir! I'll teach you what it is to impose upon me with your sham sicknesses, and your cheques for doctors' bills that you never had!   I'll teach you what it is to disobey me by making love to that girl!   If you were fifty sons and heirs, I'd cut you off with a shilling — I would, by George!   I'll give you a lesson, Sir!   I'll go up to Oxford at once and have you expelled the place.   I will, Sir, by —— "

"Don't swear, Sir!" said Mr. Percival Wylde, with the same imperturbable coolness and *sangfroid* that he had maintained throughout the conversation; "Don't swear, Sir, I beg! for as this is a public thoroughfare, I shall feel it my duty, as a member of society, to complain of you, and have you fined five shillings, as a warning for the future !"

"Ugh!" was all that old Mr. Wylde ventured to growl in reply: and, seeing his son pursuing his way to Wilton Crescent, he strode in the opposite direction, down Piccadilly, surrounded by the Chorus of small boys, singing "Pop goes the Weasel," turning head over heels, and making the most liberal offers to do "four wheels a ha'penny" for Mr. Wylde's instruction and amusement: offers which were not received by that gentleman with the same liberal spirit in which they were made.

CHAPTER III.

THE SICK MAN ON HIS ROAD TO THE DOCTOR.

MR. PERCIVAL WYLDE experienced otherwise than agreeable feelings when his father made his declaration of visiting Oxford; and he was too well acquainted with the paternal mode of decision to doubt that his father would practise what he preached. He knew very well that the Old Boy would at once take the rail to Oxford, and, on there being fully certified as to the imposition practised upon him, would probably cut off the pecuniary supplies from his hopeful son, even if he did not proceed to the extremity of "cutting him off with less than a shilling."

Now, as this proceeding, even in its mildest form, would be anything but agreeable to a young gentleman who had freely plunged into the most expensive habits of a University career, the thought of its being carried into execution filled Percie with alarm, and brought before his imagination a series of startling pictures, executed in the heaviest mental distemper, in which expelling Dons and threatening Duns stood forth in sternest colours. He saw at once that he must give up his cherished plan of spending the best part of the day in the society of Miss Fanny Douglas, and must betake himself to Oxford with all expedition. But yet, when he reflected that he was but a few hundred yards from the abode of the charmer, and that the Crescent lay not so very much out of his way to the railway-station, it was more than the weakness of poor human nature could bear, not to call in there for a few moments *en route.*

"It will never pay to go back without a look at Fanny," thought Percie, " after I've taken all this trouble to see her. I must manage to get a sight of her by herself, and to keep out of the reach of the rest; for I daresay the Old Boy will be making inquiries after me, and the *éclaircissement* might be awkward. It is unfortunate enough as it is; but who'd have thought of meeting him at Hyde-park Corner when he ought to have been safe in Shropshire. I wish now I hadn't sent for that doctor's cheque; but the game had done once before, and I thought it would do again; and I was so hard up, that I didn't know which way to turn. I wish Fanny had got something like a fortune, because then the Old Boy wouldn't cut up so rough about her. Her governor goes at such a pace, that he must live quite up to his means; and he'll scarcely be able to give Fanny a *sou,* — and that the Old Boy knows pretty well. *Hinc illæ lachrymæ :* hence his advocacy of Wilhelmina. I wouldn't take her if her gingerbread were doubly as thick in gilt! Dear Fanny is worth a dozen of her. I *must* go and see her. It would certainly be awkward if the Old Boy got to Oxford first, and found out my absence. I know that he would keep his word about me, and I should be cast into the den of Duns. I should have no money — Fanny would only have her father's blessing; and our marriage would be out of the question. Yet I think I shall have time to call in the Crescent. I know the Old Boy's habits well enough to make me feel sure that he 'll go and pay his bill at Morley's before he sets out for Oxford. This will delay him some time; so I can easily spare a few minutes for Fanny, and reach Oxford by an earlier train than the Old Boy. I 'll risk it. As I 'm an *æger* man, I can't do better than pay a visit to the doctor who will do me the most good."

So rapid is the process of thought, that, to arrive at the above decision was a far quicker thing in the performance than it is in the telling; and Percie had jumped into a Hansom, and been whirled to Wilton Crescent, before Mr. Wylde, senior, had reached St. James's Street.

A thundering knock and a rallying ring evoked a canary-coloured being, who, although six feet in his stockings, and blessed with undeniable whiskers, was yet affable and benignant. This condescending gentleman knew Percie well, and had, indeed, been moved to extreme affability by sundry and repeated tips administered to him by Percie, both in town, and also at his (or, at least, his master's — which was the same thing) country-seat in Shropshire. In consequence of this monetary relation that existed between them, the affable Canary looked with the eyes of encouragement upon the amatory passion displayed by Mr. Percival Wylde for Miss Fanny Douglas, and fostered it in a variety of ways — such as the transmission of *billet-doux*, and the retailing to Pinner, the maid, of various anecdotes, which served to place Mr. Percival Wylde in a favourable, if not heroic, light. These fragments of biography were collected by the affable Canary from his friends and neighbours in the servants'-hall of Mr. Wylde's establishment; and, having been properly spiced and seasoned by the faithful Pinner, were duly served up for Miss Fanny's entertainment during the several courses of that young lady's toilette.

As the young gentleman's love was encouraged by the young lady's mamma and papa — who were naturally anxious to secure a young man of position and property for their almost dowerless daughter, — and was opposed by Mr. Wylde alone, and that solely from pecuniary motives, — the whole band of Mr. Douglas's retainers headed by the affable Canary and the faithful Pinner (between whom, indeed, there were certain love passages, that led them to a sympathy with others in the same position), espoused the cause of the young lovers; and did not, as touching this subject, quarrel with, or bite their thumbs, at the retainers of the house of Wylde, after the fashion of the Capulet and Montague factions. The affable Canary, indeed, regarded the Juliet of his house with the most paternal feelings, speaking of her to his brother retainers, as "our eldest daughter" — as though she were a species of joint-stock property — and receiving her Romeo, and ushering him into her presence, with an air that seemed to express, "I give my consent — take her, and be happy."

On the present occasion, therefore, the affable Canary not only felt pleasure at opening the door to Romeo, but was also enabled to divine the object of Romeo's visit:

a divination far more readily arrived at from a superficial study of the visitor's outward man, than if the internal anatomy of the victim had been consulted.

" The missis and master have just druv off to the Cristial Palliss at Siddynam, Sir," said the affable Canary, in reply to Romeo's inquiry as to who was at home; " and the young ladies is gone a hairin' in the park, with Mamselle and Pinner; but Miss Fanny is at 'ome, Sir, and is a writin' in the drawin' room by 'erself.   I 'ope I see you well, Sir."

Quite well, thank you, Mr. Affable Canary, although I *do* happen to be *Æger*, so take up my card to Miss Douglas.

And the affable Canary takes a piece of pasteboard imprinted with the name of " Mr. Percival Wylde; " and that young gentleman, after desiring the Cabby to wait for him, trips up the stairs, softly singing a *carmen triumphale*.

CHAPTER IV.

PHYSICIAN AND PATIENT.

THE affable Canary had not deviated from the truth when he told Mr. Percival Wylde that Miss Fanny Douglas was at home, alone, and in the back drawing-room; for, there she was.

She was seated before a curly-legged, lady-like look-ing writing-table, on which were strewed, in picturesque disorder, letters answered and unanswered, together with the snowy sheets that were yet to receive the *pencillings*

of Miss Fanny's thoughts and fancies, and were destined
to carry to divers quarters all those varied sensations,
and paroxysms of confidence, that tear the breast of the
feminine letter-writer. The young lady appeared to
have at length brought to an end a painfully-becrossed
epistolary effusion; for she had folded up a letter into
its envelope, and had lighted a taper, which — according to that truthful imitation of nature that distinguishes
the generality of " Art-utilities," — was inserted into the
upright mouth of a blue-bell, obligingly held by a
Parian Cupid, who was already encumbered with a gilt
quiver and a sheaf of arrows; and there was an odour as
of the burning of scented sealing-wax, as Percie was
ushered into the room by the affable Canary.

Fanny was so engrossed with her occupation, that she
had not heard the footsteps of the approaching visitor
— muffled as they were by the moss-like carpet of the
front drawing-room — and she was not aware of his
entrance until the words, " Mr. Percival Wylde, Miss ! "
fell gratefully upon her startled ear. She started round
as the affable Canary placed Percie's card upon the
table, and ushered its late proprietor into the room; and,
in another moment, her hand was clasped in that of her
lover's. Then — the affable Canary having discreetly
closed the door — a little pantomimic performance was
gone through, which, though brief, was doubtless amusing and satisfactory, notwithstanding that it was accompanied by the exclamations: " there ! — don't ! — you
rude thing ! — suppose some one should come in ! "

" Why ! *can* it be you ? " at length said Miss Fanny
Douglas, when the pantomime had been brought to an
end.

" Oh dear, no ! " replied Percie; " it is n't me ! it 's a

man very like me.   Perhaps it's my wraith — like the
gentleman who so inopportunely appeared to Mrs. Auld
Robin Gray.   'I saw my Jamie's wraith, but I could
not think it he, until ' — etcetera and so forth ! "

" At any rate," said Fanny, laughing, " I am quite in
her position, for I can scarcely think it you.   It is only
just now that I was certified of the fact that you were,
at the present time, some seventy miles from here."

" Yes ! but don't you remember the Corsican Brothers ?
and have you forgotten that never-to-be-forgotten night
of happiness when we went to the Haymarket, and saw
Planchè's capital burlesque, and heard that killing imitation of Charles Kean —

> ' *I* am *his* spirit, come to show *me* how
> *He*, that is, *I*, *was* killed *to-morrow* — now ! '

Have you forgotten that puzzling position of pronouns ?
There are queer things in the drama of life, as well as in
that of the stage; and perhaps, after all, I am *not*
myself ! "

" Well ! if it *is* you," laughed Fanny, " I hope I see
you well — as people say; for I was certainly under the
delusion, not only that you were at this present time in
Oxford, but that you were very ill there."

" And so I am, my dear Fanny ! " replied Percie,
with mock gravity; " so I am — very ill indeed — *æger*.
But my ghost, who is now addressing you, is pretty
well, thank you."

" I am pleased to hear it, Mr. Ghost," said Miss
Fanny; " for your Ghostship's Papa left this room not
half-an-hour since, after giving me a most touching and
affecting narrative of the malady under which your
Ghostship was supposed to be labouring; and," con-

tinued Fanny, as she pointed to the letter she had been sealing, " I had even been giving myself the trouble to convey to you my condolence on your serious indisposition.   It seems that I might have spared myself such useless labour."

" Dear me, no ! " said the Ghost; " pray give me the valuable document, and I will see that it is duly conveyed to Percival Wilde, Esquire, who is now pining on his Oxford bed of sickness.   The sight thereof will be unto him as the sight of the goddess Hygeia, and will raise him from his *æger* couch — *æger*, my dear Fanny, being a Latin word, that signifieth sick, ill, or indisposed."

" Thank you, Mr. Ghost, for the translation;   and, having given me one translation, perhaps you will favour me with the explanation of another; and will condescend to explain why I am thus so unexpectedly honoured with the translation of an *æger* gentleman from Oxford to London."   And Miss Fanny puckered up her eyes and lips, and looked unspeakably roguish.

" Certainly, my dear Fanny," replied the Ghost; " though in as few words as possible; for my time, like your own sweet self, is very precious.   I was so ill — at least, not ill, but *æger*, you understand — that I found I must run up to town for the very best professional advice on my case.   Now, we have it on most excellent authority, that the best Physician is a certain Doctor Love ; so I naturally called at this house, where I knew he was to be found; and, ' Here we are ! ' as the clown says in the Pantomime — Physician and Patient.   The Patient having stated his case, what is the advice of my Doctor Love ? "

" That you immediately go back to Oxford, Sir, where

you know you ought to be now, you naughty boy!"
replied the Doctor.

"Is that your advice?" asked the Patient.

"Yes," said the Doctor.

"Thank you," rejoined the Patient; "I feel indebted
to you.   There is Dr. Love's fee!" and the Ghost positively seized upon the young lady, and kissed her!—at
least he *appeared* to kiss her; but we had rather not
commit ourselves to the declaration that his osculatory
intentions were fully carried out.

"There, Sir! that is quite enough!   I did not ask
you to pay me in that fashion!" said Dr. Love, with a
quickened breath, and a heightened flush — (so, perhaps, after all, the Ghost *did* kiss the young lady!) "It
is fortunate for you that you did not meet your Papa
here.   What ever would he say if he knew you were in
London — much more in Wilton Crescent?"

"Oh! he *does* know it," said the Ghost, calmly; "I
met him at Hyde Park Corner, and, thinking that honesty
was the best policy, I told him that I was on my way to
Wilton Crescent."

"I admire your boldness!" remarked Doctor Love.
"And was he *very* angry?"

"Not more so than the Old Boy usually is on this
subject," replied the Patient.   "He roared me 'an'
't were any nightingale.'   Ahem! Shakspeare!"

"But," asked Doctor Love, "was he not horrified to
find your Ghostship in London, when he thought you
were lying ill in Oxford?"

"Slightly horrified, and fearfully disgusted!" replied
the Ghost.   "But then, you see, my dear Fanny, that it
was not *me* that he met.   At least, *he* would have it that
it *was* me.   But it must have been some one very like

me; for, of course, it could not be me, because I was, at that very time, keeping an *æger* at Oxford."

"Of course not! but explain the riddle, Sir Ghost!" said Doctor Love.

The Ghost did so, in that jerky, Alfred Jingle style which he had before made use of at Hyde Park Corner; which style is a particularly useful one when you want to get over the ground quickly. In fact, it would be very advantageous to the devourers of the three-volume thirty-one-and-sixpence class of romantic novels, if the food of their imagination was drest up in this literary short-bread fashion, for it would save them the consumption of a great deal of unnecessary indigestible matter.

"So that's the state of the case, my dear Fanny," said the Ghost, as he brought his rapid narrative to a conclusion. "And now, having gained my point in seeing you, and having been considerably refreshed thereby, and having had the excellent advice of Doctor Love on my distressing *æger* case, I must be off as quickly as possible to Oxford, before the Old Boy can get there."

"Decidedly the best thing you can do, Sir," said Doctor Love. "Don't let me keep you another minute; but, if you are really my patient, take my advice and go."

"And with your advice I should like to take thee! as Lover sings, and your lover says — eh, Doctor Love?" said the patient, who appeared to be in a humour for composing impromptu parodies; for he immediately added, "'My cab is at the door, And my bark is on the sea, But before I go, Astore! I've a double kiss for thee.' And," continued the Ghost, as he gave the young lady a practical illustration of the beauties of his parody,

" don't let your Mammy or Daddy, or any one else, know of this visit. And, pray be cautious, my dear Fanny, and don't split ! "

And, with this final injunction, — which seemed to intimate that there was some danger of the young lady coming to an untimely end, after the fashion of tight dresses and unseaworthy vessels — the Patient warmly embraced the Physician (so great was his gratitude !), and the Ghost vanished.

CHAPTER V.

THE PATIENT SPELLS PATIENCE.

As the patient left the room, Doctor Love rang the bell; and the affable Canary, obedient to its summons, paused in his perusal of an exciting narrative of a " Marriage in High Life," — recorded, for the instruction and amusement of mankind, in the pages of the " Morning Toast," — and slowly, but (of course !) gracefully, proceeded to place himself in communication with the gentle spirit who had evoked him from his cell.

As drifting straws will show the viewless courses of the winds, so this willingness on the part of the affable Canary demonstrated the power that Miss Fanny exercised over all who came within the range of her fascinations. For, the affable Canary, when summoned by Miss Fanny's ring, had just reached the most interesting and exciting part of the marriage narrative, wherein the Bride's dress was described in language that would have made the heart of a milliner thrill with ecstasy; and it

was only some strong fascination that could have torn
him from his enthralling occupation. But, in Society,
— that is to say, in the world of Art, — as in the world
of Nature, we meet with whirlpools into whose depths
people are sucked irresistibly, and glide round and
round without the slightest control over their own wills;
and it is not improbable but that the affable Canary, —
who was a creature of impulse as well as of affections,
— had been unconsciously drawn into the vortex of his
young mistress's whirlpool of fascinations. Yet, be that
as it may, at *her* summons, " he stayed not for brake,
and he stopped not for stone," — he did not pause for a
second or third ring, but, his duty (or whatever you
prefer to call it) rising superior to his curiosity, he
threw down the " Morning Toast," and immediately
responded to the tintinnabular call. As the affable
Canary ascended the staircase, he encountered Mr.
Percival Wylde descending from his consultation with
Doctor Love — and, as appeared from his countenance,
already greatly relieved by the Doctor's prescription.
Percie, again making use of the abbreviated Alfred Jingle style of address, briefly stated to the affable Canary
the urgent necessity there was for perfect secrecy on the
subject of the present visit, if Mr. Wylde, senior, should
take it into his head to institute inquiries thereon.

" Master and Missis bein' at Siddynam ; and Mamselle and Pinner still hout with the young ladies, no one
but Miss Fanny and me, Sir, will be aweer of your call,"
said the affable Canary, summing up the evidence as to
the feasibility of putting in a claim for that possibility
of being in two places at once, which old Mr. Weller
designated by the name of " a alleybi," and so strongly
urged upon his son as the only safe outlet for his master,

in the labyrinthine and memorable trial of " Bardell *against* Pickwick." " And you may rest heasy, Sir," continued the Canary, "that *I'll* be as mum as a hoyster!" and the faithful and affable creature closed his fingers upon the two half-crowns delicately slipped into his hand.

" In these sort of cases," thought Percie, " and with these kind of people, a little palm-oil is most efficacious in lubricating the conscience, and enabling it to slip easily into the track we have marked out for it. And Fidelity will hold true at five shillings until it be tempted with ten."

But Mr. Percival Wylde had no further time to bestow on reflections of a philosophic nature, when it was the moment for prompt action. He waved an adieu to Miss Fanny, who was watching him from the drawing-room window — and jumping into the Hansom, ordered the driver to take him to the Great Western, as though his life depended on his speed.

This injunction, as it happened, was well nigh being fulfilled to the very letter; for, as the driver made a sharp turn round the corner of Hyde-park-street, the cab came into collision with the van of a West End laundress, which was proceeding on its homeward route laden with the heavy baggage it had collected in the Square. Now, although Hansoms are warranted to " keep this side uppermost," and to preserve their equilibrium under the most trying circumstances, yet they are not exempt from those ills which cabs are heir to, when brought into sudden and violent contact with vehicles of larger growth and heavier burden; and it therefore happened, that not only was a shaft of the cab broken, but that one of its little windows was burglariously entered by the pole of the heavy van; and, by these several means, the Hansom was brought to a standstill, and its horse to a downfall. It was fortunate for Mr. Percival Wylde, that he was aware of the collision, and instinctively sprang from his seat; for, by this action, he avoided the blow on the head or poke in the face, that the van-pole would undoubtedly have given him; in which case, his adventures would, probably, have been brought to an unexpected termination, or would, at any rate, have been deprived of the chance of being faithfully illustrated with a handsome frontispiece.

" The more haste, the worst speed! " thought Percie, as he gave the Cabby five shillings and his card, and left that gentleman busily engaged in endeavouring to raise his fallen steed from the ground, and in heaping on the van-driver's head denunciations composed of

> Filthy Conjunctions, and dissolute Nouns
> And Particles pick'd from the kennels of towns,
> With Irregular Verbs for irregular jobs,
> Chiefly Active in rows and mobs,
> Picking Possessive Pronouns' fobs;
> And Interjections as bad as a blight,
> Or an Eastern blast, to the blood and the sight.

" ' The more haste, the worst speed.' What says the proverb? ' The hasty man eats soup with a fork!' When a man is in a hurry, he 's sure to be delayed. There 's not another cab in sight; so it 's fortunate that I 'm not bothered with luggage, and that I 'm not far from the Station. Three minutes will do it! Fanny did not occupy more than ten minutes, and I shall be in good time to beat the Old Boy. I know his habits

---

[1] Hood's " Tale of a Trumpet."

well ; and he won't clear from Morley's under half-an-hour. It was worth any risk to see dear Fanny. After all, stolen joys are the sweetest — danger of discovery gives a zest to love-interviews. If Romeo had been let in at the front door, and allowed to see Juliet in the front parlour, with Mr. and Mrs. Capulet's sanction, he would n't have enjoyed it half so much as the balcony."

With hurried reflections of this comforting description, Mr. Percival Wylde quickened his steps, and speedily reached the Railway Station.

" Down train to Hoxford, Sir?"

" Yes! when does it start?"

" The carriages are in now, Sir: but the train won't leave the platform for a quarter of an hour."

" Delightful! just the ticket! by the way, I may as well get my ticket. I shall do the Old Boy beautifully!"

At the very moment that Mr. Percival Wylde had come to this satisfactory conclusion, he heard a cab clatter up to the Station; and, the next minute, in walked — the Old Boy!

CHAPTER VI.

THE SICK MAN IS IN DANGER.

It was remarked by the eminent Stoic philosopher, Epictetus, in his admirable manual of morals, " The Enchiridion " — or, if it was not remarked by Epictetus, it might have been, if he had chanced to have thought of such a thing — that it is impolitic to enumerate the brood of the domestic fowl, before the process of incubation has been brought to a satisfactory conclusion.

The folly of this delusive feeling of security was exemplified in the case of Mr. Percival Wylde, when he saw the Old Boy walk into the Great Western Station. Fortunately for the son, the father was so intent upon hastening to secure his ticket, and ascertaining if he was in time for the train, that he passed within a yard of Percie without seeing him; and the young gentleman had the intense satisfaction of hearing his paternal relative order a first-class ticket for Oxford, and assured by the clerk that he had full ten minutes to spare. Of course, Percie's first and chiefest impulse was to keep out of sight of the Old Boy; a feat the more easily achieved from the fact of the old gentleman, after one promenade and stern scrutiny of the platform — during which, Percie lay hid in a lamp-room, redolent with greasy and oily compounds that would have gladdened the heart of a Russian — either designedly or accidentally, taking up his station in front of the ticket-taker's box.

"Well!" thought Percie, in the greasy recesses of the lamp-room, "this may be regarded as a fix. What must be my plan of action? To be myself, or not to be myself—that is the question. Shall I again face the Old Boy, and have a *da capo* performance of our previous entertainment? No! that would be a trifle *too* cool: it would surpass the bounds of probability for the Old Boy to fall in, on the same day, with two individuals so strikingly like me. That won't do. Stay! a brilliant idea strikes me! What if there is an express that starts half-an-hour, or even an hour, after this train, and yet reaches Oxford before it. How gratifying to the Old

Boy's feelings it would be to have his slower Parliamentary shunted into a siding, while the quicker Express whirled me past him at the rate of a mile a minute. Delightful! if it can be put into execution."

But it could not. For, on Percie carefully emerging from the lamp-room, and consulting a time-table and a porter, he gathered from their joint information, that the train, now about to start, was a quick train, and that the Express had already gone.

"It won't do at all," thought Percie, "for the Old Boy to reach Oxford, and find the *æger* man not there. It would be risking Fanny's happiness as well as my own; for he would certainly cut off the supplies, and then, the only kind of union left for us would be the Union workhouse. In my cottage near a wood, where love and Rosa would all be mine, is all very well in poetry; but the sentiment won't do when translated into prose, unless the cottage is a cottage *ornée*, and Rosa has the proper amount of pin-money. I must take steps to prevent the Old Boy from cutting up rough. Desperate diseases require desperate remedies. I must go to Oxford in the same train with the Old Boy." And, as that venerable individual continued to remain on guard at the ticket-office until the moment of the train's departure, Percie was compelled to surmount the difficulty of obtaining his ticket, by commissioning a porter to do it for him.

"Now then! take your seats, if you please. Any more going on for Oxford?"

Certainly! Mr. Percival Wylde is going on, as soon as he has seen the Old Boy safely ensconced in a first-class carriage. He sees it; and, making a dart into another first-class carriage, the bell rings—the doors are slammed

— the last cry is heard of " Mornin' papers — ' Times,' ' 'Vertiser,' 'Mor'n Post,' ' Punch,' ' 'Lustrated Noos ! ' " — the whistle is sounded — the strong-minded old gentleman, who is determined to have all that he pays for, and has gulped down his boiling soup or coffee, in true Salamander fashion, rushes wildly at the locked carriage doors — the feeble-visioned old lady bewilders the porters with incoherent inquiries — the engine gives a few convulsive snorts, like the hippopotamus rising from his bath — and off she goes !

So far so good !   But this is only the first part of the danger overcome. Mr. Percival Wylde must bear in mind that the old proverb advises him not to give vent to vociferations until he has emerged from the forest: and the dangers of the Didcot Junction have yet to be surmounted. Dangers they were, and had liked to have proved fatal to the case of the *æger* man.

The Old Boy, with a perversity peculiarly aggravating, had got into a carriage that was going on to Bristol, and out of which, therefore, he had to get at the Didcot Junction; while Mr. Percival Wylde, with a tenacity of purpose that was well nigh his ruin, had seated himself in a carriage that was going through to Oxford. This carriage was one of those peculiar to the Great Western line — divided into two compartments communicating with each other; and what was Mr. Percival Wylde's horror on seeing his father deliberately advancing to this carriage ! He had barely time to pass into the second compartment (which was empty), and pull-to the door of communication, when his father stepped into the other compartment, and ensconced himself on the very seat that he had so lately occupied. " This is all very well," thought Percie, as he drew a long breath; " but, suppose the Old Boy

takes it into his head to pay a visit to this compartment!
'The thought, it is madness, deceiver, to thee!' as the
song says. I will sell my life as dearly as possible." Mr.
Percival Wylde, therefore, silently, but firmly, clasped
the handle of the door, and pulled it towards him; and,
with a beating heart, listened to the gaspings, puffings,
and mental ejaculations with which the Old Boy was
amusing himself on the other side.

In this way the father and son reached Oxford, side by
side, and yet, to all intents and purposes, far distant from
each other. But though he had reached Oxford in
safety, yet the *æger* man was not yet out of danger; even
Doctor Love would not have pronounced him free from
a relapse. The sick man had still to get into his College,
and that, before the Old Boy could arrive there.

Now, the railway traveller may chance to remember,
that the " Down " side of the Oxford Station is on the
further side from the city; and that, on alighting on the
" Down " platform, to proceed to the city, he has to pass
over a bridge that spans the line — by which proceeding
a greater amount of ground has to be traversed than if
he had set out to the city from the "Up" platform. This
problem of mensuration was at once apparent to Mr.
Percival Wylde, and also the benefit that he might derive
from its immediate solution. He had no sooner, therefore, seen the Old Boy clear out of compartment No. 1,
than, darting from compartment No. 2, with his coat
collar turned well up over his face, he ran across the
line, jumped on to the " Up " platform, and, in defiance
of policemen and railway regulations, vaulted over the
iron-work fencing, that — in a manner believed to be
peculiar to the Oxford station — performs the super-
fluous duty of an useless barricade against nothing, and

utterly confounds elderly females, who, having once got within the railings, can't get out again, and regard them much in the same way as they would look upon the maze at Hampton Court. In less than a minute, Percie was in a cab; and, in less than five (minutes, not cabs), was put down at the end of the lane at the back of St. Boniface, having, by this stratagem, fairly distanced the Old Boy.

Surely, the Fates had befriended him! for he gained his rooms as he had left them, unseen by other than friendly eyes; and was received by Mac with those grins and double-actioned wriggles by which a Skye terrier is accustomed to express his joy.

CHAPTER VII.

THE SICK MAN'S SYMPTOMS ARE DUBIOUS.

THE Old Boy was as good as his word, and at once made his way to his son's rooms. It was not the first time that he had visited them, so that he had not to inquire his road, but, with unfaltering memory and with unswerving steps, walked across the correct "quad.," laboured up the correct staircase, and paused to regain breath at the correct "oak," which was surmounted with the name of "WYLDE."

"Come in!" cried a faint voice, in reply to the tap at the door; and, saluted by the furious barking of "Mac," the Old Boy walked into the room, and immediately gave vent to exclamations of the greatest surprise at the very unexpected *tableau vivant* that met his gaze.

Percie had made the best use of the few minutes that intervened between his own and his father's arrival, and had produced a stage effect that proved his dramatic powers to be of no ordinary kind. The scout being fortunately in the way, a basin containing a gruelly compound had been extemporised, and placed judiciously upon the table, in company with a stout physic-bottle, and a wine-glass. Drawn up to the table was a sofa; and, reclining languidly thereupon, his feeble body supported by the pillows from his bed, was the figure of Mr. Percival Wylde, denuded of coat, waistcoat, neckcloth, and boots, and clad in a loose dressing-gown and slippers. His pallid features betokened, either the rapid inroads of his malady, or the superficial use of a certain cretaceous tooth-powder. A close scrutiny would, perhaps, have enabled the spectator to determine under which head he might assign the *palor;* but the window-blind was drawn down, and a dim religious light pervaded the apartment. As the Old Boy entered the room, Mr. Percival Wylde was lying back upon his pillows, apparently engaged in sipping the gruellous compound.

"Why, Percie! good gracious! can it be you?" gasped the Old Boy.

"Why father! good gracious! can it be *you?*" responded Percie, in a weak voice, like an echo in a consumption.

"Why — how — eh — what — you — eh!" gasped the Old Boy, in a fit of unintelligible monosyllables, which, if they were meant to express what was passing in his mind, ought to have been expanded into these words: "Why, how did you get here, when I have just left you in London? Can I have been deceived after

all?   Was it really a stranger to whom I spoke at Hyde
Park Corner?   And yet, it was a very great likeness.
But then, there *are* great likenesses in the world.   Oh!
of course, it *must* have been a stranger: my own son
would not have denied himself to his own father.   Bless
my life! how I have wronged the poor lad by my suspicions!   And so wretchedly ill as he is, too!   How shall
I forgive myself?   But, am I obliged, therefore, to confess my mistake to my son, and expose my own head-
strong blunder?   Shall I show him that I have suspected
him without a cause?   No! I must let him suppose that
I am come up to see him solely in consequence of having received the information of his illness.   Poor lad!
how I have wronged him, to be sure."

The Old Boy was assisted to the conclusion of his
mental plan of action by Percie saying, "It was very
kind of you to run up to see me; but, when I wrote to
tell you that I was *æger*, I had no thought that I should
thus put you to the trouble of coming up to Oxford, or
I would not have said a word about my illness."

"Trouble! my dear Percie," said the Old Boy, really
relieved at his son putting this construction on his visit:
"as soon as I knew that you were ill, I could not rest
until I had seen you."

"That's a thumper!" thought Percie.

"And so, I said to your mother, I don't feel at all
comfortable about Percie, until I have seen that he has
got proper advice."

"That's another!" thought Percie.

"So I at once came up to Oxford, without delay —"

"Thumper the third!" thought Percie.

"And I am quite grieved to find you such an invalid,
and looking so miserably pale."

" The tooth-powder is a success! " thought Percie.

" I am afraid you have been studying a great deal too hard. You should be careful about yourself, Percie, and not overtax your constitution. You should n't burn the — what is it? — the midnight oil, too much, you know." And the Old Boy said to himself, " Bless my life! how I have wronged the poor lad! "

"Oh! I am much better," said Percie, making a show of an attempt at cheerfulness, and thinking that the Old Boy would probably have changed his idea of his son's use of the midnight oil, if he had been one of the wine-party that had tenanted that apartment last night, and had clouded the midnight oil with the fumes of tobacco until the small hours of the morning; — " I am much better, though still on the *æger* list, and under the Doctor's hands, as you see. But I hope this is my last day of living on slops, for it is not very agreeable fare. I can't ask you to join me ; but I will soon get you something from the Buttery, or the Confectioner. At any rate, I can give you a glass of something better than this ; " and Percie indicated the medicine bottle. " By the way, it is my time for taking it. But, no! I will postpone it for awhile — I think I may throw the Doctor over this once."

" Certainly, my dear Percie," said the Old Boy; " ' throw physic to the dogs ' — as What 's-his-name says in the play — and take a glass of port instead. You look as though you wanted something strengthening. Those doctors are always on the lowering system : it makes good for their trade."

" Well! I really *should* like a glass of port," said Percie, with the air of a man whom circumstances had . compelled to be a stranger to such a luxury: " and I think I may venture on one, if it's only to drink your good health."

"Of course! certainly!" said the Old Boy; "it can't do you any harm, and it may put some colour in your checks. Your mother would be quite distressed if she were to see you looking so pale. Where have you felt your chief pain?"

"Chiefly here," replied the sick man, with a subdued smile, as he laid his hand over the region of his heart, and placed the port wine upon the table. "The symptoms have been unusually severe to-day. Let me fill your glass."

"Thank you, Percie! and fill your own also; I'm sure it won't do you any harm. And here's to your better health!" said the Old Boy. And as the wine gurgled in his throat, he thought, "Bless my life! how I have wronged the poor lad. His mother would be quite distressed to see him."

And thus Mr. Wylde senior was filled with the deepest repentance for the imaginary wrong he had done his son, in supposing that he had met him at Hyde Park Corner, when he had been lying so ill and pale in his Oxford rooms. And after the Scout had cleared away the remains of the dainty little banquet that had been sent in by the Confectioner, — in which feast Mr. Percival Wylde did eat more than was benefiting for the character of an *æger* man; excusing himself, however, on the presumptive medical fact, that heart complaints brought on great voracity of appetite — when this banquet had been brought to a satisfactory termination, and when the Old Boy had been well warmed with a further supply of port — a generous beverage forwarded from his own cellars — he, then and there, in order to make an atonement for his unworthy suspicions of his son, did, in the noblest manner, fill up for him a cheque for double the amount he had asked for.

"But you will soon throw the doctor over," said the Old Boy, as he looked at Percie, whose face had been cleared of the tooth-powder. "These doctors always keep to the lowering system. You already look fifty per cent. better for having had a good dinner and a glass of wine, instead of slops and physic; and I hope that to-morrow I shall be able to take home a better account of you to your mother."

And the Old Boy did so; for Mr. Percival Wylde, who professed himself to be greatly benefited by his father's visit — which, at any rate, he was as to purse — with the Old Boy's departure was at once restored to perfect convalescence. And, as it happened, this was the last time that Mr. Percival Wylde was "*æger.*"

CHAPTER VIII.

MR. PERCIVAL WYLDE IS DOING WELL — NO FURTHER
BULLETINS WILL BE ISSUED.

IT was shortly after this that Mr. Percival Wylde took his degree. He was one of the last who went in under the old regulations, and he thanked his stars that he came under the *ancien régime*, instead of the modern system.

It was at this important epoch, also, that a certain maiden lady deceased, having bequeathed to her niece, Miss Fanny Douglas, the sum of twenty thousand pounds, invested in the five per cents.; and as this legacy slightly altered the complexion of affairs, the Old Boy was graciously pleased to withdraw his prohibition against his son's union with the fortune-possessing Miss Fanny, who in due process of time, and with all due ceremony and rejoicing, was converted into Mrs. Percival Wylde.

It is believed that it was on the evening of their wedding day, that the arrangement was finally agreed upon which terminated in the affable Canary withdrawing Pinner from Mrs. Percival Wylde's service, and constituting her the hostess of that old-established house, and well-known resort of the Belgravian livery—" The Polyphemus and Squint"—to the good-will of which he had just succeeded.

And it is believed, that although Mr. Percival Wylde is continually attended by Doctor Love, yet that he is no more "*æger*" than he was on that memorable morning when he encountered the Old Boy at Hyde Park Corner.

A LONG–VACATION VIGIL.

CHAPTER I.

WHICH, INTRODUCES THE HERO.

THE Commemoration was just over. My mother and sister Nelly, who had never seen its glories, had been spending the week in Oxford, and were thoroughly fatigued with their severe round of sight-seeing and lionising. Like a dutiful son and brother, I had shown them everything that was worth looking at: had given them select breakfasts and luncheons in my rooms at Brazenface — promenaded with them in the Broad Walk on the Sunday — got them good places in the Theatre, where, indeed, Nelly had to blush in the front row, as one of " the ladies in pink " — procured them tickets for the Amateur Concert — taken them on to our college barge to see the Procession of Boats — gone with them to Worcester College to see the Horticultural Show and the Fireworks — introduced them at the Ball in the Town Hall; and, in short, had generally acted as a walking catalogue to all the sights and notabilities of my Alma Mater. These were fatiguing pleasures to all; and I was not sorry when they had come comfortably to their end, and the spires and domes of Oxford had been left far behind us.

I had been anxiously looking forward to the Long Vacation, for the end of it would see me going in for my degree. What with boating, cricketing, and other summer idlenesses, I had put off reading so long, that at last I had come to the conclusion it would be better to lay aside books altogether till Term was over; and that in the quiet of the Long Vacation, I should have abundance of time for my reading. So I had laid this flattering unction to my soul, and, having thoroughly enjoyed the Term, I thought I could as thoroughly and easily settle down to work now that "the Long" had commenced. Big with this resolve, I went so far as to unpack my books and lay them upon my study-table; but the exertion seemed to exercise a weakening effect upon me, and I deemed it best to brace myself up for work by a dip in the sea, and to spend a few days at the quiet little watering-place of Westcliffe, whither my mother and sister had gone with all the juveniles. Finally, I resolved that I should be in the best trim for reading while enjoying the quiet and the sea-breeze; so I packed up some books, and determined to stay at Westcliffe some few weeks.

The next week, armed with my classical weapons, I made a descent on my family, who had taken up comfortable quarters at the Royal Hotel. Like many hotels in similar places, it was so constructed that it had private entrances for those families who might take a suite of rooms; and my mother had preferred this to the usual lodgings. The hotel was on the outside of the little town, fronting to the sea. For the first few days I got on very well; and I had just come to that point when I thought how jolly it would be, when I began work next Monday, to lie on the cliff, with a weed in my mouth, and get up Aristotle, and watch the sea-gulls skimming about, and the ships sinking in the distant west, when an event occurred, which, for a time put all my logic to flight.

CHAPTER II.

WHICH INTRODUCES THE HEROINE.

ONE afternoon, when Nelly and I were returning to the hotel to dinner, from a long ramble over the cliffs, a travelling carriage and four dashed by us. Who could it be? Westcliffe was a very quiet little place, and a carriage and four was not an every-day arrival. "And how strange," said my sister, "there is neither maid nor footman in the rumble;" and, as it went by us, I looked for the coat of arms (Nelly is great in heraldry), and they had evidently been painted out. "Whom can the carriage belong to?"

"Most probably to that grey-haired old gentleman, who is just getting out of it," I replied; for the carriage had drawn up at the door of the hotel. By the time that the gentleman had assisted a middle-aged lady to descend, we had approached them (for our private door was next to the public entrance), and I had a full view of the third occupant of the carriage. She was a young lady of not more than twenty years of age, with a pale face of rare beauty, to which an air of deep melancholy gave a peculiar charm. As she stepped from the carriage a book dropped from her hand and fell under the wheel. I picked it up and returned it to her. With the old gentleman I interchanged a salutation of hats, with the young lady I interchanged a mere glance. But what will not a glance effect when one is yet a child in the eyes of the law, and when the thermometer is at 90 in the shade? From that moment, I was that young lady's slave.

With another glance, and we had passed side by side into our respective doorways, and I had only the lovely vision of her features to console me. Eating dinner under such circumstances was a mockery and a jest; I went through the ceremony merely as a solemn duty which I owed to custom and to my family. I was glad when I was able to get away on to the beach, and meditate by moonlight on the fair unknown. How her features were impressed on my mind, though I had seen her but for a few seconds! But there are some faces to be met with once or twice in a life-time, which can never be forgotten, but which will rise in all their freshness and beauty before the charmed spell of memory, without any effort or will of our own to call up the several features. And so it was with the lady of my tale. I can see her before me now — " in my mind's eye, Horatio " — as distinctly as I could in my lover's fancy when I walked that night on the sea-beach at Westcliffe, and, according to my wont under great excitement, talked to my Skye-terrier Trap, on the subject that engrossed my thoughts. Trap was my college dog and constant companion — the recipient of all my secrets. If all depositors of secrets made a similarly wise selection in their confidantes, the Mrs. Candours of the world would find a greater part of their occupation gone!

The beach lay shining before me; the sea came dashing and rolling in with its grand, everlasting music; and I — like Demosthenes shouting his orations to the waves — paced up and down the beach, and, amid the roar of the waters, told all my fancies to Trap. "Was n't it a face to haunt you in blissful dreams — eh, Trap? Did you ever see such an expression, Trap? — not one of those senseless wax-doll faces, but a calm, pensive look, with a winning gentleness and soft melancholy that reaches your heart at once — does n't it, Trap? It is the sort of melancholy air which leads you to suspect ⸴ that she has never told her love, but let concealment ——' you know the rest, Trap. But, when I picked up the book, did you see the sweet smile that played around her mouth, and lighted up her face with a sunbeam of beauty — did you see that, Trap? And then her eyes! did you ever see such eyes, Trap? such deeply, darkly, beautifully, blue eyes, Trap? Swimming in their own liquid fascinations, Trap!"

My enthusiasm was carrying me rather out of my depth; but Trap wagged his tail, as though he perfectly understood and appreciated my remarks. I therefore continued my poetical metaphor.

"Did you ever see eyes of such a liquid blue? a blue, blue sea, from which the Queen of Love comes forth to dower you with all her charms, Trap? What sea-nymph ever had such cerulean eyes, Trap? What Nereid, what dweller in the coral caves beneath this wide-resounding sea" ——

My soliloquy is disturbed by a gentleman, who suddenly, and to my vast surprise, emerges from the very midst of the waves, and announces himself to be — not Neptune, or even a Nereid — but a shrimper! In the

most unromantic and offensive way, he suggests that
shrimps and prawns form an excellent appendage to a
well-regulated breakfast-table; and further hints that he
— he, the disturber of my solitude, and soliloquy — by
name, Tom Barr, but familiarly known as Old Barnacles,
will feel it a honour to wait upon a party as smokes such
good tobaccer. Of course, I give him a cigar, and an
order for the family breakfast; by which time, as my
weed is nearly out, and my chain of ideas has been
rudely snapt, I return, in a ghostlike, dreamy way, back
to the hotel.

"To-morrow," I thought, "I shall see her!" and,
comforted by this pleasing thought, I turned off to bed.

CHAPTER III.

DISCOVERIES AND BEWILDERMENTS.

I OUGHT to have dreamed of her, and should probably
have done so, had not the low murmur of the waves
lulled me into too sound a sleep for a visit to Dream-
land; but I devoted my thoughts to her during the
whole time I was shaving, and, as that included the risk
of a razor-cut, I began to think that I was decidedly,
and madly, in love.

After breakfast, I descended into the precincts of the
Bar, in order to have a gossip with our landlady. Mrs.
Rummell was always particularly obliging on this point;
and I therefore experienced no difficulty in leading
the conversation on to the subject of yesterday's arrival.

The landlady's communicative tongue soon put me in possession of the intelligence I was so anxious to obtain.

"The gentleman's name is Spencer," Mrs. Rummell said, "the gentleman told me so himself, and said that all letters directed here in that name were to be brought to him; and he said that, Sir, just as though they was n't to be given to either of the two ladies. The oldest lady is his wife, because he called her 'my dear'" (Mrs. Rummell's logic was conclusive); "and the young lady is his daughter, because, when I offered to assist her in taking off her travelling-dress, the other lady said 'Thank you, but my daughter needs no assistance:' and I heard her call her, Amy." (Amy! what a sweet name!) "They have very grand manners, and are grand people, I 'm sure, Sir; but I think there 's something rather queer with them. It is n't often that gentlefolk of their quality, especially where there are ladies, travel without their servants; but that 's nothing to do with *me*, if they want to save expense. And they don't let the waiter be in the room at meal-time, no more than is necessary to change plates, and put the things on the table; but *that's* nothing to do with me, if they wish to be private. And, last night, when the chambermaid went to unfasten the ladies —— "

"Unfasten them!" I cried in surprise. "Why, you don't mean to say that they are chained up?"

"Oh, law no, Sir!" laughed Mrs. Rummell, in good-humoured horror.

"Then, do you mean that the two ladies are taken to pieces every night?"

"Ah! you are fond of your joke, I see, Sir; but, of course, you know what I mean well enough; that the chambermaid went to assist the ladies in unlacing their dresses, and so on."

" Oh! I see! and what happened? "

" Well, Sir!" answered Mrs. Rummell, "she was only allowed to unfasten Mrs. Spencer; and she did n't so much as set eyes upon the young lady. And it was just the same this morning, when she went to fasten the ladies; she only saw Mrs. Spencer; and, when she asked if she should go and help the young lady, Mrs. Spencer said, 'No! I will attend to her myself.' Putting this and that together, it almost looks as if the young lady had been doing something wrong, and they were keeping her under lock and key; for, when they came, Mrs. Spencer said to me, 'We shall require two bedrooms, and they must communicate with each other.' I happened to have such rooms as she required, with an inner door opening from the one room into the other, and an outer door to each room opening on the landing. So I showed the lady these, and she said they would do very well; and then she examined the lock of the outer door of the young lady's room, and she locked it, and told me that she would keep the key as long as they remained here. Of course, Sir, I could make no objection to this; but it almost looks as if the poor young lady was a sort of prisoner."

The landlady's tale roused my curiosity, and added (if possible) to the interest I already felt in the fair stranger. Poor Amy! since Amy, it seems, was her name; what could she have been doing to require such strict guardianship? It was a mystery; but it accounted, doubtless, for that sweet melancholy which gave such a charming character to her beauty.

The more I thought upon the subject the greater became its fascinations. My head was full of Amy, and busy in devising schemes for her deliverance; for that she was a prisoner, I had at once decided; and, moreover, that I was to be the chivalrous knight who should rescue her from imprisonment. I felt within myself that the age of chivalry was *not* dead, in spite of what Burke had said to the contrary.

CHAPTER IV.

DEEPER AND DEEPER STILL.

WHEN my sister and I went out for our morning's walk, Nelly was very curious to know who the arrival of the previous day might be; so I confided to her all that Mrs. Rummell had told me about Amy.

Yes! *Amy;* for I could not call her Miss Spencer. No! when a man is really in love (and I felt that *I* was) it is the lady's christian name that always leaps to the lips, and hangs lovingly upon the tongue.

And even while we were speaking we met her with her mother. They were coming up from the sands, and Amy had evidently been bathing, for her long, damp, dishevelled hair was streaming from under her plain cottage bonnet, and was lost in all its luxuriant richness under the folds of her shawl. She glanced towards us, and looked confused (at least, I thought so) as she met my earnest gaze. She sees that I love her, I whispered to myself. I was in hopes that, for the slight courtesy I had shown them on the previous day, the lady-mother might vouchsafe to recognise my existence, but she passed on to the hotel, and " made no sign."

Later in the day we were out, far away on the cliffs, when, at an angle in the narrow path, we suddenly came upon Amy, walking with her father and mother. Of course she saw us, and — she smiled! *smiled*— there was no mistaking that agreeable fact! — but the paternities put on the similitudes of Dragons guarding a priceless treasure, and they hustled her past us, and got out of sight as rapidly as possible.

Three days passed in this (to me) most unsatisfactory manner. Amy bathed in the mornings, and walked out in the afternoons, but was always under strict surveillance. And the same mysterious dragon-ship was maintained over her in-doors — so Mrs. Rummell informed me: none, except her parents, had interchanged a word with her since she had been in the house. But hers were eyes which had a dumb language of their own, far more expressive than even the words of some people's lips; and, when we met her in our walks, those pleading eyes seemed to say to us " I am persecuted and helpless; oh! be my friends!" And her sad, touching look of melancholy would so work on my excited feelings that I many times asked Trap if I should be justified in laying violent hands upon the Dragons, and delivering the unfortunate Amy from their thraldom. But my sage attendant would not commit himself to an opinion on this delicate subject.

Of course, while my mind was in this excited state, it was impossible to settle down to hard reading. I tried to do so one morning, and opened my Thucydides; but I could see nothing in the Greek characters but " Amy, Amy; " and her calm face and deep blue eyes swam between me and the page. I must " cram " at the last, I said, and make a shot for my degree. I was a bachelor, in danger, not only of losing my heart, but my B. A. also.

The fourth day came. I had inspected Mr. Spencer's carriage, in the coach-house; but the coat of arms had been so completely painted over that I was unable to make out anything. The carriage was nearly new — why should the arms have been obliterated? I rubbed off some of the paint with my thumb, and I discovered that the arms were surmounted by an Earl's coronet. Stranger still! Was Mr. Spencer travelling under false colours? or, was he a *parvenu* who had bought the carriage at a sale, and therefore painted out the heraldry? But the appearance of the whole party was against this supposition. There was an air about the Dragons which showed them to be Dragons of gentle blood, while, as for Amy, she was every inch a lady! The mystery was increasing; and to all appearance, was as far from being solved as ever — at any rate by me.

What with the heat of the weather, and the fervency of my passion, I should have been completely prostrated with the oppression of this mystery, if the burden had much longer remained upon my mind; but, that same afternoon it was destined to be removed in a very unexpected manner.

CHAPTER V.

A CLUE TO THE MYSTERY.

NELLY and I had gone out for a stroll, and had reached a part of the cliff, down whose steep side there wound a narrow pathway to the beach. We were nearly half way down, when we saw Amy and her father and mother coming up. The Dragons looked as though they would have turned when they saw us; but, if that was their first resolve, they changed it, and came on towards us. As they slowly approached, toiling up the steep path, we both noticed the unusually bright look of joy which lighted up Amy's face. She was leaning on her father's arm, while her mother walked at her side, but slightly behind, the path being narrow.

"Look, Nelly!" I whispered, " she is evidently showing us a letter!" and my heart throbbed quick, like the bell of an electric telegraph machine — for I thought the letter might be for me.

"She is, indeed!" whispered Nell; "and see, she conceals it under her shawl, that her father and mother may not see it. And look how earnestly she is gazing at me!" ("and at me!") "And she puts her finger on her lip — that means secrecy. She must mean the letter for me;" ("or for me;") "But how will she convey it to us?"

There was no time to speculate on this point, for we had reached the trio. I pressed Nell's arm as a signal, and we drew on the one side of the narrow path, so as to allow the others to pass us. We each looked earnestly at Amy, while Nell (so she tells me) threw into her face as great an amount of sympathy as she could express.   Amy also looked at her (for it was at *her* — there was no mistake about it!) with a look of almost tearful supplication; and, as she passed, evidently trembling, there fell from underneath her long trailing shawl, a letter.   Her father seemed to hear the slight rustle of the paper, and quickly turned; but I was too quick for him.   The letter had no sooner reached the ground than it was covered by my foot, and the Dragon saw me earnestly engaged in pointing out to Nelly an interesting steamer which was trailing its smoke in the far distance.   I suppose he was satisfied, for they continued to ascend the cliff.   I secured the letter, and, watching my opportunity, as Amy slightly turned her head towards us, I gave the document, with stage effect, into Nell's hands, while Nell waved her handkerchief as a friendly signal of " All 's right."

Then we went down to a sequestered part of the beach, and, sitting upon a fragment of rock, Nelly read the letter to me.   It was addressed " To Miss ——," and was written in pencil, in a neat, elegant hand.   It ran thus: —

" Pardon this, my friend — for oh ! let me call you friend, though I know not even your name; but, something tells me that I have not read your kind face in vain, and that you will indeed be a friend to me.   I steal the minutes to write this; and, as I write, I know not how I may convey it to you; but, I must trust to the God of the helpless to aid me, and I pray that this day, on which hangs my fate, may not pass away without these lines being in your hands.   I must burden you with my sad tale, in order to explain the request which I shall have to make to you; but I will be very brief.

" My father is the Earl of Glenarvon; I am his only child; he has great estates which, if I outlived him, would be mine. They are joined by the estates of Lord Gurdon; and my father's cherished plan has been to unite the Gurdon with the Glenarvon estates. For that purpose an arrangement was made which betrothed me to Lord Gurdon's eldest son. I had known Philip Gurdon from a boy; but I could not love him. I never did love him. Ah! my friend, they cannot order the affections—they cannot say to them 'Go there,' or 'Stay here.' No! They are like the waves that are now murmuring in my ears, and no sovereign power, except the Great Supreme, can rule the mighty tide of love.

" My heart was not my own to give. I had entrusted its keeping to another. But, when my cousin, Captain Alvanley, proposed for my hand, my father would not listen to him; he had set his heart on marrying me to Philip Gurdon, and he would hear of nothing else. He is a kind father, and loves me; but he is cold and stern; and when I wept upon his bosom, he told me that I *must* marry as he wished me, and must forget my cousin. I pleaded strongly, and with tears; but in vain. Henry, also, had one more interview with my father, but was dismissed — even with insults. I was in despair —I had no one to counsel me, or speak words of hope; and in my wild grief, and deep, deep love, I consented to fly that night from my father's house, and be married to Captain Alvanley at Gretna. He was to bring a carriage to a private door in the park wall, and I and my maid (for I had confided my secret to her, and she had promised to go with me) were to meet him there. I made my preparations, and counted the minutes until I should be with Henry; but my maid played me false, and, at midnight, as I was preparing to leave the house, my father met me on the stairs. He upbraided me with my disobedience, and I fell fainting into my mother's arms. It was a terrible scene.

" My father still feared that I should fly with my cousin, and he determined to remove me to some spot unknown to Captain Alvanley. Travelling privately, and under feigned names, they have, therefore, brought me to this place; and they keep a constant watch over me to prevent my communicating with Henry. But 'Love is strong as Death,' says the Holy Book — 'many waters cannot quench it, neither can the floods drown it.' My father intended his purpose to be kept secret from me ; but, before we left home, I by chance heard a conversation between him and my mother, and learnt the name of our destination. I discovered a trustworthy messenger, and immediately wrote to my cousin ; and it was arranged that he should bring a carriage *this very evening* at midnight, to the environs of Westcliffe. As I knew not where we should be, I promised to send some one (on whose secrecy I could depend) to meet him. My mother, I was sure, would take measures to keep me to my room, and I knew that I should have ·to escape by the window. Henry was to bring a rope-ladder for the purpose.

" But whom can I send to meet him? In whom can I confide? I am alone, and among strangers — watched and guarded. I throw myself, then, upon the generous kindness of yourself and the gentleman whom I suppose to be your brother. My deep love emboldens me to break down the barriers of form, and to ask assistance at the hands of strangers. Oh ! if you would secure the happiness of another, and save her from sinking into misery, forgive the freedom of her appeal, and aid her in what she asks. It is this : that the gentleman (your brother?) would this evening, at midnight, meet Captain Alvanley where the Avenue-road by the hotel joins the Northern-road, and would inform him where I am to be found. My room is at the side of the hotel towards the Avenue-road. I shall be at my window, dressed, and in readiness ; but the greatest silence must be observed, as a door only divides my

room from my mother's.   Of the outer door she has the key;
but this we had expected.   The ladder will be of silk, and I
can secure it without noise.

"I know not how to apologise for the boldness of my
request; but I ask of your brother, as a man of honour, not to
betray the confidence of this communication, but to aid me in
changing my present misery into joy, for the sake of him who
is dearer to me than life itself.   And that God may bless
and reward you, and smile upon the love that is dearer and
nearer than love of father, or love of brother, is the sincere
prayer of

"AMY FRANCES DARNELL."

Such was the letter, but it was not without many
interruptions and comments, that Nelly read it to me.

CHAPTER VI.

PLANS AND PREPARATIONS.

HALF an hour had passed; we had re-read the letter,
and had carefully considered every word of its remarkable disclosures.

"Poor thing!" at length sighed Nelly; "what is to
be done?"

"Done!" I cried; "why, what she wants, of course.
'Lives there a man with soul so dead who never to him-
self has said'—it's my duty to help a female in distress?
What's to be done!   Why, of course, I shall go to meet
Captain Alvanley, and shall help them all I can.   That
is what is to be done, Nelly."   I said this with quite a

Spartan firmness; for, as Amy was really another's, I had only to make a virtue of necessity, and nip my love in the bud with the best grace I might.

"Poor thing!" again sighed my sister; "no wonder she looked so sad; and, when she *might* be so happy, it seems hard to refuse to help her. But would it be acting right towards her parents?" I think that Nelly in her secret heart was rejoiced at the very prospect of assisting in an elopement; but I suppose she considered it proper morality to make an objection.

"Her parents!" I answered hotly (and I don't wish to defend what I said; I only record it because I said it); "her parents, indeed! Have *they* acted right towards *her?* Did that dragon father of hers care more about uniting *her*, or the estates? Hasn't he set title-deeds and dowries in the place of love and affection? Hasn't he proudly placed his own family aggrandisement as superior to his child's happiness? Doesn't he look upon her wedding-ring merely as a symbol of a ring-fence? Doesn't he want to make the holy estate of matrimony an estate of broad acres, and to sink love in the land-tax? Is marriage only a matter for lawyers? Can you write on hearts like parchment, and endorse them like bills, to be made payable at sight to any one you please, changing 'I love you' into an I O U? Must poor Amy be a ' puppet to a father's threat? ' as Tennyson says."

"Dear me," said Nelly, whose breath was almost taken away by my impetuosity; "you treat me to quite a little homily."

"Why, suppose," I continued, " that *you* were placed in a similar position with regard to Fred." (my sister was engaged to Fred. Temple, so I knew that this was an *argumentum ad hominem*, which all her filial logic would not be able to resist); "and suppose you threw yourself on the confidence of a young girl of your own age, what should you think of *her* if she refused to assist you; and what would Fred. think of that young lady's brother if he followed his sister's example? Fred. would call him out at once. So, as I don't want to go out with Captain Alvanley, I shall meet him with pacific intentions at the cross-roads at twelve o'clock to-night."

Nelly did not require more persuasion, so we both agreed to help poor Amy all we could, and not to mention the subject to my mother, for fear she should side with the parents, and disclose the projected elopement to Lady Glenarvon.

"Captain Alvanley," mused my sister as we wandered back to the hotel, "I cannot but help thinking that I have heard his name, and that he is a friend of Frederick's, and in the same regiment."

Now that my sister mentioned it, I had some dim recollection of the same thing; and though we could neither of us fully determine it as a fact, the mere supposition of its truth made us, if possible, more earnest in Amy's cause. We had no "Army List" to refer to, to settle the point; but when we got back to our rooms, Nelly turned up Lord Glenarvon's name in the "Peerage" (my mother never travelled without the "Peerage," and "Johnson's Dictionary") and, sure enough, we there found the name of his "sole child and heiress, the Lady Amy Frances Darnell, heir-presumptive to the barony of Darnell, born ——, (Amy was barely twenty). And it further stated that the "heir-presumptive to the Earldom and Barony of Arvon," was "his Lordship's eldest brother," whose son, the Hon. Henry

Algernon Alvanley, was " Captain in the —th Light Dragoons " (Fred.'s regiment).

This discovery was exceedingly agreeable to our feelings, as we had now an additional incentive to aid poor Amy. Nelly entered heart and soul into the scheme; delighted at being able to assist a friend of her affianced husband.

Both she and I remained in a great state of excitement all the evening, longing for midnight to arrive. "It will be impossible for me to go to sleep," said Nell; " so I shall take a book to my room, and sit up till you can come and tell me the result of the night's adventure."

To Mrs. Rummell, I said " that I was going out, and should not be back till late : would she give me a latchkey? and that would prevent any of the servants' sitting up for me."

" Oh, certainly, Sir, with the greatest of pleasure; it was n't every gentleman that had so much thought for servants."

All being prepared, as the hour of midnight drew nigh, I sallied out with Trap, and commenced my vigil. The hotel was situate on the outside of the little town. Its front (where was our suite of rooms) looked over the cliffs towards the sea; its north side (where Amy had told me was her bedroom) was bounded by the Avenue-road, a road overhung by lime-trees, which led towards the inland, and which, at the distance of between three and four hundred yards, met at right angles, the North-road. It was at this point that I was to meet Captain Alvanley.

CHAPTER VII.

ALVANLEY TO THE RESCUE!

IT is a midsummer night of rare beauty. The dew lies heavy upon the grass, telling of the morrow's heat. The broad moon is at the full, making a light almost equal to that of day. The air, which has been so sultry, is now cool and refreshing, and comes floating through the lime-tree boughs with the most delicious perfume. The quivering leaves of the overhanging trees are stirred by its rich breath, and throb as though with rapture. Through the dewy screen of leaves and interlacing boughs, the wandering moonbeams pass, dancing and leaping, and making bright floating circles on the shaded floor of the road beneath. In the hedgerows honey-suckles hang their links of sweetness, and mingle their odours with the scent of the newly-mown hay: the rip-ening corn gently sways in the soft night breeze; sea-gulls are settling down into their rocky nests; and the querulous note of a quail reaches me from a distant meadow. A little wayside brook comes babbling on toward the sea, with a light musical song of ferns, and foxgloves, and flowering heather; while the sonorous roll of the ocean, breaking on the beach below, fills up, with its deep diapason, the summer-hymn of Nature.

I look down through the vista of chequered light and shade, and I see the great cliffs, and over them the wide expanse of sea, and the blue-paved heaven thick inlaid with its " patines of bright gold ; " and, though the dense foliage over-head shuts out the moon from view, I see her beams reflected in the waters in a long line of streaming light, that insensibly takes my thoughts back to one, who, in the days of Earth's youth, laid him down to sleep in the lonely desert, and, in a vision, saw a ladder of light that reached to heaven, and the angels ascending and descending the shining stars of glory.

Midnight is proclaimed from the old church tower. The reverberations of the last stroke become fainter and fainter ; and I listen attentively for the sound of carriage-wheels.   I hear nothing but the babbling brook and the distant breakers.   I light a cigar, and ask Trap to favour me with his opinion of Lord Glenarvon.   There is no danger of our being interfered with, and told to " Move on ! " by the police.   Westcliffe can't boast a guardian of the night ; we have the Queen's highway all to ourselves. The North-road lies bare and white in the moonlight ; and I could see a carriage at three miles' distance — could hear it, at more.   Captain Alvanley is decidedly not a punctual man !   I think that if *I* had a girl like Amy waiting to fly off with me, and be my wife, I should be rather before my time than after it.   I am not at all cold ; on the contrary, out-of-doors is more refreshing than in, this hot weather ; but I dance a polka, merely for a little amusement and change.   Trap sits in the middle of the road, and gravely watches me from under his shaggy eyebrows, as I polk round him.   " What ! can't you make it out, old doggie ? "   He evidently takes me for a lunatic ; but I explain the matter to him, and he rubs his cold nose in my hand, to show that his confidence in me is restored.   I pause from my exertions, and sit on the mile stone, smoking my weed ; while Trap

turns out an unfortunate field-mouse, and amuses himself to his great satisfaction.

One o'clock! No carriage, no sound of wheels. Captain Alvanley, Sir! what are you thinking about, to
keep a gentleman and lady waiting in this way? I will
walk down the Avenue-road, to see if Amy is on the
watch. Softly! there she is! bonneted and shawled,
sitting at her open window. How the moonlight falls
full upon her face! Captain Alvanley, if you could
now see that face, and its intense expression of anxious
expectation, you would give your post-boys any fabulous fee to whirl you the sooner to your Amy's side.
She sees me at once as I emerge from the avenue, and
I come softly under her window. She points within, as
though towards her mother's room, and lays her finger
on her lips. No talking allowed; I take the hint, and
am speechless. She looks full upon me with those
deep-blue eyes, and she lays her hand upon her heart,
and bends towards me. She is thanking me for my
vigil. Then she folds her hands together, and looks
inquiringly. I shake my head in reply, and point
towards the North-road. Then we go through a little
ballet of action, and I am almost inclined to pirouette
on one toe, as I signify to her that I will return to my
post, and keep on the watch. And so I turn away while
she dumbly expresses her thanks.

I walk back to my mile-stone, and light another weed.
Trap don't understand it at all, and sits in the road, and
yawns; so I throw stones to divert him. But even this
lively pastime fails on too great repetition. Still no
carriage! I watch the scented smoke curling lightly
from my lips, and I begin to think of "Locksley
Hall:" —

"Then her cheek was pale and thinner than should be for one so
    young,
And her eyes on all my motions with a mute observance hung,
And I said, " My cousin Amy, speak, and speak the truth to me ;
Trust me, cousin, all the current of my being sets to thee."

If Captain Alvanley thinks so, why does n't he come?
" O, my cousin, shallow-hearted ! " Tennyson must decidedly alter his verses, and make the gentleman the one
who is " falser than all fancy fathoms."

Two o'clock strikes, and no sight or sound of carriage.
I pace again down the Avenue-road. There is faithful
Amy, still at her window — still on the watch. She looks
as though she had been weeping, and I try, by friendly
signs and nods, to comfort her. " She speaks, and yet she
says nothing. What of that? Her eye discourses." As
I look up to her, I wish that " I were a glove upon that
hand, that I might touch that cheek ; " and, of course, I
think of " Romeo and Juliet," and the Balcony Scene.
But where *is* her Romeo? Are his " love's light wings "
impeded by a yellow post-chaise? Once more, I silently
go back to my mile-stone.

I hum operatic snatches, and go through the chief
part of my vocal performances ; but Trap has a delicate
ear for music, and he howls down my attempts. Another
hour slowly passes, and still no Captain Alvanley.

I steal under the shadow of the trees, and I see poor
Amy looking so sad, that I have scarcely the heart to
approach her without good tidings. I go back, therefore, to my mile-stone ; and my comforting cigar-case is
being rapidly diminished. Only one weed is left, for I
did not calculate on such a lengthened vigil — so I husband it ; but, at last, it is smoked out, and I am cigar-
less. And still there is no carriage — no Captain
Alvanley !

Something must have surely occurred to prevent his coming. Perhaps he cannot obtain leave of absence from his regiment. If this is the case, I can fancy what his state of mind must be just about the present time.

Four o'clock strikes. Once more I go to Amy's window. She is still there, and, being ready dressed for her departure, I feel almost inclined to propose an elopement on my own account, and so, provide a substitute for the Captain; but my mirth is checked as soon as I have seen her sad, sad features. She weeps outright this time — bursts into a silent agony of tears, that I can well understand. My heart is touched with pity, and I scribble on a piece of paper — " He may not be able to get leave of absence. He will probably come to-morrow night, and I will watch and meet him. Be of good cheer." I toss this up to her, and as the morning is breaking, there is sufficient light for her to read it. She cheers up directly, and smiles and waves her hand to me. I signify to her that I shall continue on my watch till five o'clock, and then I go back to my mile-stone.

But, when the hour has passed, no Captain Alvanley has arrived; and I see that to prolong my vigil would be useless, for it is broad day now, and people are beginning to move about to their boats and their work; so, much to Trap's satisfaction, I turn my steps towards the hotel. Amy is still at her window. She thanks me as much as any one could thank me without speaking. She again reads my scrap of a note, and looks towards me with a cheerful face, as though she depended upon the fulfilment of my promise; and then she noiselessly lets down her window and blind. Having seen this, I quietly make use of my latch-key, and pass up-stairs to my sister's room.   She has not gone to bed, but has fallen asleep in her chair, from sheer exhaustion.   I tell her the result of my night's vigil, and am presently in my own room, and a sound sleep.

CHAPTER VIII.

A MIDSUMMER-NIGHT'S REALITY.

THE next day passes wearily.   In the morning we see Amy go to bathe, as usual; and, in the afternoon we pass them on the cliffs.   Amy looks pale and anxious; and her eyes seem heavy with weeping and watching. When we are close to them, I pretend to be talking in a loud tone of voice to my sister; and I say — meeting Amy's eyes as I say it — " he will be quite certain to arrive, and I shall be there to meet him."   I think this a Machiavellian stroke of policy, and I am delighted with myself at my ready wit.

As evening advances the sky becomes overcast; and, as I let myself out of the hotel, at half-past eleven o'clock, big drops of rain beat against my face.   I send Trap indoors again; it is evidently going to be a night not fit to turn out a dog in, and Amy will have but rough weather for her departure, though the noise of the wind and rain will favour her escape.   I put on a rough boating coat, light a weed, and sally forth to my vigil.

The thunder comes growling up from the west, and, presently, bursts into peals like the discharge of heavy artillery.   The lightning gleams vividly through the lime-trees overhead; and, for a moment lights up the tumbling waves, that are white with foam. Soon the rain comes down in a perfect sheet, and even penetrates the dense mass of foliage above me. It is, indeed, a rough night for a vigil. But hark! the carriage-wheels! I run out into the North-road, and meet — the blinding, hissing rain. I listen again: there is no sound of carriage; it was but the rattling rumble of the thunder.

It must be some time after midnight; but the violence of the storm overpowers the sound of the church clock. I keep under the half-shelter of the dripping trees, and twice or thrice I run forth as before to meet the carriage, but with no better success; the wind and the rain together always deceive me.

At length the storm subsides, and the thunder dies away in distant peals. I shake the wet off me like a Newfoundland dog coming out of the water. There is a grateful sense of coolness all around; the thirsty earth has drunk in the refreshing moisture; the July storm is over. Soon the moon shines out, ghastly and pale, through the dark, driving clouds; and only the rain-drops patter from the leaves. I light a fresh cigar and wait till two o'clock strikes. No Captain Alvanley! So I walk down the avenue towards the hotel. Faithful Amy! there she is at her open window, on the watch, just as she was last night. She still looks very pale and sad, and she is evidently listening intently for the sound of the carriage wheels. As soon as she sees me she bends and greets me as an old friend. I have provided myself with a sheet of paper, and I scribble on it in large letters, "The violence of the storm must have delayed him. No horses could face such a tempest. By this time he is on his road." I throw this up to her, and she catches it as nimbly as a cricketer. It seems to console her; so again I return to my post, or, to speak correctly, to my mile-stone; for I take my seat thereon, and smoke placidly. I rather miss Trap, for he was a companion; but I know that Amy is sharing my vigil;. so what more can I desire?

Three o'clock, and still no Captain Alvanley. This is getting strange. Can he have played her false? I will go and take a quiet look at Amy. She is still at the window — still gazing out anxiously towards the North-road, with a sad, sad face. I have not the heart to go towards her; for what can I say?

Another hour passes slowly and wearily, and no sight or sound of carriage. · Surely Amy could not have made any mistake as to the night? It is not probable; but I will go and ask her. She is at her open window; but clouds have floated before the moon, and it would be impossible for her to read anything that I may write. I, therefore, essay to speak to her. She leans forward out of the window and we converse in whispers. " Are you quite sure that he fixed last night?" I ask.

"Quite sure," she answers; " he mentioned the night and the hour. I could not be mistaken."

" Perhaps he has not been able to leave his regiment; perhaps it has been called out by some sudden riot; there may be a hundred reasons why he cannot come " (*I* could not think of them!) " and, of course, he could not write to you. But do cheer up and take courage " (for tears were beginning to fall); " I will watch again to-morrow night — and — "

And our *tête-à-tête* is suddenly brought to an end by the appearance of Lady Glenarvon, attired, *Lady Mac-beth*-like, in her *robe-de-chambre* and *bonnet de nuit*.

Amy gave a scream as she turned and saw her mother standing at her elbow. Lady Glenarvon advanced to the window — stood there for a moment (regardless of her costume), while she mentally took my portrait in very stern colours, and then, without saying a word, drew down the window and the blind.

I waited to see if more would come of this; but as there did not, I returned to my mile-stone to ponder over the *contretemps*, and inform Captain Alvanley, should he arrive, of the state of the case. But he did not arrive; and, wearied and somewhat sick at heart, I went back to the hotel, and to bed.

CHAPTER IX.

MYSTIFICATIONS AND EXPLANATIONS.

I was so tired out by my two nights' vigil, that the sun had been up several hours when I awoke, and it was late when I got down stairs. "Good morning, Sir!" said Mrs. Rummell, who was the first person I met. "Mr. Spencer, Sir, has left this note for you. He asked me your name, and he directed it here, in the bar, Sir."

"Mr. Spencer! And pray who *is* Mr. Spencer?"

"Why, the strange-mannered gentleman, Sir, as come with the two ladies in a carriage and four."

"Good heavens!" I cried — for I had forgotten Lord Glenarvon's incognito — "you don't mean to say that she — that they are *gone?*"

"Yes, Sir," said Mrs. Rummell; "they went quite sudden, just after eight this morning; and I'd barely time to make their bill out. I suppose, Sir, they must have heard of the death of some relative."

"Very like, very like!" I muttered in a dream-like way, as *Hamlet* does when they tell him of the *Ghost;* and, tearing open the note, I read this: —

"Sir, — When you again assist a young lady to break through her ties of filial duty and obedience, I should advise you to first ascertain if the young lady is a free agent.
Yours truly,
J. SPENCER."

"A free agent, indeed! Well that *is* cool of the old Dragon, when he knows what a tight prisoner he 's kept her." And — metaphorically speaking, of course! — I foamed at the mouth with fury and excitement.

When Nelly heard the news, she was as much astonished as I had been; and when the post had come in, our mystification was still further increased; for, she received a letter from Fred. which had been written on the morning of the day when the elopement *ought* to have taken place, in which he said (referring to some people my sister knew) "the J.'s have got a picnic in hand for to-morrow, in which I expect some of ours will be ingloriously taken captive. Bessie J. is to bring all her battery of charms to bear upon poor Alvanley, whom we have forcibly compelled to accept the invite. He has been 'all in the downs,' lately; and we thought that a dose of Bessie's flirtation would do him good. So, perhaps, you may hear of *your* friend being engaged to *my* friend; but I trust she will not deprive herself of the pleasure of being your bridesmaid."

And so it seemed, that while I was keeping my vigil, and pacing my lonely round, and while Amy was on the watch for her lover, Captain Alvanley was either snoring between the sheets, or dreaming of flirtations with Bessie J.! Nelly and I were altogether mystified. Had Amy been imposing upon us, and was the Dragon really a Mr. Spencer, and not an Earl? Had Amy been really expecting some one to elope with her, to whom she had given a name out of the Peerage? or was the whole affair a practical joke on her part, to relieve the tedium of a dull watering-place? But this could not be. To solve the mystery, we determined to write at once to Fred., and submit it to his tact to find out if there was any connexion between the Captain Alvanley of his regiment, and our mysterious beautiful Amy.

It was some time before the matter was perfectly cleared up. Captain Alvanley himself wrote to me a very long and sad letter, which put us in possession of all the particulars relative to his engagement with his cousin Amy. All that she had written in her letter to my sister was quite true, up to the point of the discovery of the projected elopement; beyond that, it was the mere invention of a disordered brain.

After Amy had fallen fainting into her mother's arms, she had been seized with delirium and fever. This, together with the wild excitement through which she had gone, partially unsettled her intellect. As in many other similarly sad cases, the chief feature of her disease was a settled melancholy, and a derangement only on the one point that had brought on her illness; she was under the belief that her cousin had planned another night for the elopement, and her mind dwelt upon this, as though it were a fact. Hence her letter to my sister; and hence her plans of escape. It is needless now to explain the watchful care of her father and mother;

they were too well aware of the peculiar phase which their daughter's aberration of intellect had assumed, not to fear lest she should escape in the night to the imaginary assignation. Change of scene and strict retirement had been advised as the most effectual way to prevent the increase of the malady, and it was by the doctor's counsel that Lord Glenarvon had maintained an incognito when he had brought his daughter to Westcliffe, in order that she might derive all the benefit that could be gained from sea-bathing and the fresh sea-breeze.

The effects of my vigil, and her unfortunate acquaintance with us, had added to her disorder; and her father (as Captain Alvanley afterwards discovered) had removed her from Westcliffe to the south of France, and from thence to Italy. There, under judicious treatment, her mind gradually recovered its healthy tone; and, though the shock upon her nervous system had been so great, she returned to England, after a little more than a year's absence, in perfect health and strength — the same Amy that she had been when she won her cousin's love.

CHAPTER X.

BRIEF, BUT SATISFACTORY.

THE twelve months that saw Amy's gradual progress towards health, also witnessed the occurrence of three other important events.

In the first place, the Long Vacation had ended; and despite the interruptions to my reading, I had taken my degree.

In the second place, Lord Glenarvon had been taught a lesson on forced marriages that he was not likely to forget.

And, in the third place, Philip Gurdon, when he learnt the cause of Amy's illness, had transferred his affections to another lady, and had married her.

As the possibility, therefore, of joining the Gurdon to the Glenarvon estates was now at an end, the Earl did what he easily might have done in the first instance, gave his consent to his daughter's union with her cousin, Captain Alvanley.

They were married about a month since. If any one is curious to see how the bride was dressed — what was the worth of her *trousseau* — how many bridesmaids she had — and what notabilities figured at her wedding, he has only to refer to the " Morning Post," which devoted nearly half a column to these women-absorbing topics. You will not find *my* name there, as I was unable to get back from my Swiss tour in time; but you will see Nelly's and her husband's name — " Captain and Mrs. Temple."

Amy's wedding-cards are lying on the table as I write this. I have not yet seen her; but, as they are expected to be at Glenarvon Castle in a fortnight's time, and as I am invited to meet them, I shall soon have an opportunity of judging whether, as Lady Alvanley, Amy looks as sad and melancholy as she did on the nights of my Long Vacation Vigil.

THE ONLY MAN LEFT IN COLLEGE ON CHRISTMAS DAY.

CHAPTER I.

THE CHRISTMAS "COACH."

I'LL never do so again! If I do, may I be plucked for my "Greats!" And that, my Masters, is a big oath; for this is the Oxonian for "Great Go;" which in its turn, is the equivalent for the "Examination in *literis humanioribus* for the degree of B.A." So that you may suppose I am terribly in earnest when I say, I'll never do so again!

When I came to the resolution of staying up in Oxford during the short Christmas Vacation, and spending Christmas-day in the deserted halls of Brazenface, I had no suspicion that I should be left there as solitary as Robinson Crusoe. I had not the most remote idea that I should be the monarch of all I surveyed; that my right there could be none to dispute; that, to the Master's Lodge over the way, I should be the only poor desolate brute. But so it was! And relentless fate must have had a delightful time of it, when she saw me register that resolution.

Willoughby, Collins, and I, having hunted, and idled, together for the last twelve months, had taken it into our heads to forswear Suppers and "Wines;" and, in their stead, to open our cob-webbed Lexicons, to spread over the table with Greek Plays and Aldrich, and old " Thicksides " (as we profanely called "Thucydides "), and to start a reading " coach," of which I was constituted the " unicorn," or leader. Like all similar coaches, we went off at a slapping pace, scarcely staying for meals; and at the end of a fortnight found ourselves so blown, that we were fain to bait with a wine party. This threw us back at least a week, and when we had started once more, we found we were obliged to retrace our steps over a good deal of the road along which we had come so merrily. In another fortnight just as we had got into condition again, and were beginning to pick up flesh, Term ended. So we held a virtuous debate, in which it was unanimously agreed upon, that the Christmas festivities, and pretty girls we should meet at home, would most undeniably and effectually disperse the heavier classical and logical awkward-squad we had with so much difficulty marshalled into our respective brains. The stern resolution was therefore adopted, that the Reading Coach should run through the Christmas Vacation; and the next day we got the necessary licence to allow this.

When we had seen the last team of men off from the Mitre, and the last train leave the Station, and had walked up the deserted High, and had come back across the now dreary and silent Quad. of Brazenface to my snug rooms, we sat down by the firelight, and there talked as Martyrs may have talked — as Curtius may have talked, the night before he leapt into the pit in the

Forum, — as Coriolanus may have talked, when he went out to war against his wife and children, — as Mr. John O'Connell may have talked, when he was about to die for his country on the floor of the House, — as any one may have talked, who, as our popular Comedians express it, have " been and gone, and done it," and voluntarily given themselves up to disagreeable alternatives.

All went on well till Christmas Eve. Like cloistered monks, we buried ourselves within the college walls, and only issued forth for rapid constitutionals. As Indians at the stake are said to relieve their pains by biting through their tongues, so we felt a certain relief in violent reading, and in thus revenging ourselves on those studies which kept us from so many pleasures. On Christmas-eve, Collins and I had gone out together alone for our diurnal constitutional, Willoughby having pleaded a headache; and when, after a stiff header round Hillingdon Hill, we had returned to my rooms, what was our surprise at reading the following laconic epistle, which was lying on the table : —

" Dearly beloved Charley and Collins, — By the time you read this, I fervently trust I shall have got clean away from Alma Mater. The nearer we came to Christmas-day, the more undutifully I thought I was acting in not going home to see my own Alma Mater, who, I 'll be bound for it, has been sobbing her eyes out, at the thought of having to eat her plum-pudding without her young Hopeful to help her. Excuse me putting a *ruse* upon you, but I was afraid you would lay violent hands on me, and detain, against my will, in this dreary Brazenface,

" Yours elopingly,

" W. Longueville Willoughby."

I'm not quite sure what we said on the occasion, but, though I know we both agreed that he was the most ungrateful reprobate that the confiding arms of Friendship had ever embraced, I yet think we entertained a very strong, though unexpressed, idea, that we should only be too glad to follow his example. But if my surprise and indignation were great then, they were still more greatly excited the next morning.

CHAPTER II.

THE CHRISTMAS DINNER.

I HAD lain rather late, having no horrid bell to rouse me up for chapel, so it was after ten o'clock in the morning of Christmas-day before I went to Collins's rooms to breakfast, for he and I always boiled one kettle between us. There was the breakfast laid out, certainly, but only for one. And, to increase my wonderment, on diving into his bedroom, where I heard somebody moving, whom should I see but old Mrs. Tester, the bedmaker, busily employed in cramming linen, clothes, and a heterogeneous mass of articles into the portmanteaus that were gathered around her. The fearful truth at once flashed upon my mind! Collins was gone!

"Tell me — tell me the worst!" I gasped out, and old Mrs. Tester handed me the following note: —

"Dear old Charley, — It's really too bad, upon my honour! But what else could I do? I dreamt about Willoughby all night, and the first thing this morning got a letter from my sister to say what a Beast I was for not going home on Christ-

mas-day, — and that all kinds of things are going to be done,
and that no end of people are there, — Fanny among the rest,
— and what an awful state she's in about my preferring staying up here to going down there, and all that sort of thing.
Now, who could stand this? Especially when he thinks of
the intense dulness of this hole. So I have made up my mind
and my carpet-bag to go by the 8.50 train, and I shall get to
Hammersleigh in time for dinner. Mother Tester is to send
off the heavy baggage by the next train. Quicken her about
it, there's a good fellow, for I want to come out strong at our
county ball on the 31st, and all my Sunday-going toggery can't
be stowed in my carpet-bag. And do go home yourself, old
fellow, by the next train; it's the proper thing to do: and,
depend upon it, too much reading is bad for the lungs; I feel
mine going already; and don't victimise yourself with the
brutalising books, but get away home to the women, and have
a bit of polish, and you'll ever bless the advice of yours, in a
railway hurry,

                                   "HENRY COLLINS."

I would much rather pass over the events of the day.
I should not like to expose myself in the eyes of the
public, as I feel I did in the eyes of the respectable Mrs.
Tester. But I did *not* go home by the next train; I
stayed where I was. I laughed a hollow "Ha! ha!"—
like I had heard the Stage Pirates and Villains do; and
I rather think I wished myself a stage villain, that I
might do somebody an injury, and expend the fury of
my gloomy anger. Hall-time came, and I slank across
the Quad. for my dinner. There was a cloth laid for
me across the end of one of the long tables, and the
nearest chandelier had two of its lamps lit for my
special benefit. Of course there was no High-table;
any of the Dons, who were still in residence, would dine

together on *that* day ; and now Willoughby and Collins were gone, I was positively the only man left up — the only man. left in College on Christmas-day ! " Ha ! ha ! " Desolation had marked me for her own.

Our Dining-Hall at Brazenface is, as every one knows, one of the largest in Oxford, and the feeble light from the two solitary lamps only made it appear the more vast and solitary. When I peered into its farthest depths, and thought of the brilliancy, and crowd, and laughter, and loud hum of conversation, that, during the Term, reigned there at that time, I cut into the roast beef before me with a savage energy. At least, I had the proper Christmas dinner ! They gave me that ! But I think it only made me worse : if I had had other dishes, I might possibly have forgotten the day, and not felt so wretched. The cook, however, in his mistaken kindness, decorated the plum-pudding with a large piece of holly ; and there was no forgetting that it was Christmas. My scout waited upon me : to do so, he had been obliged to leave a party of his fellow-servants, and was sulky, accordingly. He told me of this, and asked my permission to rejoin them, as soon as he had put my tea-things ready against I wanted them. So even *he* was going to a merry party, and would be in company, and enjoy himself ; whilst I —— " Ha ! ha ! "

The very eyes of the Founders and Benefactors seemed to be fixed upon me, from their canvas, as I ate my solitary dinner. It was soon over : it was not at all the sort of thing I wished to linger upon : and I walked out of Hall, and through the Second Quad. to the cloisters of our Chapel. It was the most lonely place I could find, and it harmonised with my thoughts and condition.

There, busy Fancy took me back to past Christmas-days, and showed me all their joys and pleasures. I saw the happy groups of home, the family meetings, the hearty-welcome of long-loved faces, the greeting of well-remembered friends, the gathering round the social table, the laughing faces of the children, the light-hearted smiles of all, the cheerful fire-side, the gleaming holly-berries and shining leaves, the mistletoe hanging enticingly from the ceiling, the noisy games, and the merry dance, — I saw all these; and, my classical reading not yet having converted me into a stoic, resolution gave way before nature; and within an hour I had packed up a few things, followed Willoughby's and Collins's example, and was being whirled away by the Express Train, every moment farther and farther from Oxford. I never before was so glad to leave it!

Thanks to the blessings of the railway, and the pace we went, I got home that night, much to the astonishment of the assembled party, in time to bid them "a merry Christmas," before they broke up; and in time, too, to kiss Helen Clifford under the mistletoe!

I don't think that Mrs. Tester will ever again be able to say of me, that I was the only man left in College on Christmas-day. If she can, may I be plucked for my Greats!

THE END.